Pl ase return
Y

FEAR ON FRIDAY

FEAR ON FRIDAY

Ann Purser

Severn House Large Print
London & New York

This first large print edition published in Great Britain 2006 by
SEVERN HOUSE LARGE PRINT BOOKS LTD of
9-15 High Street, Sutton, Surrey, SM1 1DF.
First world regular print edition published 2005 by
Severn House Publishers, London and New York.
This first large print edition published in the USA 2006 by
SEVERN HOUSE PUBLISHERS INC., of
595 Madison Avenue, New York, NY 10022.

British Library Cataloguing in Publication Data

Purser, Ann
   Fear on Friday. - Large print ed.
   1. Meade, Lois (Fictitious character) – Fiction
   2. Cleaning personnel - England – Fiction
   3. Country life - England - Fiction
   4. Detective and mystery stories
   5. Large type books
   I. Title
   823.9'14[F]

ISBN-13: 9780727875396
ISBN-10: 0727875396

Printed and bound in Great Britain by
MPG Books Ltd, Bodmin, Cornwall.

Deceive boys with toys, but men with oaths.
Lysander, Spartan, d 395 BC

Prologue

A man in a long, dark-coloured coat stood outside the narrow shop window and stared in. Stick-thin models draped in black shiny macs stared blankly back at him, their lifeless hands arranged to smooth the tactile rain-wear. *RAIN OR SHINE*, said the discreet sign above the shop. A small smile of pleasurable recognition crossed the man's face.

He looked furtively to right and left. Nobody about, except for a postman, slowly approaching, from the far end of the terraced street. It was very quiet. Then a motorbike turned the corner and roared past him, its rider anonymous inside the oversize helmet. The man turned his face back to the window, and the shopkeeper, glancing out, saw him and recognised a familiar face.

'Hi, there! Got your letter, thanks. Come along in. Got some new stuff to show you...'

The man followed the shopkeeper, shutting the door quickly. The customer relaxed. 'Right then,' he said, his eyes brightening. 'New girlfriend, new games ... what's new with you, young Fergus?'

One

Letters in the post can be dangerous. From a handful of envelopes in the morning post, most are junk. But there is always a potential disaster, that one particular envelope examined back and front, and opened gingerly with a butter knife. Even so, given that possibility, most of Long Farnden residents would still rather have the postlady walk neatly up their path and deliver. No mail at all is an insult, a confirmation that the world has forgotten you.

The postlady never missed Rupert Forsyth's house. There were always letters for him, from all over the country. He easily came top of the list of those who got the most post in the village. What's more, they were *real* letters, with handwritten addresses and stamps stuck on by hand. Occasionally, there were names and addresses of senders on the backs of envelopes. This singled him out from the rest of the village, and was duly noted.

Josie Meade had been postlady in Long Farnden for only a short while, but she was fascinated by this one exception to the general rule. She was the daughter of Lois Meade, who was proprietor of a cleaning business, New Brooms, and an experienced amateur sleuth on the side. Josie, her mother and grandmother, had taken on the village shop and post office, when the old couple who ran it were more or less forced out of business by neglect and financial decline.

'It'll be your job,' Lois had said to her daughter. 'If you and Rob want to come back and live in the village, we'll all chip in and buy it, and you can run it. It'll be an investment. I've enough to do with cleaning, but I'll be around if you need help. And there's always Gran.'

There *was* always Gran, stalwart mother of Lois and a reliable prop for the whole family. She had been thrilled at the idea of taking on the shop, and in a quiet way proved to be a backstop in many ways. Rob, Josie's partner, though with a job of his own in Tresham, worked shifts, and was often able to give a hand. This way, Josie could be postlady and shopkeeper, and was in her element.

In no time at all, Josie had had everything under control, and with Gran manning the shop first thing, the early morning post delivery was the best time of the day for her. The birds were singing, the air fresh, roads empty. Rupert Forsyth, almost alone of her calls, was always up and about, and opened the door of No 2 Albert Villas, holding out his hand for his fat packet of post.

Rupert and his wife had moved into the village six months ago, buying a house which sat solidly on a plot in a side road off the main street. Albert Villas had been built by a nineteenth-century farmer for his best workers, using a plain, no-nonsense red brick, and the Forsyths had known at once that this house, four-square and reliable, was exactly what they wanted.

This morning, Rupert Forsyth appeared at the door in his shirtsleeves. 'Lovely morning, Josie!' he said. 'The forecast is good for the weekend, too. You'll be off on your bikes, I expect.'

Josie nodded. Rob was a biking enthusiast, and had given her an amazingly speedy model with twenty-five gears, every possible gadget she could need, and a safety helmet that made her feel like an elongated snail. She handed Rupert his letters, and warned him against going out with too little protection against the wind. 'Still sharp, you know, Mr Forsyth,' she cautioned. 'You know what my Gran says: "Ne'er cast a clout 'til May be out." And it's only the twenty-sixth today.'

'I do indeed know what your Gran says,' Rupert laughed ruefully. 'A very great deal! Not a lady to meet if you're in a hurry.' His tone was pleasant, but Josie bridled.

'She's wonderful for her age,' she said.

'Been a widow for ages, and helps Mum no end, as well as me. I couldn't manage without her. And anyway,' she added, 'most people in the village like her. They come in just for a chat, and then buy something. Very good for business, is Gran.' Which is more than you are, Mr and Mrs Rupert Forsyth, Josie said silently to herself. I see you coming back on a Friday afternoon with your bargain buys from Tesco's. I'm lucky if you buy a box of matches from me.

She walked smartly back down the path and out into the road. 'Shut the gate, please!' called Rupert, but Josie pretended not to hear and cycled off without looking round. It's not his place to criticise Gran, she thought angrily. He's not been here five minutes. Who cares about his stupid letters? But she had to admit that, along with the rest of the village, she could not resist speculating about the Forsyths.

Two

Lois Meade, Josie's mother, sat in her office and chewed the end of her pen in the comfortable family house that had once belonged to the village doctor. New Brooms, her cleaning business, had expanded, and she was seriously considering opening a branch office in Tresham, the nearest big town serving Long Farnden. But how to staff it? Accustomed to absolute freedom herself, she hated the idea of being stuck all day in an office. Perhaps it could be done on a part-time basis?

One of New Brooms' first cleaners, Hazel Thornbull, had recently had a baby, and was now itching to get back to work. With her mother-in-law close by, and only too ready to help, for lively-minded Hazel it would be an opportunity to get away from the farm and back to the variety of New Brooms' working life. Much as she loved her young husband, cows and sheep had nothing much to say, and Hazel loved to talk.

Could Hazel manage some hours in an office in Tresham? She was certainly the best candidate, bright and experienced. She'd stand no nonsense, but was good with people. Lois thought on. Did she need another office? She'd always managed from home, but lately had begun to think she'd like a small place in town, with New Brooms over the door, where clients could walk in and discuss their requirements in person.

'Lois? You there?' It was Derek's voice from the kitchen. A self-employed electrician, he should have been at work.

Lois yelled, 'What are you back for?'

Derek appeared at her door. 'Forgot something,' he said. 'Any coffee going? No sign of Gran. I expect she's at the shop.' He missed the warm presence of Gran, always ready in the kitchen with a cup of this or that and slice of home-made cake. Lois was just as likely to tell him to get his own.

'You can make it, and bring me a cup,' she said.

'You know what they say,' he grumbled, 'y'don't keep a dog to bark yerself.'

'Huh!' Lois grinned, walked over to him and kissed him warmly. 'Well, this old dog's not barking for nobody. How's about making it together? Josie's always goin' on about togetherness. Reckon we could manage it without bickering. You get the mugs, and I'll put the kettle on. And then we'll have a cosy chat just on our own, for once.' Gran's new role as shopkeeper had its good side for Lois.

Sometimes two women in one kitchen was not a good thing.

'Chat about what?' said Derek suspiciously. He distrusted Lois's cosy chats. They always involved something he didn't want to do, or didn't like the sound of. And though they had an agreement that Lois could carry on detecting, provided he knew about it, he still dreaded the signs: Lois abstracted, doors banged shut to keep phone calls private, Gran frowning and Lois snappy. But this time, it proved to be an innocent enough plan.

'I've bin thinking,' said Lois, 'that I might open an office – just a small one – in Tresham. Just so's people could come in and talk face-to-face with one of us. Now we've got so much work, and bigger clients, I reckon it'd be a good idea.'

A few years ago, Lois had been a solitary cleaner living with her family in Tresham, when one of her clients, the doctor in whose house she now lived, had become involved in a murder scandal. When he moved away, nobody had wanted the house, but Lois and Derek had seen a bargain, and the grim associations didn't bother them. It had seemed like paradise after the estate semi they'd lived in with three children and Gran down the road.

New Brooms had been a logical development for Lois. She'd recruited a team, and discovered that the demand for their services was great. An added bonus was that instead of one snoop, she now had half a dozen and more. Not that they knew they were snooping ... at least, Lois never spelled it out.

It had all started when she'd fancied being a Special Constable, and been turned down by the police. A middle-aged policewoman had patronised her, and said she had too much responsibility already with children and a job. She should wait a few years. Lois was stroppy, stubborn and did not take kindly to being patronised. Already convinced that a cleaner's job was ideal for what she liked to think of as investigations, Lois decided to go it alone. But when a murder involving several of her clients struck Long Farnden, her unique position was quickly recognised by local Detective Inspector Hunter Cowgill, and, in a sparky partnership, they had worked together ever since.

Hunter Cowgill, from the beginning, had – not to beat about the bush – lusted after Lois. He had never said a word of it to anyone, and wouldn't. She knew it, of course, and used it against him at times. It was a hopeless, from afar kind of attraction, and had not dimmed with time. When the need arose to ask Lois for help, Cowgill's pulse quickened, and his normally dour countenance softened. But Long Farnden had been peaceful since a particularly nasty fire at the vicarage, and Cowgill was reduced to staring out of his third floor office window in Tresham, hoping he might see Lois striding by on her way to market. Sometimes she turned and looked for his window. He'd wave casually, and she would laugh up at him, causing him to curse himself for being an old fool.

Now Lois was bored. While Derek thanked God for a peaceful life and a normal household, Lois was restless. Taking on the shop had been exciting, but Josie was competent and confident. Nothing there for Lois to get her teeth into. At least the New Brooms office in town would be a challenge, and perhaps a financial risk. Lois began to plan.

Three

In the Town Hall in Tresham, the Mayor's Parlour was a suitably impressive place for the most important citizen of the town. Panelling in a mellow dark wood, heavy velvet drapes, and an impressive desk the size of a billiard table, all were an appropriate setting for the present incumbent of the office.

Howard Jenkinson, sixty-eight and still handsome in a heavy, thick-set fashion, stood at his window looking out at neatly landscaped gardens, and smiled. How fortunate he was! Lately retired from a successful timber merchant business, he and his wife were able to remain in their large Tudor-style house in the best part of town with no financial worries about the future. Howard had, of course, a down-to-earth watchful nature, and had been brought up not to neglect the pennies. But now his concern with matters financial was a close interest in observing the stock market, making shrewd moves where necessary.

His wife now, as in all their married years, took no interest in money. 'I always leave money matters to Howard,' she would say comfortably, and then laugh. 'I've not much alternative, actually...'

Doreen Jenkinson was, most of her friends agreed, the perfect wife, mother and Lady Mayoress. Her two daughters were suitably married, had provided both grandsons and granddaughters, and apart from a few creaky joints and a growing reluctance to tackle energetic jobs around the house, Doreen was in the best of health.

A knock at the parlour door brought Howard out of his reverie; his smile widened as he saw Jean Slater, his old friend Ken's wife, bearing cups of steaming coffee. How fortunate he was. His school friend still his best mate, and Jean an efficient and, at one time, very attractive secretary who had worked for him for years in the timber business, and whose transfer to the Town Hall he'd been able to arrange with little trouble. A lot to be said for the old boys' network!

'Doreen's been on the telephone,' she said. 'Asking me about finding help in the house. Seems old Edna's given in her notice. I looked in Yellow Pages and came up with a cleaning service that sounds good. New Brooms, with a Long Farnden number. Doreen says she'll give them a ring.'

'You're a wonder, Jean,' Howard Jenkinson said. 'What would I do without you?'

His secretary nodded. 'Not very well,' she said, with a smile.

'Anyway,' continued Howard, 'I'm glad Edna's finally packed it in. She's been worse than useless since her op. " 'Ad it all out, dear," as she embarrassingly told me. We didn't like to give her the old heave-ho, but now she's going, so great. Well done! What else have you got for me? The St Christopher's School fête? Right. All set. Doreen loves fêtes, so no doubt I shall be footing the bill for a new hat.'

The telephone rang from the outer office, and Jean disappeared. Now, said Howard to himself, what had she said? New Brooms?

Good name. Let's see what I can find out about them. He reached for his dark blue blazer and set off for the County Club, where he could find a few old chums and have a good lunch.

The County Club had been established more than a hundred years ago by the solid citizens of Tresham, and still exuded an air of conservatism in business, recreation and life in general. Originally for men only, it had been more or less forced to add a ladies section, and this had added a frivolous touch to the décor. Pastel colours had crept in, spectacular flower arrangements, perhaps a little rigid, were placed at strategic corners, and pleasant toilet facilities had been installed.

Howard seldom brought Doreen here. He liked to think of it still as a male sanctuary from domesticity. 'I love my home,' he'd say waggishly to Ken Slater, 'but I love to get away from it too! These women ... sometimes a bit of peace and quiet and sensible conversation is very welcome.'

Ken and Howard had not only been at school together, they now played golf together, and, with their wives, they occasionally made up a foursome on the course. Every year the four went on holiday together to a leisure development in Spain, where they were happily insulated from all things

Spanish, except the hot sun and cheap Spanish wine.

Now Howard ordered himself a pint of best and settled at a small table in the bar to wait for Ken, who was joining him for lunch. Ken would know about New Brooms. He managed the Tourist Information Office in town, though there was precious little tourism in Tresham, and as a result was a mine of information. It was not a job with prestige, nor an impressive salary, but Ken had leaflets on everything. He'd be certain to have one on New Brooms, and be able to update Howard on their reputation.

'Ah, here we are then, boy!' he said, beaming at Ken, who had walked silently into the bar. The very reverse of Howard, Ken was balding, and wore rimless glasses that gave him an unmerited air of studious abstraction. He had left school with Howard when they were fifteen, and worked for the County Council ever since. He too approached retirement, but was hoping to extend his working life by becoming a freelance tourist agent. A certain low cunning and ability to see the way the wind was blowing in any situation involving the Council had stood him in good stead, and he had connections. Although Howard was in a different wealth league from him, on the surface they remained at ease with one another.

'New Brooms?' he said now, as they sat

21

down in the dining room. 'That cleaning business over in Long Farnden? Yes, I know it. Been going for a quite a while. Run by a woman ... now, what was her name? Meade, it is. Louise, or something like that. Why d'you want to know? Some deal you're cooking up?'

Howard laughed. 'Questions, questions,' he said. 'No, it's very simple. Our Edna is leaving, thank God, and we need a new cleaner. New Brooms sounds professional. Might be a good idea. Edna's been off sick more than she's cleaned for us lately. I presume this lot would send a replacement if the regular couldn't come.'

Ken nodded. 'Friend of ours in Long Farnden uses them. I'll see what I can find out.'

'Long Farnden?' Howard frowned. 'Isn't that where the vicarage went up in smoke a while back? Nasty business, that. I hope New Brooms had no part in that!'

They both laughed, and picked up the menu. 'Ah, good,' said Howard. 'Apple pie and custard. Only place in town where you can still get proper Bird's custard. I shall have the roast, then, followed by apple pie.'

'Your usual, then,' said Ken, without the trace of a smile.

Lunch with Howard always put Ken in a bad

mood. He supposed it was Howard's obvious superiority in position and wealth which chafed on a raw spot that had never really healed since they had been a pair of lads at school with similar ambitions and equal skills. In fact, if anything, Ken had been the cleverer of the two. Howard's cunning streak had come in useful at exam time, and he had learned fast how to manipulate friends to his own advantage. That included Ken, of course, whose memory was infinitely better than Howard's. Oh yes, Ken remembered only too well the history exam where he and Howard worked out a hand signal code that supplied Howard with necessary dates and names. He'd been so busy keeping Howard happy that he'd not had time to finish his own paper, and the rotten sod had got better marks.

Then there was a matter of personality. Howard had been a bluff, confident businessman by the age of twenty-five. And then there had been a business to step into, founded by his grandfather and growing with each generation.

Ken walked down the High Street towards the Tourist Office, but stopped suddenly. No, he could not go straight back to his cramped office, where there were never any surprises. He took out his mobile and spoke to his assistant. 'Raging toothache, dear,' he said. 'Got an emergency appointment with

23

the dentist, so I'll take the rest of the day off. Looks like the tooth has to come out, so I shall be in no fit state to work! Back tomorrow, without fail. Cheers.'

He retrieved his car, and drove off, but not to the dentist. He headed out of town towards the pleasant premises of Tresham Gun Club. He had been a member for years, was an excellent shot and had won many competitions. Target shooting was his forte, and he enjoyed superimposing faces of his enemies on the one-dimensional targets in his sights. He boasted to his patient wife Jean that far from diminishing with the passing years, his skill seemed to be ever better.

'Lucky old you,' she had said. 'Such a constructive hobby ... shooting at targets. Some men build cupboards, dig vegetable plots, construct cars from kits, paint their houses. But mine? He shoots at targets, and very good he is too. Wins cups. Has a jolly social life with other shooters. Family days are fun too, with everybody talking about shooting at targets and who is the best. Often it is my Ken!'

'All right, all right,' he had replied. 'I get the message. But we do play golf, too, and you like that, don't you?'

Jean had nodded. 'Especially in the winter,' she'd said, 'when the wind freezes your fingers and feet, and your glasses steam up so you can't see where the little white ball is going. I suppose it is marginally better than lawnmower racing.'

He sighed now, wishing Jean was a little more pleasant about his enthusiasms. Like Doreen, Howard's wife. Nice little woman, that one. Seemed to take pleasure in everything Howard did, and was very cuddly into the bargain.

He parked his car and joined a friend heading for the clubhouse. 'Lovely day,' the friend said.

'Very,' said Ken, his mind elsewhere.

'Taking the day off, or are you on leave?' His friend was also a civil servant, and used the old jargon.

Ken nodded. 'Officially at the dentist,' he said, suddenly grinning. 'How about you?'

'Business trip up north,' said his friend, smiling in return, and together they went in to enjoy an afternoon in complete harmony.

Four

The next day the post was delayed, and Josie finished cleaning the shop early. She wondered if there was time for a quick coffee, but no, the door opened and she moved behind the counter to greet her first customer.

'Morning, Mrs Reading,' she said. She smiled warmly at Bridie Reading, mother of Hazel and fellow member of New Brooms. 'How's the little one today?' Bridie had heaved a three-wheeled pushchair up the shop steps and now proudly leaned over and drew back the cover to reveal her sleeping grandchild.

'Isn't she a poppet!' Josie said. Babies were not much to her liking, though she trusted she would grow to them later on. But she knew what was good for business, and Bridie was a regular customer. Lois and Bridie had been at school together, and seen some hairy patches during their respective marriages. Bridie looked now at Josie, a very attractive young woman, and remembered when she'd been a rebellious teenager. Always loyal to

Lois, Bridie had decided to patronise the village shop more than before, to give Josie a chance of making a success of it.

'What's her name again?' said Josie, weighing out potatoes.

'Elizabeth. Lizzie for short,' said Bridie. 'Hazel named her after her grandmother on my side ... Hazel's grandmother, that is, not Lizzie's ... 'cause that's me!'

Now losing interest rapidly, Josie decided to change the subject. 'Where's Hazel today? Is she back working for Mum?'

'Yes, just started. They're off to Tresham to look at a possible office. Your Mum's hoping to get it going soon, and Hazel might help run it.'

'It'll soon be New Brooms Euro,' said Josie caustically. 'I hope Mum's not overreaching herself.'

Bridie was about to leap to Lois's defence, when the shop door jangled open to reveal Rupert Forsyth, out of breath and red in the face.

'Where's my post?' He elbowed Bridie to one side and slapped his hand on the counter.

'Excuse *me*!' said Bridie. 'I was here first, and I haven't finished my shopping!'

Rupert Forsyth stared at her, as if seeing her for the first time. 'Oh, oh dear,' he said, deflating like a pricked balloon. 'I'm so sorry, my dear. It was just that ... oh dear, I

27

do apologise.'

'S'all right,' Bridie said huffily. 'If you're in a hurry, you can go ahead.'

'No, no. I just wondered what has happened to my post, Josie? I am expecting a very important letter.'

'It came late,' said Josie calmly. 'Strike in Tresham. He's sorting it in the back right now. As soon as Gran gets down here, I'll be out delivering.' She looked at Rupert Forsyth and noticed his hands were shaking and now he had gone very pale. 'Here,' she said. 'Sit down on this stool for a minute. You shouldn't've run so fast at your age.'

For a moment Rupert considered challenging this, but instead perched himself gratefully on the edge of the stool. 'My letters are my business, you see,' he added. 'The wife and I have only the state pension, and without supplementing it we'd have trouble managing.'

Most do, thought Josie. But she nodded and offered him a cup of tea to calm him if he was feeling shaky.

'No, no thanks,' he said. 'Must be getting back. The wife will be worried. We shall see you soon, then, with the post.' He looked at Bridie, and said again, 'So sorry, my dear. Do forgive me.'

'Smarmy bugger,' said Bridie, when he'd left the shop. 'And *what* business, anyway?'

Josie shrugged. She had her own idea of

what was in those letters, but kept it to herself. It was more than her postmistress job was worth to discuss letters with anybody. This did not stop her listening, however, and she looked encouragingly at Bridie.

'If you ask me,' the older woman said, 'from my experience ... letters of that sort – an' he gets a lot, doesn' he? – are up to no good. Plain brown wrapping, an' that. You know what I mean, Josie. That's what most people in the village think, anyway.'

Josie laughed. 'Not my place to guess,' she said lightly. But she knew exactly what Bridie meant, and had come to much the same conclusion herself.

Daisy Forsyth watched her husband walking slowly up the path and sighed. If only he wouldn't lose his rag so easily! He'd always been the same. Calm and reasonable most of the time, but now and then a sudden burst of rage that terrified her. It was the letters, of course. She wished he'd never started the business! But that was years ago, when they were both fairly young and still foolish. She had helped him then, doing all kinds of things that were new and sometimes scary. It had all changed now, but she still helped with the admin, sending out stuff and being a general dogsbody. She laughed at that thought, and relaxed. He'd be fine now, once the storm had passed. Josie Meade would have calmed him down. She was a nice girl, and worked hard. Very like her mother, village people said. Straightforward and honest. You knew where you were with her, even if sometimes she was a bit sharp.

'Hello, dear,' she said, opening the door to her panting husband. 'Come and sit down and have a nice cup of tea. Just made. Did you sort it out?'

Rupert collapsed on to the sofa. 'Yep,' he said. 'I made it quite clear we required our post first thing in the morning. A strike at Tresham, apparently. Fellers don't know when they're well off,' he added, and took his tea. 'Sugared?' he said, eyebrows lifted.

'Yes dear,' she answered. 'Just as you like it.'

Five

Lois drew up outside the To Let sign in Sebastopol Street, and turned off the engine.

'That's one plus, anyway,' said Hazel, 'you can park outside without having to pay a fortune.'

'You get what you pay for,' said Lois. 'This is not exactly a town centre site, is it? Still, you're right. It could be a point in its favour.' She looked at the dingy shopfront, with its fly-blown window and peeling paint. 'Not too promising, is it?' she said.

'Let's get out, Mrs M,' Hazel said. 'Walk around a bit. Get a feel of the area. After all, you don't want a scruffy image for a cleaning business.' She was not at all sure at first sight. The street was narrow and quiet, with long terraces of red-brick Victorian buildings either side. Hazel knew Tresham very well, since at one time she had worked with the police as an expert – from personal experience – on the never-ending war against drugs. This part of town was known for being the haunt of dodgy dealers, but it had been cleaned up and the houses were being bought and restored by young couples with not much money but high ambitions.

The shop to let had sold electrical supplies, but had clearly gone out of business some time ago. Lois and Hazel peered through into an interior littered with lengths of cable and ancient electric fires. 'Brought in for repairs, I expect,' said Hazel. Lois, whose Derek would have shuddered at the sight of these dangerous objects, replied that they'd need a skip for that lot.

'Hazel Reading!' A loud voice interrupted their gloomy thoughts, and Hazel turned to see a girl with a pushchair grinning broadly at her. 'It is, isn't it?' the girl continued.

'God, I haven't seen you since school!'

Hazel stared, and then gave an answering smile of recognition. 'Maureen! Fancy seeing you! D'you live round here? And is this...?'

'Robert,' the girl said. 'Six months old and a holy terror. Yep, I live next door to the shop. You married?'

Hazel nodded. 'Hazel Thornbull now,' she said.

'Blimey!' said the girl. 'Very rural!'

After this, Lois walked tactfully away, and let them get on with reminiscing. She was expecting the estate agent to meet her, and glanced about for a sign of him. She looked at her watch. She had deliberately arrived early, but now he should be here. A small, jazzy car approached and pulled up behind Lois's van.

'Mrs Meade?' The agent was young and confident. 'Very pleased to meet you,' he said, shaking her hand vigorously. Lois nodded, and said she didn't have too much time, so could they please get on with it.

Hazel heard this, and parted from her friend with promises to keep in touch. 'She lives next door,' she muttered to Lois. 'Could be useful.'

Lois's spirits did not rise as they picked their way through the shop to the 'excellent facilities' – even the agent had difficulty making this sound convincing – at the rear.

A small storeroom and disgusting toilet occupied the rest of the ground floor, and up a narrow stairway they came to a largish front room with a boxroom behind. A window, so dirty that Lois had to rub a patch with old newspaper in order to see out, looked over a small backyard and behind that a derelict warehouse.

'It's a dump,' she said flatly to the estate agent. 'A real dump. You're asking far too much rent, and I wouldn't dream of paying it. You have wasted my time showing me this place, and I'll be trying another agent in town.' She marched down the stairs and out to the shop. 'Come on, Hazel,' she said. 'Let's go.'

Hazel frowned. She was surprised. Her first impression had changed. Surely a good clean-out and new paint throughout would make a world of difference. And it was not a bad position, on the corner of crossroads and visible from all sides. With a good sign up, it could be not half bad. Then she saw Lois looking at her, and knew she was up to something. 'Right,' she said. 'I reckon we should try that new lot in the Market Square.'

'Wait, wait, wait!' spluttered the young agent. 'Let's just talk about this one. I agree with you – though I shouldn't – that it looks a dump now. But it could be fixed to look good. This obviously means expenditure for you, but I think I can promise you some accommodation on the rent.'

'You mean I can have it cheaper,' said Lois, coming to the point. 'How cheap?'

The agent named a figure, and Lois shook her head sadly at Hazel. 'Shall we go?' she said.

This galvanised the agent, and he blurted out, 'Well, Mrs Meade, what would you consider a fair rent?' He knew only too well that this property had been hanging about on the market for quite a while, and he could see a potential customer slipping rapidly out of his grasp. Finally they reached a compromise that Lois would accept. 'If,' she added, 'if I decide to take it ... I'll let you know tomorrow.'

'We'll hold it for you until then,' the young man said, sighing with relief.

'Queuing up for it, are they?' said Lois lightly, and she and Hazel left him standing on the pavement as they drove off in high spirits.

'Tell me about your friend Maureen.' Lois could see Hazel was bursting with news. 'She says the whole place is designated for improvement,' she said. 'The new ring road'll make it one of them desirable areas. That old warehouse at the back will be a new leisure centre, and it's all goin' to be landscaped and whatnot.'

Lois said, 'We got a bargain, then, d'you

reckon?' The agent had told her all this on the phone, and she'd been sceptical. She knew about Council plans, she'd said. Might never happen. But she was not about to spoil Hazel's enthusiasm. She smiled at her. 'Fancy working there, then?' she added.

Hazel nodded. *'And,* what's more, Maureen said she'd baby-mind for me when Mum's working and can't help. So what a piece of luck, hey?'

They walked out into the quiet street. 'Not many casual passers-by,' said Hazel.

'Won't matter to us,' said Lois. 'At least they can park outside. Anyway, there's another shop over there.'

'What, that one with the macs? Looks dodgy to me. You name it, they stock it. What d'you think, Mrs M?' Laughing, and in celebratory mood, the two of them set off for the supermarket and bought a bottle of champagne – on offer – to share with the team.

The business of the meeting done, Lois said she had an announcement. She looked at them sitting in a semi-circle. Old friends and loyal team members. Sheila Stratford, farm worker's wife and one of her originals, and solid as a rock. Enid Abrahams, quiet and mouse-like, but with a core of steel that she'd needed not so long ago. Bridie and Hazel, who she'd known for ever. Bill, her stalwart cleaner cum vet's assistant. And Sharon, blonde and cheerful, with not much sense but a willing learner. With several occasionals, they were her business as well as her closest friends. For once, Lois felt almost sentimental and was annoyed to find her eyes misting over. She prided herself on a cool, practical approach, and it wouldn't do to let them see her weaken.

'You know we're doing pretty well now,' she said firmly. 'And I've decided we'll have a proper office in town. It'll be good for business, somewhere where people can drop in and discuss their requirements. And we'll feel more professional, all of us. Hazel's going to work part-time there, and I'll do the rest. Any questions?'

There was a moment's silence, and then Enid said quietly, 'What a good idea, Mrs M. And where will our office be?'

Lois told them, admitting that at the moment it was a wreck. 'But Derek and his mates'll see to that in no time,' she added.

'I can see it now,' said Hazel dreamily, 'with New Brooms over the door in gold letters, and me sitting at my desk with a big smile for customers comin' in...'

'What about Lizzie?' said Bridie, looking worried. This was going to take more of Hazel's time than she'd bargained for. But when she heard about Maureen living next door, and Hazel's plan to take her up on her baby-minding offer, she relaxed. They were all talking together, and excitement was in the air.

Lois stood up and went to the door. 'Gran!' she yelled. 'You can bring it in now!'

As they stood and toasted the new office, Josie appeared at the door. 'Just popped in to see Gran,' she said, nodding at the assembled group. 'Blimey, what're you lot up to?' she added.

There was a thimbleful left in the bottle, and Josie drained it and smiled. 'Makes up for being in the doghouse with old Rupert,' she said. 'Better get going now. Post was late and I'm just delivering. He blew his top when he didn't get his bumper pack first thing.'

'Not surprised,' said Bill quietly. 'He would not want them drifting about, maybe getting lost. Not old Rupert. Not those letters.'

Six

'She's coming at five o'clock tomorrow, dear. Will you be here?'

Howard and Doreen Jenkinson sat in their pleasant sitting room, drinking coffee in the cool of the evening. The French windows were open to their immaculately groomed garden, and the liquid song of a blackbird floated in on cue.

'Depends,' said Howard. 'There's the tournament tomorrow, and if I do well I might still be at the club. Ken and me did quite well last year, so we're hoping for great things.'

'I'm sure you'll win it, dear,' Doreen said comfortably. 'Anyway, I'm quite capable of interviewing a cleaner on my own.'

'Not necessarily the cleaner you'll be getting,' Howard warned. 'Mrs Meade is the boss. She'll assess your requirements and choose the best cleaner for the job.'

'Crikey!' said Doreen. 'Chars are getting a bit uppity, aren't they? I don't want a business plan. I need a reliable woman who works hard, doesn't talk too much, and is willing to get down on her hands and knees if there's a call for it.'

Howard stood up and stretched. 'Just going up to my den for half an hour or so,' he said. 'Oh, and by the way,' he added. 'Make sure this woman knows nobody goes in to clean my den. I do it myself as always. Don't forget, Doreen!'

'You keep it locked anyway, Howard,' Doreen said quietly to his retreating back.

'A *man*?' said Doreen next day. She had decided to interview Mrs Meade in her kitchen. Start as we mean to go on, Doreen had decided. Now she looked at the confident, attractive woman sitting on the other side of the table, and repeated, 'A man to come and clean for me? Good gracious, I can't have that. What would Howard say?'

Lois smiled patiently. 'I don't know, Mrs Jenkinson. It isn't all that unusual these days. Bill has worked for me for quite a while, and has always given satisfaction. He's the son of a farmer in Yorkshire, and as well as working for me, he helps out at the vets. There's nothing odd about Bill.'

But Doreen frowned. 'Is there no woman who could come?' she said.

'Certainly,' Lois said, realising she was up against a person used to having her own way. 'But perhaps you'd like to give Bill a try? Then we could send someone else if you

weren't happy with him. Anyway,' she added, getting to her feet, 'why don't you talk to
your husband about it, and give me a ring
tomorrow? I have some very experienced
women on my team, and there'd be no
problem in sending one of them.'

'Very experienced?' said Doreen. 'In what
way? Surely it doesn't take much experience
to do a bit of dusting and hoovering. We
don't make a lot of mess, just the two of us.'

Lois looked at her watch. 'We take our
cleaning very seriously, Mrs Jenkinson, and
our clients appreciate that. I'm sure you'll
find we do a good job. Our aim is to make
you happy. After all, it's your home and you
live in it. No,' she added, 'don't disturb
yourself. I'll see myself out, and look forward
to hearing from you tomorrow.'

'Oh, no, I'll see you to the door,' Doreen
said, hastily following her out of the kitchen.
'And there was one other point – an
important point. My husband does not like
anyone going into his den. Even me! He
keeps it locked, as he has important papers
in there. He cleans it himself, so he knows
nothing will be disturbed.'

Does he now, thought Lois, but she nodded and said, 'Fine. We'll remember that.
Hear from you tomorrow then,' she smiled,
and walked briskly out to her van.

On her way home, she called in to see Bill.
He had just returned from his least favourite

40

job at Farnden Hall, and was making strong tea for himself and his long-time partner, Rebecca.

'I hope I'm not interrupting,' said Lois, accepting a cup of Bill's brew. 'Just thought I'd let you know that you'll be cleaning for the Mayor and his lady wife as from next week.'

'Wow!' said Bill. 'They don't come any grander in Tresham. Old Howard Jenkinson? I've heard he's a wheeler-dealer and one to beware of. A real Treshamite of the old school. Tough and unforgiving. Charming on the surface, and ready to crucify you if necessary.'

'Where'd'you hear that?' Rebecca said. She taught in Waltonby village school, and was not well up in town gossip.

'These things get around,' said Bill. 'We hear all sorts in the vets' waiting room. Apparently the Jenkinsons used to breed those poor little squashed-face dogs, and were tight as ticks when our bills were sent. Always quibbled. Wanted discounts. You know the sort, Mrs M.'

Lois smiled. 'We'll be ready for 'em, then,' she said. 'Mrs J has to clear it with her husband – she's not at all sure about having a male cleaner. You know, the usual thing. But I think it'll be all right. If not, I'll send Enid.' She bravely downed the dark orange tea, and drove off. Sounds like we've got awkward

41

sods with the Jenkinsons, she thought. Still, it would be worth keeping them sweet. They know everybody in Tresham, and everybody knows them.

Seven

The man from the Council Planning Department knocked on the Forsyths' door and waited. He quickly checked that he had all the papers concerned with the application, and put on his serious face. Almost all applications, if not turned down in this conservation village, had to be modified, and he believed in making it quite clear that whatever the applicant was planning, it was not just a case of what suited them, but how it affected others in the village, their close neighbours, and the Council's own overall plans for the area.

Unless, of course, it was a plan for development by the Council itself, like the school extension in Waltonby. There, in spite of strong local protests, they had cheerfully felled a perfectly healthy hundred-year-old sycamore which had sheltered generations of schoolchildren from sun and rain in the school playground. This was to make way for a couple of extra classrooms, because local elections were coming up, and money was made available suddenly for school building extension. Rebecca Rogers had watched the tree come down from her classroom window, and felt sick, as if observing a particularly brutal murder. One of her small students had tucked her hand in Rebecca's, sensing her distress. Bill had stood at the playground railings, taking before and after photographs, and the butchered stump haunted Rebecca's dreams for days afterwards.

None of this had made any impression on the Council official standing at Rupert Forsyth's door, and he had half a dozen other applications to see to in his document case. Uppermost in his mind was the worrying fact that it was his wedding anniversary and he had forgotten to buy his wife a present.

'Good morning,' he said briskly, as Daisy Forsyth opened the door. 'County Planning Office, Mr Collins.'

'Oh, yes,' said Daisy quickly. Rupert was upstairs in the bathroom, but she ushered Mr Collins into the sitting room and went off to make coffee. Mr Collins looked around, then walked over to the windows overlooking the garden. The application was for an extension – quite substantial – and he checked the intended use again. 'Seating area, cloakroom and boot room.' Boot room? He hadn't encountered this before.

'You learn something new every day in this job, Mrs Forsyth,' he said accusingly. 'What on earth is a boot room?'

Rupert appeared and said firmly, 'Where we put our boots, Wellington and walking, muddy and wet, also umbrellas, walking-sticks, folding garden chairs, sunshades—'

'All right, all right,' said Mr Collins. 'I get it. Now, let's have a look at the plans.' He walked to a drop-leaf table by the wall, and Daisy rushed to open it up. The plans were spread out, and the two men pored over them.

'Is this supposed to be a sort of conser-vatory seating area?' Mr Collins asked. 'And if so, why in brick and with very few win-dows? Why not have a perfectly good prefab, wooden framed job in a style harmonising with the house? You're much more likely to get permission.'

Silence. Daisy looked nervously at Rupert, praying that he wouldn't have one of his explosions.

'Ah,' he said calmly. 'Now, Mr Collins...' He spoke slowly, as if to a dim child. 'If I had wanted an off-the-peg, gimcrack conserva-tory, with flimsy Victorian trimmings, I would have asked for one. This is an extension carefully thought out to meet our requirements, mine and the wife's, and we are hoping the Planning Department will approve it as such. Of course, if there are small adjustments suggested, then we shall be only too happy to co-operate.'

He beamed good-humouredly at Mr Collins, who did not smile back. We've got a right one here, he thought to himself. Well, we'll see just how happily Mr and Mrs Forsyth co-operate when they get the Council's decision!

Secure in the knowledge that his report and recommendations were all-powerful, he left the house and immediately dismissed the Forsyths from his mind. He remembered the village shop, and pulled up in the forlorn hope that it would offer something suitable for his wife.

Nothing in Long Farnden went unobserved. Josie had seen Mr Collins's car arrive outside the Forsyths as she cycled back from delivering. Now he had parked outside the shop and was coming up the steps. A strange car. Who was he, then? And what did he want with the Forsyths? These thoughts were routine in the village. Everybody had them, and the answers fed the network of information that kept the gossips going.

'Morning! Can I help you?' Josie was always cheerful.

Blimey, thought Lois, coming in behind

Mr Collins. Can this really be our Josie, the sulky teenager who caused us so much trouble? She waited discreetly until he had wandered round the shelves, not seeming to know what he was looking for.

'I don't suppose you have any ... er ... any special chocolates, flowers, or...'

'A present?' said Josie. 'For your wife?' Oops, she thought. Is that a step too far?

But the man nodded. 'In the doghouse,' he said, with the trace of a smile.

'Right,' said Josie briskly. 'You're in luck. I can just hear the flower van out the back, so there'll be fresh flowers. And over here...' She walked across the shop to shelves in the corner. 'Over here we have our Swiss chocolates. We put them away from the window. First mistake I made,' she added chattily. 'I put some new stock on the front shelves so's people would see them, and the afternoon sun melted the lot.'

When Mr Collins had paid and was about to leave looking infinitely more cheerful than when he came in, Josie asked lightly, 'Are you a stranger round here? Need any directions?'

Mr Collins gave a gravelly laugh and shook his head. 'No, I'm from Tresham. Been to see about plans for an extension.' It was said with a purpose. You never knew what useful information would result from a word in the right place.

'Oh, you mean the Forsyths,' said Josie cheerfully. 'Yeah, we know about that. Looks quite a good idea, for him and his letters! Needs a new building to house that lot!'

'Letters?' said Mr Collins, his nose twitching like a rat's. Was this a business Rupert Forsyth was intending to conduct from his home? If so, there would be regulations to consider. Regulations were meat and drink to Mr Collins.

'Oh, just a joke,' said Josie hastily, seeing exactly which way the wind was blowing. 'Now, if you'll excuse me, I must see to the flower man. You had the pick of the lot! I hope your wife's pleased. Have a nice day.' And she disappeared from Mr Collins's prying eyes.

He reluctantly left the shop and climbed into his car, but did not start the engine straight away. Letters, eh? Maybe he should go back and have another word with the Forsyths, just to make sure. Then he looked at his watch. Oh Lord, he'd only just get back in time to take his wife out to lunch. He couldn't risk two scenes in one day. There'd be time later to see the Forsyths, he decided, and drove off towards Tresham and humble pie.

Eight

Bill's car crunched slowly up the curving drive to the Jenkinsons' house, and parked round the back, as instructed. He looked at his watch. Nine o'clock on the dot. Mrs M was very particular about punctuality, and he got out and walked swiftly to the back door.

'Good morning, Mrs Jenkinson,' he said cheerfully. 'Lovely morning.'

Doreen looked at him suspiciously. 'Are you from New Brooms?' she said.

'Yes, that's me, Bill Stockbridge. How d'you do.' He extended his hand and shook her reluctant one.

'I wasn't expecting...' Her voice tailed off.

'Weren't expecting a bloke? Surely Mrs M told you?' Bill's voice was light and unfussed. He was used to this kind of reception at his first visit, and prided himself on putting the client at ease in no time at all.

'No, no,' she said. 'You don't look like what I was expecting, I suppose,' she added lamely.

Bill laughed heartily. 'I'm just a Yorkshire

farmer's son,' he replied. 'And I've got a steady girlfriend, who's used to me going cleaning. I love it, Mrs Jenkinson, and I can see you love your home. You can trust me with it, that's for sure. Now, where would you like me to start?'

Doreen hesitated. She was not at all sure about this strongly-built young man with a determined chin and disarming smile. He was not at all what she had been expecting. So what *had* she been expecting? Well, she thought, leading him through to the kitchen, perhaps a gentle, sensitive lad with delicate hands and ... and ... well, somebody not quite so *masculine*.

Doreen opened a cupboard door and said, 'Look, there are all the things. Our last cleaner kept it in a bit of a muddle, I'm afraid, but seemed to know where to find things.'

'Don't worry about that,' Bill assured her. 'We bring our own equipment and supplies. All you need to do, Mrs Jenkinson, is show me round the house, say if there's any routine you'd like me to fit in with, and then relax. Make a coffee, walk the dog, phone a friend, go shopping ... whatever. I'm here to make life easier for you, not to give you a headache.'

This was a spiel he had worked on, and had had very caustic comments when he'd tried it out on Rebecca. Still, it worked with most people, and as Doreen gave him the conducted tour, he noticed her visibly relaxing, and soon she was showing him photographs of her grandchildren.

'This is my daughter,' she said. 'She lives locally, and has two boys. Look, this is Sam and this is George. Aren't they lovely?'

Bill peered closely. Two perfectly ordinary, nice-looking lads. 'How old? Ten and eight?' he asked.

Doreen nodded delightedly. 'How clever! Exactly right. Well, they're our pride and joy, of course. Very fond of their grandfather, and he spends hours with Sam over his stamp album. Not many boys these days are interested in stamps, but Sam is very keen. Howard saves up interesting ones for him.'

'How wonderful,' said Bill, walking purposefully on. 'Now, I must get started, otherwise you won't get your money's worth.'

This was enough to send Doreen smartly ahead of him, up the stairs and towards a closed door off the landing. 'First of all,' she said, remembering Howard's stern strictures before he left for the Town Hall. 'This is my husband's study, and nobody but him is allowed in it. Not even me,' she added sourly.

'Ah yes,' Bill said in an even tone. 'Mrs Meade told me about that. You can trust me absolutely.' Though if I catch him in there, he thought to himself, I shall probably

50

blunder in, because forbidden doors are irresistible to the curious. What could a retired timber merchant have in there that made him so anxious to keep it secret?

They continued around the bedrooms and bathrooms, and Bill admired everything and saw that Doreen was now completely happy with him. Right then, that was the first hurdle crossed. The next would be to persuade her that he knew best. Most women had their own ways of cleaning, but New Brooms had its own. The team was trained, and they all stuck to what they had been taught.

At coffee break time Doreen called Bill into the kitchen. 'Sit down,' she said, and he told her that he was allowed five minutes only. 'Plenty of time, Mrs M says, to drink a coffee and get back to work.'

Doreen raised her eyebrows. She'd been looking forward to a bit of a chat with this polite chap, to find out some more about him. His job with the vets, his girlfriend, family up North. All that. Ah well, he'd settle into the job, and then they'd have some good chats later on.

Bill was on his feet on the dot of five minutes, just as Howard let himself in through the front door. The big man jangled his keys in his pocket and marched through to the kitchen. 'Morning,' he said dismissively to Bill. 'Coffee fresh, Doreen?' he added, turning his back on Bill.

And good morning to you, too, thought Bill, as he climbed the stairs and started to clean an already immaculate bathroom.

'You're back early,' Doreen said, pouring out coffee and handing Howard the biscuit tin.

'Jean sent me home. Nothing for me to do, she said. But I've brought some papers to attend to, so I'll take the coffee upstairs. Where's that bloke got to?'

'Landing and stairs next, he said.' Doreen looked closely at Howard. What was he up to? He never came home early, preferring to stay in the Mayor's Parlour and spend the morning fixing up games of golf, checking the stock market, looking in on various offices and obstructing work in progress. He was known for being one of the most 'hands-on' mayors that Tresham could remember. Most of the Town Hall staff counted the months to the end of his term of office.

'You remembered to tell him, Doreen!'

'Course I did. For heavens' sake, Howard, anyone would think you've got a body in there!'

'Don't be ridiculous,' he snapped. 'A man can have a bit of privacy without being constantly got at by his wife, I hope! I'll be up there 'til lunchtime.'

He left the kitchen in a whirlwind of self-righteousness, and Doreen heard him fling a couple of words at Bill before slamming the door of his den behind him. She sighed, and picked up a package that had come in the post. Addressed to Howard, but no clues as to what it was or where it came from. Oh well, it could wait. She was damned if she was going to trail upstairs like some servant. All the euphoria engendered by nice Bill had evaporated, and she decided to call her daughter and fix up a shopping trip. That would have the advantage of annoying Howard on two fronts – wasting telephone time, and spending money on fripperies. His favourite word, that. Fripperies, fripperies, said Doreen to herself, and felt a little cheered.

Nine

Some days later, Lois took Derek over to see the shop, and he cast a professional eye. 'Needs re-wiring,' he said. 'Shouldn't be too bad. Then me and the lads can redecorate throughout.' The lads were Derek's fellow Tresham United supporters, who met regularly at Farnden pub, and supported not only the team but each other as well. 'We'll go through this dump like a dose of salts,' he said reassuringly to Lois. Privately he was not at all sure it was a good idea, but he trusted Lois's judgement, and was very sure that anything that kept her away from Inspector Cowgill and dangerous sleuthing *was* a good idea.

They went cautiously upstairs, with Lois sniffing hard. 'Somethin's died in here,' she said. 'Must be a rat in a cupboard.'

'Leave it to us,' said Derek, opening a window overlooking the street. 'Let in some air. Soon sweeten it up.'

Lois moved beside him and peered out. 'That shop over there,' she said. 'The one opposite. Look, it's got somebody goin' in and out. So people do come to this part of town.'

Derek grinned. 'Yeah, well,' he said. 'That ain't just rainwear they sell, m'duck.'

'I weren't born yesterday,' retorted Lois. 'And it doesn't bother me. Many a marriage has bin saved by them kind of shops.'

Derek laughed loudly. 'Right you are!' he said. 'Reckon I should call in on me way home?'

Lois turned on him. 'If you think,' she said, 'that I'm going to dress up as a maid in frilly cap and apron—'

'—and black fishnet tights,' chipped in Derek, grabbing her round the waist. He kissed her roundly, and a minute or two later

54

they turned again to the window. A young man was standing in the dark doorway of the shop, staring up at them. As they watched, he smiled and waved.

'Cheeky devil!' said Lois.

But Derek said, 'Can't see him very well, but there's something ... haven't we seen him before somewhere? Isn't it old Rupert Forsyth's son?' Then he waved back and yelled out of the window, 'See yer later, mate,' and started off down the stairs with a huffy Lois following. After they'd been out at the back of the shop, and Derek had investigated the unsavoury outbuildings and a narrow yard, Lois said she reckoned they'd earned a drink. They locked the shop door behind them and walked towards the van. Lois suddenly stopped dead. A familiar dark-coloured car had drawn up outside the rainwear shop, and a man got out. He looked across and remained on the pavement for a second or two. Then he crossed the road, and Lois frowned. 'What are you doing here?' she said. 'Not following me, I hope.' Derek hung back, his face thunderous.

'Just thought I'd pass the time of day,' said Detective Inspector Cowgill smoothly. 'Morning, Derek. And no, Lois, I'm not following you. Just a regular call at the shop opposite.'

Lois pounced. 'Never've thought it! *You* of all people!'

Hunter Cowgill did not smile. 'In the line of duty, Lois,' he said firmly, and added, 'When you move in, it'll be very handy if I have a job or two for you.'

'She'll be much too busy,' snapped Derek. 'Come on, Lois, we're late already.' He took her arm and headed for her van.

'No need to pull,' said Lois irritably. 'And anyway,' she muttered, 'how did Cowgill know I was taking that shop?'

'Snoopin' is his job. Just ignore him,' Derek advised, with little hope of Lois taking any notice.

Hunter Cowgill watched them drive off and allowed himself a small smile. Yes! – what a piece of luck Lois being so handy. He walked into Rain or Shine and greeted the owner. 'Morning, Fergus,' he said. 'What've you got for me this week?'

Upstairs, in the tiny back room of the Forsyths' house, Rupert sat at his desk opening letters. All around him were boxes stuffed to the gills with invoices, old catalogues, packs of photographs yellowing at the edges, newer piles of videos and books. He sorted the letters into small heaps and sighed. That bloke from the Council hadn't been very forthcoming. He hadn't given them any reason to hope – or otherwise, come to that. It was a difficult one, Rupert reflected. He needed extra space urgently, and no doubt could find somewhere to rent in the village. But security and confidentiality were essential to his business, and he could not trust anyone but himself and Daisy to have access to this lot. He looked around. This small room represented years of building up connections, enlisting outworkers, finding storage space and a shop in town when they moved from London – generally oiling the wheels of a business that had been a nice little earner. They had to keep up with the times, of course. What with the internet, and more and more retail outlets appearing, he had to think of new ways of marketing. Daisy was good at that. She had ideas that he would never think of, never in a million years! Even at her age!

'Rupert!' Daisy's voice reminded him they were going shopping in Tresham. He stacked the now empty envelopes in a small pile and put them together in a plastic bag. He could drop them in to Howard Jenkinson's secretary whilst they were in town. Some interesting stamps this morning, some from foreign parts. Old Jenkinson's grandson would be pleased. Whistling softly to himself, he shut and locked the door, and went downstairs.

That evening, in the Jenkinsons' large and well-tended garden, Howard felt at peace with the world as he stood by the big pond feeding his goldfish. 'All well, dear?' said

Doreen, coming up and taking his arm. 'How's the new shubunkin?'

'Fine, of course, Doreen,' Howard replied. He extended a fine mesh net across the water and scooped up a dead leaf that had had the temerity to land on the sparkling surface. 'I can never understand,' he continued firmly, 'why other people have such trouble with ponds. Take Ken. His wife gave him one of those pond liners – rigid things – and it's only the size of a baby bath. You'd think he could manage that. But no, the water's like green soup, and every week there's a bloated body floating on the surface. He's been through more shubunkins than you've had hot dinners!'

'I've never eaten a shubunkin,' said Doreen, with a perfectly straight face. She liked Howard to think she was stupid. Over the years of their marriage she had found it a useful role to play, encouraging him to be protective and indulgent ... well, as indulgent as he could ever be. She smiled to herself. 'Perhaps it's too small. Not suitable for fish ... maybe he should just have plants, then he'd not have any more bloated bodies ... ugh! I hope he gives them a decent burial.'

'Gives 'em to the cat,' said Howard with a smirk.

'Oh dear!' Doreen's mock concern fooled Howard once again. 'I always did think Ken Slater had no heart.' Except when he spotted me in me nightie early one morning, she thought, then his heart was going fast enough. That had been the start of it...

They strolled arm-in-arm around the garden, admiring Howard's flower borders and not mentioning the gardener who came in every week and tackled the tough jobs. 'Time for drinky-poos?' Doreen said, and they walked through the French windows and into the sitting room. Howard opened the drinks cupboard and inspected a crystal glass closely. It passed inspection, and Doreen said, 'Everything's really clean in the house now, dear. Such a relief having Bill. Can't fault him. Are you sure you wouldn't like him to give a quick dust round your den? He's absolutely trustworthy, I'm sure.'

Howard rounded on her. 'How many more times, Doreen? Nobody, nobody at all, is to go in my den. Very confidential papers in there, and it's all organised so I know exactly where to find everything. On no account is Bill whatever-his-name-is to enter that room!'

'No need to shout, dear,' said Doreen comfortably. 'Just a small one tonight, please. I had lunch with our lovely daughter, and I'm afraid we got a bit giggly. Now—' she added, picking up a programme paper, '—what's on the telly for our delight tonight?'

'You choose,' Howard said. 'I'll be upstairs

for a bit. Oh, and by the way, I've got some more stamps for Sam. Jean had them ready for me in the office. Interesting ones, I think.'

'Where does she get them from?' Doreen said curiously. She'd always known about Jean and Howard, but had thought the best policy would be to say nothing. It had worked with all the others.

'Goodness knows,' said Howard carelessly. He had warned Forsyth that there was to be no discoverable connection between them. 'She's got a big family. All around the world. She's always telling me news of far flung cousins, but it goes in one ear and out the other – you know me, Doreen.'

'Yes dear,' she replied, 'I know you. Um, perhaps I'll just have one more tiny drink, after all.'

Good old Doreen, thought Howard, and poured her a large one.

Ten

At the Town Hall, Jean Slater settled wearily into her chair and looked over the tidy desk. It had been a hectic weekend, with visitors staying and endless cooking of food their children wouldn't eat. Still, there was nothing much to do this morning. Howard had said he would not be in today, but would telephone her to make sure he had the details right for his visit to a school with a good cultural mix. She had primed him well, but was still uneasy about what he might say off the cuff. Sometimes, in private, he still referred to 'darkies', and 'wogs', but she was hopeful that he had enough instinct for self-preservation to suppress the prejudices of his youth.

She opened a folder and took out a used envelope. It was one of the bunch that Rupert Forsyth had brought in yesterday. As usual, she had cut off all the stamps and disposed of the envelopes, but this one she had kept back. The connection between Forsyth and Howard was supposed to be a secret, even from her, but over the years

61

Howard had surrounded himself with secrets, and she knew the truth of most of them. His world was like that, and she accepted it. She was well aware of the nature of Rupert Forsyth's business, and looked at the envelope again, unable to believe that anyone would be so stupid. But yes, there it was, the address of the sender written in small letters on the reverse side of the envelope. Rupert could not have noticed it, otherwise she was sure he would not have brought it. The handwriting was not all that clear, having been smudged by heavy rain at some stage in its journey from the north, so perhaps he'd thought it was part of the post mark.

She reached for her handy magnifying glass, used for referring to the Tresham street map when Howard had official calls to make. Now it was clearer. N.F. Stevenson, 11, Dale Court, Colcombe, Manchester. Good grief! Jean closed her eyes and thought about Norman. He had been one of the directors of the timber business and had moved up to Manchester under some sort of cloud. He was now in charge of the yard there. She was sure he lived in the suburb of Colcombe. Yes, that was it. Norman Stevenson. She'd liked him well enough, but he and Howard had had a major row. Ah well, she'd better not let Howard see it. She was about to return the envelope to the folder when a knock at the door surprised her. She was usually left undisturbed when Howard was not in. 'Come in,' she said. The door opened gently, admitting Doreen Jenkinson, Lady Mayoress, carrying an expensive-looking dress-shop carrier bag.

'Doreen! How nice. Come on in and have a cup of coffee.'

The two women were friends, in spite of knowing about former betrayals. Neither fully trusted the other. There were still secrets carefully guarded and subjects which were tacitly avoided. 'I've been shopping,' Doreen said, 'and I knew Howard wouldn't be here, so thought I'd drop in and show you.'

'Oh, Doreen, that's lovely! Did it cost the earth? That colour really suits you.' Jean's enthusiasm was genuine. She knew Howard was a stingy old sod, and admired Doreen for her determination and wiliness in getting more or less what she wanted out of him. But this time, Doreen was having second thoughts. She had never before spent so much money on a dress, and was uncomfortably aware that the balance in her account would not cover it. Howard would not allow her to have credit cards, and she'd always seen the sense of this. She earned nothing, and was totally reliant on the allowance he gave her. Credit cards would be too much of a temptation. But this morning she had lost her head. Perhaps it was something to do with Bill, who'd arrived before she left. Silly to blame it on her cleaner! But he treated her like a person of importance, and Howard never had.

'Are you really sure, Jean?' she said. 'Is it worth risking Howard's wrath? I shall have to ask him for some extra this month...'

Jean looked at her. 'Doreen,' she said patiently, as if to a child, 'your Howard is rich. You have looked after him all these years, given him children, a comfortable, well-run home, and turned a blind eye when necessary.' Here she paused, wondering if she had gone too far.

But Doreen smiled straight at her, and said, 'Yes, Jean, I have done all those things. And so have you, for Ken, but here you are earning your own money. I've never done that.'

'No, but Howard wouldn't have wanted it. You know that. So now you deserve a few treats. He can afford it. And I know you'll get round him! Go for it!'

She picked up the phone to order coffee but could get no reply, and so said she'd fetch some for them both. 'Back in a jiff,' she said smiling, and left the room.

Doreen put the dress back into the bag, and looked around. This was where Howard and Jean had had their tête-à-têtes, exchanged endearments, planned assignations.

Oh well, good luck to them, she thought cheerfully. I had some good times with Ken, too.

She looked at Jean's neat desk, and idly picked up the empty envelope left there. She turned it over in her hands, and noted it was addressed to somebody called Rupert Forsyth in Sebastopol Street. Wasn't that where Mrs Meade had her office?

She turned the envelope over in her hands, and read the smudged name and address on the back. She couldn't decipher the name, but the town was vaguely familiar. Colcombe, perhaps. That was where Howard's one-time fellow director had been sent, wasn't it? The one he'd quarrelled with? He'd been a bit of a pest for a while. She smiled. Such a long time ago. But she remembered the suburb of Manchester he had moved to. How odd! She heard Jean's footsteps approaching, and a well-developed suspicion of anything odd to do with Howard made her slip the envelope into her handbag and walk quickly to look out of the window.

'Here we are then,' Jean said. 'I got us some doughnuts, too ... and don't look like that! Weight-watching is nothing to us now. Here, help yourself.'

The sun came out from behind heavy clouds, and shone straight into Jean's office, lighting up the two women delicately making short work of the doughnuts, and smiling happily at each other. It was not until Doreen had gone that Jean remembered the envelope. She hunted around for a while, and then her telephone rang. It was Howard, and he was stuck in traffic. 'Get a message to that old folks' home, Jean,' he said. 'I shall be a bit late. Say all the right things, as always. See you later.'

By the time she had smoothed down ruffled feathers at the retirement home, the empty envelope had gone completely from her mind. At home, much later, she remembered it, and shrugged. The cleaner would put it in the bin. It didn't really matter.

Eleven

It was Saturday, half-day for Fergus Forsyth, who was consequently in a good mood. He looked out from behind the shiny raincoats at the derelict shop over the road and smiled. His father, Rupert, had told him that a Farnden woman who ran a cleaning business had taken the shop as an office. A couple of burly blokes had carried in boxes of tools and large tins of paint, and had opened all the windows wide.

It could only be a good thing, he reflected. This part of town was very quiet, and had been the attraction for Dad. Customers were happy to call in with little fear of being spotted. But for Fergus the time passed slowly when there were no customers. Dad insisted on doing all the paperwork, and kept all records, addresses, and anything confidential, at home in his small workroom. Fergus had disagreed with Rupert over extending the Farnden house. Why couldn't they move all the paperwork to the shop? They could make sure it was secure, with new locks and stuff. But Dad was adamant, saying he would have it all where he could keep a constant eye on it. Fergus had argued that he could help out with admin – answering letters, organising orders etc – while the shop was empty. But Dad wouldn't have it. Still, with a new business opposite, things should liven up a lot. Fergus had noticed the two women arriving in a New Brooms van the other day, and he'd seen young Maureen come out with her baby and the fond reunion. Fergus missed very little of what went on outside his shop window. That would have been the boss and her assistant, he guessed. Both good lookers, though the assistant looked more his age. Then there was Maureen. She was one of Rupert's out-workers, and was always good for a lark. Yes, things were definitely looking up.

Doreen Jenkinson drove round the back streets of Tresham, taking books to old people who were housebound. She hadn't much charitable instinct, but agreed to do it to enhance Howard's public image. She wondered, not for the first time, how she was going to pay for the new dress. She had not told Howard, and as the days went by, she was increasingly reluctant to do so. There must be a way of adding to her bank balance without telling him. Perhaps she could borrow from her daughter? No, that would never do. She had always preserved the fiction that their father was a generous, warm-hearted man. The perfect father. It wouldn't do to destroy the illusion now. She pulled up outside a terraced house in Sebastopol Street.

After a ten minutes talk with an old man living on his own, she emerged into the street and saw opposite the rainwear shop. Rain or Shine. A nice name. A shiny, sky blue jacket in the window attracted her attention, and she crossed the road to have a closer look. Not that she would consider buying it. She mustn't spend another penny until next month. Still, she thought, gazing at it, it was very pretty and would be useful for summer showers. No harm in trying it on. Maybe it wasn't her size. And anyway, if it was right for her, she could always get it next month. She opened the door and went in.

Once inside, Doreen looked around until a young man came in from the back room. 'Morning, Madam,' he said pleasantly, eyeing her up and down. 'You just caught me before I shut up shop.' Oh dear, it was one of the occasional old ducks who wandered in without realising. Or would she surprise him? He would be closing soon, and it was always pleasant to make a sale at the last minute.

'It was that jacket, the blue one in the window,' Doreen said. She glanced around quickly, and couldn't see much in the way of clothes display.

'Very pretty, that one, and so smooth to the touch,' said Fergus. 'Would you like to try it?'

Doreen looked at herself in the long mirror. It certainly suited her. Brings out my blue eyes, she said to herself.

'For hubby, is it?' Fergus said, with a knowing smile.

'What did you say?' Doreen frowned. 'No, of course it's not. It's for me! Anyway,' she added, feeling more and more uncomfortable, 'I'll have to think about it. I come this way quite often, so I'll look in again.' She took off the jacket, picked up her handbag and scuttled out. Something very odd about that place! For the moment she had forgotten her worrying overdraft, and turned back to check she'd shut the door. She didn't want the man thinking she was alarmed. It was then she noticed the name over the door. There it was: R. Forsyth. The name on the envelope. Maybe Jean would know more about it. Perhaps she would own up to filching the envelope, and ask Jean more about it.

Then it clicked. Of course! She coloured with embarrassment. Rainwear! Smooth to the touch! Was it for hubby? Oh my God, Doreen, she accused herself, you are a silly fool – it was one of *those* shops! What on earth had that young man thought of her? She felt hot all over, and got into her car, grating the gears as she set off as if pursued by bears.

When she was home and settled with a calming cup of tea, she pondered again on the name Forsyth, on the shop sign, and on the envelope with its stamp destined for her grandson. And the sender. She looked again, and could hardly make out the name. NF S something? ... N ... Colcombe ... Norman! Norman Stevenson. A long-time customer of Rain or Shine? Or an errand-boy? She knew Howard kept in touch. There were telephone calls from the den. Was Howard up to something? Of course he was. He always was.

Twelve

Oddly enough, it was Lois who discovered what Howard was up to, though in an accidental way. Now that her new office in Sebastopol Street was open, and Hazel was happily installed as manager four days a week, Lois often called in to pick up new contacts. One day a week, and at other times when Hazel needed time off, Lois took over, and admitted to Derek that she thoroughly enjoyed herself.

'Beats going to see stroppy new clients in their homes,' she said. 'When they come into the office, they're usually desperate for a cleaner. Very polite and nice. Later on, when they see a perfect stranger around the house, poking into their private things, they can get nasty.'

'Not, of course, that your cleaners poke, do they, me duck?' grinned Derek.

''Course not,' said Lois. 'Not unless asked.'

'Huh!' said Derek. He knew that Lois used New Brooms to collect up information for Cowgill, and he privately thought she sailed pretty close to the wind at times. Still, that was her business.

Now, with no clients in the office for the moment, she stood at the window chatting to Hazel, and looked across at Rain or Shine. She had not yet spoken to the young bloke who was there every day, but she had looked curiously at the men – usually men – who were his customers. Some marched to the door with great bravado, and disappeared inside, emerging later with plain carrier bags. Glancing to right and left, they marched equally swiftly off up Sebastopol Street and disappeared. Others hugged the inside of the pavement, overshot the shop at first, then turned and came back, finally scuttling inside with face averted. Yet others arrived by car, and parked away up the street. Then they walked nonchalantly up to the window and peered inside, as if wondering idly whether to go in. Then in a sudden dart they would open the door and disappear, like a mouse into a hole.

All this amused Lois, especially as she had been told by Hazel and her friend Maureen that the shop's stock covered a wide range of sex aids and toys. Maureen was one of many outworkers who made up raincoats, nurses' uniforms, bodysuits and much else. 'Most of 'em want PVC these days,' she'd said knowledgeably, 'rubber's out.'

'What else does he do in there?' Lois said bluntly. 'What goes on upstairs?'

'Nothing much – Fergus Forsyth uses it for storage, Maureen says.' Then she added, looking hard at Lois, 'You know Fergus is Rupert's son?'

'Rupert Forsyth, you mean? His son? Well yeah, Derek thought he recognised him.'

'Rupert and Daisy live in Farnden. He gets all the letters. Rupert owns the business. I could find out more.'

Lois remembered the day she had seen Hunter Cowgill outside Rain or Shine. What was it he'd said? 'In the line of duty, Lois.' What kind of duty? She supposed Fergus Forsyth would be a good source of information. No doubt some of his business verged on the dodgy.

'Well, don't pry, Hazel,' she said. 'Just if it comes up in the course of conversation. Might be useful. You know what I mean.' Hazel knew exactly what Mrs M meant, and made a mental note to steer Maureen round to the subject when she went to collect Elizabeth at the end of the afternoon. The arrangement was successful, with the babies getting on well and Maureen grateful for the extra money. Her partner had gone off one weekend and never returned, and she found it hard going at times.

'Well, I'd better get going,' Lois said. 'See you, Hazel. Give me a ring if there are any problems.' She turned to the door, and stopped. A big car drove slowly by, and pulled up

73

two or three hundred yards up the street. After a minute or two, a uniformed chauffeur appeared and went quickly into Rain or Shine. In less than a minute, he reappeared with a parcel, and half-ran back to the car, which he drove off at speed.

'What car was that, then?' said Lois. 'It had a sort of coat of arms on the door. Have you seen it before?'

Hazel made a face. 'Certainly have,' she said. 'Talk about corruption in high places! That car is for the use of the Mayor of Tresham. Old Jenkinson, to be exact. Interesting, Mrs M?'

'You'd think he'd be more careful,' Lois said.

Hazel shook her head. 'He's thought of that. What that chauffeur buys at Rain or Shine is for himself. Fergus told Maureen—'

'—who told you,' smiled Lois. 'Anyway,' she continued, 'do we believe that? And if not, how does Howard Jenkinson persuade his driver to carry the can?

'Very influential, is old Jenkinson,' said Hazel, looking at her watch. 'Very influential indeed. Now, I must do a bit o' paperwork before I collect Lizzie.'

'And I must be going,' Lois repeated. 'Take care, then. See you tomorrow.'

In the Town Hall, Jean Slater finished

Howard's letters and took them in for him to sign.

'Morning, lovely Jean,' he said.

Oh God, thought Jean. Not that old thing. Who'd stirred him up this morning? On cue, there was a knock on his door and he said, 'Come in!' in a firm voice.

A girl in her twenties, blonde and slender, walked tentatively into the office and looked at Jean. Then she said, 'You wanted me, Mr Jenkinson?'

I'll say! thought Howard, but he nodded, turning to Jean. 'Just sorting out a problem with the staff,' he said. 'If you'd give me a few minutes with Sus— er, Miss Jacobs?'

'Jacob,' said the girl. 'Susanna Jacob.'

Jean glared at her, collected up the signed letters and left the office, banging the door behind her. Surely he was past all that? But no, they were never past it. Her old Dad, who'd had a roving eye all his life, had almost lost his wits in the final old folks' home, but that hadn't stopped him propositioning a buxom nurse. 'I've booked us a room at a luxury hotel, my dear,' she'd heard him say confidingly to her one visiting time. 'Keeps 'em going, you know,' the nurse had said afterwards to Jean.

So what would Doreen say? Well, she need not know.

Thirteen

'Bill? Mrs M here. Can you stay on for a few minutes after the meeting today?'

Monday morning, and the team were meeting at midday. Lois put down the telephone and shuffled her papers. There were already several new contacts from the office in town, and she had begun to think seriously about the need for more cleaners. Now that Hazel spent most of her time in Tresham, she was finding it difficult to spread the team efficiently. She would bring it up at the meeting, see if they had any ideas. A recommendation from one of them was more useful than any number of ads in local papers.

As she had hoped, at the end of the meeting the team had several useful suggestions. One of them – the most likely – was a girl from the nearby village of Round Ringford, a niece of Sheila Stratford. She was working at the Town Hall at present, but Sheila had been talking to her mother, who'd said that she was looking for another job where she'd meet more people, and did not have to sit in front of a computer all day.

'Fair enough,' said Lois. 'Give me her particulars, and I'll get in touch.'

They settled a few last problems, and then dispersed, leaving Bill standing awkwardly by the door. 'You wanted to talk?' he said, looking apprehensive.

'Yeah, close the door,' Lois said. Gran was lurking somewhere, she knew, and this was going to be a very confidential matter. She wasn't sure why she wanted to know, except for a nagging curiosity about a potentially explosive matter. But why? It was none of her business, and for sure no crime had been committed ... yet.

Bill shut the door, and turned to face her. Lois laughed. 'Don't look like that,' she said. 'There's nothing wrong. Just wanted to ask you about the Jenkinsons. Well, about that room of his. Have you had a look inside?'

Bill shook his head. 'Always locked,' he said. 'But I think our Doreen would like to know ... she was hovering outside the door the other day when I went up to do the bedrooms. Asked me if Howard had mentioned having it spring-cleaned. I said no, and she went off. But I reckon she's dead curious.'

'With good reason, if I'm guessing right,' Lois said, and told Bill about the mayoral limousine.

Bill was unimpressed. 'Nothing much wrong in that,' he said. 'Bit of an old fool, but not exactly a dangerous secret. Anyway, it's between him and her, Mrs M, as you're often tellin' us. We don't get mixed up in clients' private business.'

Lois felt rebuked, and snapped back, 'And quite right too. Glad you remembered. Still, I have a reason for asking.' She hadn't really, nothing concrete, but continued, 'So if you notice anything about that room – door left open by mistake, Howard gets taken short, that kind of thing – and you spot anything odd, let me know.' She sat down and began collecting up papers, dismissing him.

Bill grinned. 'Yes, Mrs M,' he said. 'You on to something again?' he added. Lois did not answer.

Later that afternoon, Josie looked at her watch and was surprised to see it was half past five, closing time. The shop had been busy all afternoon, especially around school turning-out time. The junior children first, running in with pocket-money to spend, taking hours to decide how to spend it. Then the school bus arrived from Tresham, spilling out the seniors, who sloped up the street and into the shop for cans of drink and peppery crisps. Occasionally, one of the tall lads would take off his school tie on the bus, then walk into the shop nonchalantly and ask for cigarettes. Josie knew them all now, and dealt with this summarily. There was nothing she could do about the gang who collected outside the shop and rolled their own with sweet-smelling substances, and so she looked the other way. Remembering her own teenage days, she trusted they'd grow out of it.

She went out to the street now to bring in the sandwich board she had on the pavement. It had been Rob's idea, and was useful for chalking up bargain offers. She looked along the street, checking who was about. Villagers always did this. It was a way of telling who were real village people and those who were incomers, moved out from towns, and not yet schooled in the ways of Long Farnden. Josie was not a born-and-bred villager, of course, but was now completely accepted.

She saw the Forsyths' car approaching and sighed. Old Rupert, no doubt, wanting stamps. He got through dozens every week. Should she quickly put up the Closed sign? No, he was a good customer. She went back into the shop and waited. It was Daisy Forsyth who ran in. 'Are you closed, Josie?' she asked breathlessly. 'Rupert will be so cross with me – I completely forgot about the stamps today.'

'Don't worry,' Josie reassured her. 'Post Office is shut, but I've got stamps in the till. How many d'you want?'

Daisy sank down on the stool placed by the

counter for the elderly and infirm, and sighed with relief. 'Thank goodness,' she said. 'He's a bit of an old sod when he's cross,' she added.

'I know,' said Josie. 'When the post is late, for a start.'

Daisy nodded. 'It's the letters, you see, dear,' she said. 'Our livelihood, they are. And we can't keep the needy waiting, can we?' She burst out laughing, an unexpectedly fruity sound.

'In need of what?' Josie said innocently.

'Ah, that'd be telling, wouldn't it,' Daisy said, paying for her stamps and heading for the door. 'But I'll tell you this,' she added, pausing on the threshold, 'it ain't a cure for rheumatism or arthritis we're selling!' And she laughed again, so infectiously that Josie joined in, although she wasn't sure of the joke.

This time she managed to bring in the board and lock up before any more last-minute hopefuls – 'runners', Rob called them – got a foot in the door. She pulled down the window blinds and walked through the darkened shop to the small garden at the rear. Derek had given her young plants, and she lingered with a watering can, savouring the fresh air after a day indoors.

I wonder, she thought. I wonder what exactly old Rupert supplies? She had a pretty good idea, but was intrigued by Daisy's part in it. Such a respectable, round little person, with her neat skirts and blouses. Ripe for the WI, Gran had said, and sure enough, Daisy had joined soon after arriving. But Josie guessed none of them had heard her laugh like that, a jolly, unrestrained hearty chuckle, suggesting another, riskier side of Daisy Forsyth.

Josie tipped the last of the water over the garden, and speculated. Maybe I can get her talking one day in the shop, when nobody else is in, she thought. I'm getting quite good at that. Chip off the old block!

'Oh gawd,' she said aloud. 'Just as Rob predicted ... Josie Meade back in the village and turning into a real old shop gossip.' She put away the watering can and set her mind to what they were having for supper.

Fourteen

Friday in Colcombe, a respectable suburb of Manchester, and Norman Stevenson, middle-aged, overweight and losing his hair, looked at himself in the bathroom mirror and wondered what he could do with the freedom of the coming weekend. It had come to this. He dreaded weekends. His wife had gone off with one of his young employees, children were busy with their own lives and seldom in touch. His girlfriend was losing interest, and no wonder, since his prowess was more than a little diminished lately. He doubted if she'd want to see him. The two days stretched ahead of him interminably.

The downward slide had started years ago, he considered, when he'd had that major row with Howard Jenkinson. It had been about the timber business, of course, and Howard had been so cunning he'd managed to put all the blame on Norman for irregularities which had come to the notice of the Inland Revenue.

Since then, he'd managed the Manchester depot, but was always aware that he'd been sidelined, and the best he could do was to keep his head down. And keep quiet. That was the big thing. Short of threatening him, Howard had made it quite clear that if the slightest whisper of anything, business or personal, came to his notice, Norman would be out on his ear, with his name blackened so thoroughly that he might as well emigrate.

Now that Howard had retired, Norman had wondered if the bonds would at last be loosened. But no, the new Mayor of Tresham had renewed his vows. Now that he was a public figure, it was even more vital to protect his spotless image.

The business scandal had been a long time ago now, but on the personal side, Norman – a fellow customer of Rain or Shine – knew much that Howard would do anything, *anything*, to keep secret. Norman's last meeting with Fergus Forsyth had been difficult. Questions had been asked, prying questions, and he hoped he had given nothing away. Fergus had remembered his connection with Howard Jenkinson, but then, he must know many people with closer connections than Norman. Perhaps his curiosity about Howard was idle. The young bloke never seemed to have enough to do. But his questions were persistent, and Norman hoped he had given nothing away.

Taking a clean shirt from the drawer, he sighed again. The buttons were tight across his stomach, and he cursed. Better sign on for another session at the gym. How he hated it! But he hated loneliness even more, and if, with the help of Fergus Forsyth, he could brighten his relationship with the girlfriend, life might be worth living.

He heard the post landing on the door mat and went down stairs. Mostly junk, as usual. But here was a more interesting-looking envelope. Norman's name and address written by hand, and PERSONAL, underlined in red, prominently in the corner. He put it by his breakfast plate, and went quickly through the other mail. Two bills, and a charity appeal. The last went straight in the bin, and the bills he tucked behind the clock on the kitchen shelf. He sat down, poured himself a cup of coffee, and slit open the handwritten envelope with a knife.

The message was in neat capitals, written with a blue ballpoint, and the paper had been anonymously torn from an exercise book. His heart stopped. Then began again at a thumping pace. He dropped the letter on the floor as if it was on fire, and stared down at it fearfully. He hadn't felt this dizzying fear for years, not since the big row with Howard. Finally he stooped and picked up the paper. KEEP YOUR MOUTH SHUT – OR ELSE. That was all.

With trembling fingers, Norman found the envelope. Postmarked with a London district number. So it could have been from anyone. But it wasn't from anyone. Norman had no doubts. For some God-knows-what reason, it was from Howard. Or from one of his loyal servants. Ken Slater? He was a quiet one. Never knew what he was thinking.

His legs buckling slightly as he stood, Norman lifted the telephone and dialled the Slaters' number. Might as well settle this straight away, he comforted himself, and began to speak.

Fifteen

Jean and Ken Slater trudged around Tresham golf course in the pouring rain, silently slicing balls into the rough, three-putting on sodden greens, and only speaking to discuss abandoning play and heading for the clubhouse.

'But we can't, Jean,' Ken said. 'What will Howard and Doreen say?'

'Thank God, I should think,' muttered Jean, kicking her ball out of a deep hollow. 'You didn't see that, did you, Ken?' she said.

'No, but you bet Howard did,' he answered, as he spotted the tall figure, kitted out in waterproof garments from head to foot. 'He can see round corners, that one,' he added darkly.

Sure enough, Howard loomed above Jean and looked down. 'You lose a stroke there,' he said firmly, 'but you have got a much better lie. Should get on in two from here.'

There are times, said Jean to herself, when I could fetch him one round the ear'ole with my putter. And when he was out for the count flat on the fairway, I could trample on him with my spiked shoes until he looked like he'd been put through a grater.

Cheered by this thought, she waved to Doreen, who was plodding gallantly on through the driving rain. 'Last hole,' Jean shouted. 'Then we're going in. Whatever these two say,' she added, and whammed the ball so hard that it soared into the air and landed two feet from the flag.

'Well done, Jean!' said Howard with false magnanimity. 'Now, Doreen,' he shouted across the waterlogged grass, 'let's see what you can do!'

Doreen hesitated, took a club from her bag, and positioned herself for the shot. Ken looked at her wiggling bum and felt a welcome warmth. Then she swung the club, hit the ball and watched it trickle ten yards in front of her, coming to a halt at the edge of a deep, sandy bunker. She turned and looked across at Howard, and mouthed something, her voice lost in the rising gale.

'What did she say, Jean?' asked an irritated Howard.

'Couldn't hear,' said Jean diplomatically. But she'd lip-read, and heartily agreed. 'Drop dead!' had been Doreen's succinct and heartfelt reply.

The atmosphere was not much better in the Forsyth house in Farnden. Among the usual pile of letters that morning, Rupert opened an official-looking envelope. 'Damn!' he said loudly. 'Here, Daisy, look at this. How dare they?'

Daisy took the letter and read the first paragraph. It was from the Planning people, and they had sent a list of features in the proposed extension to which they took exception. 'Well,' said Daisy, 'at least they haven't turned it down all together. We can work on the plan and have another try.'

'And that'll take another couple of years!' said Rupert, exaggerating furiously. 'Not to mention the expense of producing another set of plans, etcetera etcetera...' He snatched the letter back from Daisy and read it again, his colour rising angrily.

'Calm down, dear,' said Daisy. 'We've managed up to now, and I'm sure we can manage a bit longer.'

'Huh! That's what you always say,' Rupert shouted at her. 'If it wasn't for me, nothing would ever get done! And your son takes after you. Lazy so-and-so ... he spends all day gossiping with that girl in the cleaners' shop opposite. Pity they ever took over that place. And now if I phone, it's Hazel this and Hazel that, and nothing about how business is going or any ideas for improving it!'

He sat down suddenly, and Daisy went over swiftly to him. She took his hand. 'You really mustn't take on,' she said. 'It's not good for you at your age. Now, let's think what we can do.' She didn't argue with him over Fergus, having learned long ago that this was useless. It had been a disappointment to her that her only son had done nothing more ambitious than working in his father's shop. He wasn't stupid, and could have gone on with his education. She blamed Rupert, though had never said so to him. He had chivvied the boy, never leaving him alone to find his own way, and in the end he had taken the easiest option, following in his father's dubious footsteps.

They sat in silence for a few minutes, then Daisy said, 'What we need is someone with influence. Someone who can put in a good word. You know, the old boys' network an' all that.'

'So who do you suggest?' said Rupert sourly.

'I think you know who I'm thinking of,' said Daisy, and grinned. 'A certain person who has enjoyed our services – mine especially – for years, and still does. A certain person in a position of importance in the rapidly expanding town of Tresham? Are you with me, dear?'

Rupert stared at her. 'You mean Howard Jenkinson?'

She nodded.

'Why should he do anything for us?' said Rupert. 'He's got everything he needs in life, has recently retired to a cushy life of golf and holidays, and has more money in the bank than most of us can count. He'd not lift a finger for us.'

'Ah, now that's where you might be wrong,' said Daisy wisely. 'Just think a minute, Rupert. Yes, he's got everything his heart desires, and what he values most of all is his Mayor of Tresham chain of office. Now, I'm not stealing a gold chain, but I am suggesting we could drop a few careless words here and there which would make his elevated position very shaky indeed. Are you still with me?'

'You're talking about blackmail!' said Rupert. 'No, no, no! I'll certainly not stoop to that!'

Daisy was unruffled. 'No need for you to do anything,' she said. 'I'll do the stooping. Leave it to me, dear. I shall enjoy myself,' she added, and burst out laughing. 'I might be a little out of practice, but it won't take long to brush up the old skills. You concentrate on the changes Planning wants, and leave the rest to me.'

Rupert looked at her. Her neat body was in good shape, her hair carefully coloured and cut in a youthful style, and her clothes – though perfectly respectable – perhaps not quite so conservative as her village contemporaries. A low-necked blouse with frilly sleeves, her skirt slit so that it showed her still trim knees. All quite subdued, but a hint there of secret pleasures? Oh, for heavens sake, Rupert said to himself. They were a couple of middle-aged fogies. Whatever it was that Daisy had in mind would be decorous and trouble free. He decided to let her get on with it. He'd always respected her judgement in the past, and had no reason to doubt her now.

Things were certainly more cheerful in the small office of New Brooms in Sebastopol Street. Lois had called in to see Hazel and pick up any new client details. She also wanted to see if Hazel had any information on the applicant for the new cleaner job. All Lois knew so far was that she was Sheila's niece and wanted to get out of a bureaucratic job.

Hazel looked at the application and frowned. 'Don't think I know her at all,' she said. 'Susanna Jacob ... Posh name. I hope she's not too posh for us. Where does she live? Oh, yes, here it is ... Round Ringford. Says here she works at the moment in the Town Hall, but is fed up with sitting in an office all day. Sounds all right?'

'I've asked her to come here for interview at eleven o'clock.' Lois looked at her watch. 'Just time for a coffee before she arrives. No, stay there, I'll make it.'

She walked into the tiny kitchen behind the office, and was pleased to see that it was spotless. Hazel was proving a real treasure. She was a good administrator, and her natural acerbic tendencies seemed to have faded with the increased responsibility and respect that went with it.

Hazel smiled to herself. She was not fooled. Mrs M was checking up on her! Still, she'd do the same if she was the boss. She took the steaming mug, and said, 'D'you want me to go upstairs while she's here?'

Lois shook her head. 'No, stay here. Two heads are better than one. But I'll ask the questions.'

'Of course,' said Hazel, and got up from her desk. 'You sit here, Mrs M. I can see a girl coming down the street, looking for the right place. I'll be in the corner, where I can take mental notes.'

Lois moved to the seat behind the desk, squared her shoulders and prepared for what she did best: finding out what she wanted to know without any trouble at all.

Across the road, Fergus Forsyth watched from his window as Susanna Jacob halted outside the New Brooms' door. 'Hello,' he said to himself. 'That's a girl I know, don't I? Young Jacob? Works at the Town Hall ... caught old Howard's eye?' He chuckled, and had to turn away to answer his persistent telephone.

Sixteen

Friday came round again all too quickly for Norman Stevenson. He had spent the week throwing himself into a frenzy of work, checking up on all aspects where fault could be found, and staying in the warehouse office late into the evening. When he finally arrived home each night, to an empty house, he unwrapped his takeaway meal, turned on the television, and sat in a comatose heap until he fell deeply asleep. He did not wake up until the midnight chill forced him out of his chair and into bed.

The nagging pain that knifed him when he thought of the threatening message had refused to go away. The Slaters had denied all knowledge of the letter. Ken had been abrupt and unfriendly. After Norman had read it over a couple of times, he had impulsively torn it into small pieces, but then, in an agony of apprehension in case he should need it, had put the fragments into a small brown envelope, sealed it, and hidden it in his sock drawer.

There was nothing he could do, except put

it out of his mind, and this Friday morning, as he lay watching the early morning rain lashing his window, he knew that that would be impossible. The best he could think of would be to fill his life so full that there would be no room for brooding on a malicious anonymous missive. Well, not really anonymous, because he was convinced it had come from Howard. Good old Howard, one of the best, and saviour of the people of Tresham.

'Right,' he said aloud. 'Friday today, Saturday tomorrow, and I need a plan for the weekend. I'll ring round and fix up a game of golf for a start.' He pulled on his dressing-gown and avoided his reflection in the mirror. Exercise and fresh air might be a good idea for several reasons! Then he heard the click of the letterbox and felt the daily jolt of anxiety. From the top of the stairs he could see three letters on the mat. Two were the unmistakeable jazzy envelopes of junk mail, and the third ... oh God, the third was a square white envelope with the address in neat blue capitals.

His bare foot slipped on the top stair, and he had difficulty regaining his balance. He grabbed the banister and steadied himself. It could be from anyone – his sister in Canada, his old chum who lived in Caithness and occasionally visited him on his way down to London – but neither of them would write in neat capitals. Sprawling black letters, or a typed label, yes, but not a blue ballpoint, clear and legible as a writing exercise on the blackboard.

He took it into the kitchen and considered putting it straight in the bin. But suppose it contained more than an empty threat? He should know what he was up against, in case his plan of action, quickly put together last Friday, should need adjustment.

JUST A REMINDER, NORMAN. AND A SMALL REQUEST. CHECK YOUR BANK BALANCE AND SEE HOW MUCH YOU CAN DONATE TO A WORTHY CHARITY. DETAILS FOLLOW NEXT FRIDAY. AND DON'T FORGET – MOUTH SHUT, NORMAN. OR ELSE.

Norman Stevenson slumped down on a chair and his head fell forward. His hands closed over his ears and he banged his head a couple of times on the hard wooden table. Then his shoulders heaved, and the kitchen was filled with the sound of a large man sobbing with fear.

Howard and Doreen sat at the breakfast table, reading the morning papers. Howard had taken the *Daily Telegraph* for as long as he could remember, and without asking, he had ordered the *Sun* for Doreen. She would have preferred the *Daily Mail*, having no interest in page three girls who looked as if they'd been inflated with a balloon pump. But habit had caused her to accept Howard's choice without demur, and only lately had she begun to think of changing.

'Good heavens, Doreen!' Howard said suddenly. This morning he was reading the local paper property pages, and looked up at her in astonishment.

'Ooops,' thought Doreen. 'What now?'

'Here, look,' he continued. 'This ad for next door's house – see what they're asking for it!'

The Jenkinsons lived on the Nob Hill of Tresham, where all the large houses had spacious gardens and carriage drives and coach lamps, and all the trimmings of wealth. Howard had heard a rumour that their neighbours were moving, and now here was the estate agent's advertisement, with a large photograph and the usual overblown text.

'Million and a half!' Doreen exclaimed, peering at the paper. 'Gracious, Howard. Makes you think, doesn't it?'

It had indeed made Howard think. He suspected house prices were at their peak, and would shortly begin to fall. This house was much too big for them now, and he had begun to think perhaps he should sell, capitalise on the investment, and buy somewhere smaller, outside Tresham, perhaps. In the country, but not too far away. It would take time to find a place, of course. He would have to find out if that would rule out a second term as Mayor of Tresham. Howard had so many plans, most of them involving discreet plaques acknowledging the patronage of Howard Jenkinson as the prime mover of projects to benefit the community.

Doreen was watching his expression, and had no trouble reading his mind. 'Maybe we should think about selling,' she said. 'Look for somewhere smaller. I wouldn't mind. It'd be easier, and we'd save on cleaners and gardeners. Where d'you fancy looking?' The prospect began to look appealing. All the boring routine of her life would change. New faces, new neighbours – and not such snotty ones, with luck – and a different way of going on. Especially if they settled in a village. She was a faithful fan of radio's vintage farming soap, being as familiar with generations of the Archer family as her own, and had always had a fancy to be one of them.

Howard reflected. He knew the area like the back of his hand, he often said. 'Like the back of my hand, Ken,' he'd repeated, when they were looking for pastures new in business or pleasure. Now he remembered one particular village that had come to his notice recently. Old Rupert Forsyth and his missus, the delectable Daisy, had not long ago moved to Long Farnden. He'd met Daisy in the market, and she'd said she loved it.

'Should have settled there years ago,' she'd laughed, 'instead of all the back streets I have known!' She'd been a great girl, had Daisy. And still full of fun!

'I'll give it some thought,' Howard said. Best not to look too keen at first. He didn't want Doreen going overboard, trawling the villages for miles around. Time enough later on. Yes, he'd suggest Farnden at drinkies time this evening. 'Well, dear, best be off,' he added. 'Busy day ahead.' Including dictating a few letters to the fair Susanna, he thought with pleasure. Somehow, he had to ease Jean Slater out gently, he had decided. Not only did she know too much, but he was tiring of her familiarity, lack of respect, and the increasingly frequent mocking tone she used with him.

'I'll just feed the fish,' he said. 'Check the pond. Then I'll be away. Not in for lunch, but I hope to be home in reasonable time. Take care, Doreen. Have a nice day.'

He strode out into the garden and Doreen could see him by the pond. 'Giving the fish their orders, I expect,' she muttered. The day stretched ahead, but instead of her usual fight against boredom, she cleared the dishes cheerfully and made a list of estate agents. What fun! She'd ring Jean and see if she could get time off to view properties with her. A lovely excuse to snoop round strangers' houses, and this time she was going to decide where they lived. She would do the choosing this time. A new life, that's what she wanted, and that is what she intended to have.

Seventeen

In the excitement of a new life dangling before her, Doreen had forgotten that it was a Bill day. When he tapped at the back door and opened it, she turned in alarm. 'Oh, oh, it's you, Bill. Of course it is. Come on in. I've just finished the dishes, so you can make your usual start.' She wondered whether to open a conversation about moving house, but thought it was maybe too soon.

Bill began to collect up the newspapers from the floor where Howard had dumped them, and said, "Ello, 'ello ... what have we here? Reading the property pages? Thinking of going into the agency business?' It was a joke, and he was surprised at Doreen's reaction.

'No, of course not,' she said sharply. Then she softened, and said, 'Well, actually, Bill, we are just beginning to think about the possibility of moving out to the country. All in the very early stages of course, and I shall be needing you for *months* to come – if not years!'

Bill filled the mop bucket and tipped in a generous slurp of Flash. 'Anywhere in mind?' he said casually.

Doreen shook her head. 'A village not too far away from Tresham,' she said. 'Near enough for Howard to continue with his community work.' Then she spluttered and began to giggle.

'Mrs Jenkinson?' Bill was curious. There was a distinct difference about Mrs J this morning. Almost flirty! Oh Lord, not a menopausal client – but no, she was past all that. From his lofty early thirties, Bill saw all ladies over fifty as past everything, and Doreen knew this. Still, she could have a bit of fun with him.

'Don't worry, Bill,' she said. 'Just the thought of Howard and his community work. His idea of a good deed in the community is strictly to do with cheering up any females languishing in the offices at the Town Hall. If they're young, tall, and blonde, so much the better. Now,' she added, relishing his obvious embarrassment, 'I'll let you get on.' And she positively skipped out of the room.

At coffee time, Bill had a suggestion for Doreen. He'd been thinking about the difference in her as he went about the house. At the top of the stairs, he'd caught her looking through the keyhole of the den. She'd not even tried to pretend she wasn't snooping, but had said, 'Come here, Bill. See if you can see anything. There's a telly, and what looks like a pile of videos. I can see them, but not much else.' He had shaken his head and said it was more than his job was worth. 'If Mrs M found out, it'd be the end of my illustrious career with New Brooms,' he said.

'Who's going to tell her?' Doreen had said, not put off.

But Bill had stuck to his refusal, and walked away to finish the luxury bathroom which was all Doreen's own with its gold taps and heart-shaped bath.

Now he stood by the kitchen table, sipping coffee and listening as she nattered on about her grandchildren and the latest tooth cut by the baby. In a short pause in the monologue, he said, 'I've just remembered something that might interest you.'

She looked at him enquiringly. It was unlike Bill to initiate any topic in the conversation. 'Go on,' she said.

'It's just that there's a house for sale in Long Farnden. You know, the village where Mrs M lives. Her house was our headquarters, until the office opened in Tresham. Nice village – shop, pub, church, school. More facilities than usual. Bus three times a week. Not that you would need that,' he added quickly, unable to see Doreen climbing into the bus with her shopping bag.

'What kind of a house?'

'Old, stone-built, medium size, mullion windows, beamed ceilings – you know the sort of thing. Used to be lived in by an old man who died, then it was rented temporarily by the vicar, while they rebuilt the vicarage. Remember that fire? Well, the vicarage is ready for him to move back now, and the old house'll be on the market. No signs up yet, but I reckon if you got in there quickly, you'd get it for a good price. Needs quite a lot doing to it, but that'd be no problem for you.' He glanced around at the immaculate kitchen, thought of the rest of the prestigious property, and nodded. 'No, you'd fix it up easily.'

This was an unusually long speech for Bill, and Doreen laughed. 'Good heavens, Bill, are you getting commission from the agents?' Then she added quickly, 'But it sounds just the thing. I'll tell Howard this evening, and we'll have a look at the weekend. Thanks, Bill. And you'd stay with us, wouldn't you, even if it needed less hours?'

'We'll see about that,' he said practically, 'when the time comes.'

Howard was in a good mood when he returned. He had explained to Jean that he'd been asked to try out a new girl for possible advancement, give her a few letters etcetera, but he omitted her probable destination. Susanna had proved very efficient, demure and respectful. Lovely as ever, he'd thought, as he looked at her neatly crossed ankles. He viewed Jean's broad bottom with a jaundiced eye when she'd come into his office with a feeble excuse and a sneer on her face. The only fly in the ointment had been when he'd asked Susanna if she intended to stay on at the Town Hall. He dropped a hint that promotion might come soon. She'd been evasive, stuttering about not being sure ... possible other plans ... difficult to say at the moment. That kind of thing. Still, if he offered her the job soon, promised a hefty increase in pay, that should do the trick.

All he wanted, he told himself, was a nice pair of legs to look at over the desk, and a willing nature.

'Good day, dear?' Doreen asked him, as he took off his coat.

'Not bad,' he said. 'Rushed off my feet as usual, but you know me – I flourish on hard work. Now, ready for a little drinkie?'

He got around to the subject of looking for houses quite quickly. To Doreen's surprise, he said almost at once that he had been thinking of Long Farnden. A particularly attractive village, he had insisted, and Doreen was not objecting. In fact, when she had a chance to contribute, she told him of the odd coincidence. 'Bill was telling me,' she said, 'about an old house in Farnden that'll be on the market very soon. Isn't that strange? Must be meant, Howard. Shall we go and look at it?'

Bill had not known which agents would be handling it, but that was no problem for Howard. He knew them all in Tresham. Estate agents, builders' suppliers, architects' offices, all in the same world and all doing each other a good turn where possible. And it was always possible.

'Easy, Doreen,' he said. 'Leave it to me, pet. I'll get it all sorted tomorrow, and we'll drive over and have a look. If we like it, we should be able to get things moving reasonably quickly. There'll be no problem selling this one, anyway. I had a word with the editor at the *Gazette*, and he rang back to say our neighbours have sold already. People competing, apparently, which drove the price even higher!'

Doreen said nothing, but smiled in agreement. Inside, she was plotting fiercely. She had no intention of looking at it with Howard. First she would see it alone, or with Jean. And if she liked it, she would be prepared. Howard had little imagination, and if it was in a bad state, would probably not see the potential. A vicar, had Bill said? A man living on his own. Could be neglected, at the very least.

'When d'you reckon we could go?' she said, and when he replied that it would most likely be early next week, she decided to ring Jean as soon as possible.

'Hello? Jean?' Howard was up the garden, lecturing the fish, and Doreen made a swift call. 'Can't say much now, but can you spare an hour or two tomorrow?' She explained quickly, and the visit was fixed before Howard returned, complaining that two fish were missing. 'That heron again! Really, Doreen, you've got nothing to do all day, you could've kept an eye on the pond, chase the bugger away as soon as he landed.'

'Yes, dear,' Doreen said meekly. 'Maybe the fish are hiding under a lily pad. They do sometimes, you know. Or they could be right at the bottom. It's quite deep up one end, isn't it? Have another count in the morning, and you'll probably find they're still there.'

Howard was mollified for the moment, and switched on the television, choosing a mindless quiz game that he loved, and Doreen loathed. 'I'll just be in the kitchen for a while,' she said. 'Finishing touches to supper. I'll give you a shout when it's ready.'

She closed the kitchen door behind her, and picked up the local paper, turning to the property pages. Now, which agent was it likely to be? Oh, Lord. Could be any of them. A half-page of ads for properties in Waltonby, Fletching and Round Ringford, caught her eye. Ah, yes, and there were a couple in Long Farnden. Bill had said the house was not yet on the market, but as soon as Howard had gone tomorrow, she would ring these agents and ask. Bound to be the ones! She made a note of the telephone number in her diary, in case Howard took the paper off to the Town Hall, as he sometimes did. He loved to read over and over again the reports of his own visits to schools and fêtes and newly opened swimming pools. There were a couple of photographs of him in this issue. In one, she was there with him. They'd been invited to the dedication of a new multi-faith church in an expanding area of town. Howard had a suitably solemn expression, and Doreen saw herself unsuitably smiling at a rogue choirboy picking his nose. In the other photograph, she was not there, and now looked closely at Howard presenting prizes at the local College of Further Education. Resplendent in his golden chain, he had a fatherly hand on the arm of a nubile blonde student.

One of these days ... Doreen thought, taking a deep breath as she set two trays for supper. They would have supper on their laps, watching the telly. Then she wouldn't have to listen to his report of the day's triumphs in his Mayoral duties.

'Just coming in, Howard. Would you like a beer with yours?' she shouted.

'Good girl,' he answered. 'What should I do without my Doreen?'

And what would your Doreen do without you? she said silently to herself.

Eighteen

Lois could see old Cyril's house from her office window. She had kept the office going in the Farnden house, although some of the paperwork had been moved to Sebastopol Street. For one thing, she liked having a bolt-hole where she could escape from Gran occasionally. Her mother was a gem, but sometimes her love of gossip, and memories of the old times, were too much for Lois.

The team still met on Mondays in Long Farnden, as it was more convenient for all of them. Hazel closed the Tresham office for a couple of hours, and they all gathered in Lois's house to go over schedules of work and for a chance to say anything that was on their minds – good or bad.

Last Monday, Sharon Miller had said she'd applied for a business studies course at the college in Tresham, and might not be able to give so much time to cleaning. Lois had thought privately that she'd have serious doubts about any business run by Sharon, but wished her well, and thought how fortunate that Sheila had come up with her niece, Susanna. She'd liked the girl at interview, and they'd agreed she could start in a month's time. This would give Lois a chance to reorganise things, and Susanna could quit the Town Hall job without leaving them in the lurch.

Lois looked up and down the street in the time-honoured fashion, and saw no one. Then a car drew up outside old Cyril's house. She always thought of it as old Cyril's, although the vicar had been living there for some while. Poor old Cyril. He was much missed in the village, even though – or perhaps because – he had been such an awkward old sod.

Two women got out of the car, and Lois strained to see if she recognised them. Both were middle-aged and both well-dressed. The car was small, but Lois knew a luxury model when she saw one. What are they after, then?

At this point, Gran knocked at the door perfunctorily and came in. 'Like a cup of tea, Lois?' she said.

Lois knew this was a signal that Gran was bored, and needed someone to talk to. 'Not really,' she said. 'But come here and have a look down the street. See those women? D'you recognise them?'

Gran looked out, and considered. 'One of 'em,' she said, 'looks a bit familiar but I can't think why. Hey, Lois, they're going into Cyril's garden – and now they're peering in the windows! What's going on? And where's the vicar? He's usually at home at this time of the day.' Everybody in Farnden knew where everybody else should be at any given time of day.

'Well, they're knocking on the door now,' Lois said. 'Maybe he'll let them in.'

But the door was not opened, and the women hovered uncertainly.

Gran was galvanised into action. 'Just going to the shop,' she said. 'I need to tell Josie something,' she added, and was out of the front door and into the street before Lois had time to answer.

The telephone rang as Gran left, and Lois picked up the receiver. 'New Brooms,' she said. 'Lois Meade speaking. Can I help you?'

'I hope so,' said a man's voice, 'but I don't need a cleaner. Well, maybe I do, but that's not what I'm ringing about.'

'Who is this?' Lois was instantly on guard. Not another caller asking about yard brooms and feather dusters. The man didn't give a name, but said, 'I hope you'll forgive my ringing if I've got it wrong, but I'm told you have a detective agency on the side?'

Lois snapped. 'Whoever told you that was wrong! Completely wrong. This is a cleaning business, with a good reputation, and I have nothing more to say.'

'Hold on a minute! Don't fly off the handle,' the man said. 'I just wanted a bit of enquiring done on the quiet. An old colleague of mine in Tresham. Man in high office, all that sort of thing. Your name was mentioned once. Something to do with clearing up that business of a fire in Farnden? Young man died? Anyway, sorry if I've got it wrong. I'll try somewhere else.'

Lois put down the phone, and then immediately checked the call. 'The caller withheld their number,' said the disembodied voice. Ah well, she supposed her name had been in the local paper at the time. Cowgill had tried to keep her out of it, but intrepid journalists had come asking questions.

'Lois?' It was Gran, swiftly returned from the shop and a conversation with the two strangers. 'I asked if I could help them, and they said they were meeting someone. Quite cagey, they were. I reckon I've seen one of 'em before somewhere. Face looked very familiar.'

Lois picked up the local paper, and turned to the property pages. 'You don't think the house is up for sale, do you? The vicarage is nearly ready for Rev Rollinson to go back.'

She flicked through the paper, and suddenly stopped. A group of people outside the new church caught her eye. In the centre, standing next to Mayor Jenkinson, and wearing the chain of office of the Lady Mayoress, was the woman down the street. 'Look, Mum. This is her, isn't it?'

Gran nodded, pleased. 'Well, I'm glad we got that sorted out,' she said. 'Now then, I'm ready for a cup of tea if you aren't.'

Lois heard her filling the kettle in the kitchen, and thought she might as well be sociable. But the odd telephone call stuck in her mind. 'Man in high office,' the voice had said. High office in Tresham? 'They don't come any higher than Mayor,' she said, as she sipped her tea.

'What's that?' said Gran.

'Nothing,' said Lois, 'just thinking aloud.'

'We'd better sit in the car until the man from Schofields comes. We are a bit early, aren't we, Jean?' Doreen turned back to the car.

'Why don't we have a wander up the street and get the feel of the village?' Jean said. 'After all, the village in general is just as important as the house.' Privately, she had grave doubts about this idea of the Jenkinsons moving to a village. They were town people, born and bred, and she could not see Doreen leaving behind town amenities. Nor could she imagine her joining the WI, making jam and shopping at the little village store over the road. Still, Long Farnden wasn't that far from Tresham, and Doreen would probably continue to shop at the supermarket she'd always used. And the dress shop! Jean had felt so sorry for her friend that she'd lent her the money to balance her account without thinking of the ludicrousness of it. There was Howard, rich as Croesus, while Ken and she still had to watch the pennies. Well, she had saved a bit, and knew Doreen would pay it back without fail. She'd promised, and that was good enough.

As if reading Jean's thoughts, Doreen said, 'Should be able to pay you back next week. It was ever so kind of you.'

'No hurry,' said Jean lightly, though in fact she would need the money soon if Howard managed to unseat her from her job. She knew for a fact that he wanted her out, but she hoped it wouldn't be too easy for him.

'Oh, look, Jean! Look at that dear little shop. Shall we go in and buy something?'

Jean smiled. Good old Doreen. She could not see a shop window without wanting to get out her purse! 'Fine,' she said. 'There's still no sign of the agent. And your car is parked outside the house, so he'll know we're about.'

They went up the steps and into the shop, the jangling bell announcing their arrival.

Josie smiled at them over the counter, and said could she help? Doreen thought quickly, and said she needed a birthday card. Did they stock cards? Josie pointed to the rack of pleasant designs and busied herself with sorting out an order book. After a few minutes, Doreen came up with a card and opened her handbag.

'Are you staying in the village?' Josie said. This was the stock question for people she did not recognise, though one of the women was vaguely familiar.

Doreen shook her head. 'No, just looking around,' she said. She was not sure that the old house was officially on the market yet, and did not want to spread rumours that would attract other buyers. If Howard could be persuaded to move quickly, they could probably get it cheaply. She could see already that a lot of work was needed on the stonework and roof. But the ancient mullioned windows and heavy oak door appealed to her already. Small dormer windows indicated a third floor in use, and her imagination was busy with exciting bedrooms for the grandchildren, tucked away under the eaves. It would be a new life all together. The house would mould them into something different.

Jean walked over to the shop door and looked out. If they didn't leave soon, this girl behind the counter would certainly worm out of Doreen the reason for their visit. She never could keep a secret for long. It had been child's play to get a confession about her affair with Jean's husband Ken. Armed with this, Jean had been able to reciprocate, and the pleasant truce between them had held.

'Hey, Doreen! I think that's the person we're meeting,' she said. 'Come on, let's go before he drives off again.'

They left the shop, and Josie quickly followed them to the door. She looked across at old Cyril's house, and watched a smart young man get out of the shiny Toyota. Wasn't that...? Yep, now he'd taken off his sunglasses, she was sure. He was Sharon Miller's new boyfriend from the estate agents in Tresham. She was known to be partial to estate agents. So that was it. Cyril's house was up for sale.

Josie picked up the telephone and dialled. Gran answered, fortunately. Josie was never sure whether her mother's strictures against gossip were genuine, or just a chance to appear virtuous in a family of gossips. 'Hello, Josie dear. Nothing wrong?'

'No, just thought you might like to know those women are looking at Cyril's house with an agent. So it *is* up for sale. Yes, Gran, quite sure. Yes, see you tomorrow. Bye.'

By next morning, most of the village knew that Cyril's house, at present rented by the Reverend Rollinson, was for sale.

Nineteen

'Hello? Lois, is that you?' It was a bad line, breaking up, and Cowgill guessed Lois was on her mobile.

'Of course it's me,' she said crossly. 'You can't have forgotten my voice so soon!'

He had not. Not much in his life these days gave him the same buzz. My God, talk about unrequited passion! Cowgill steadied himself, and said, 'Signal's not very good. Can you get a better one?'

'Hold on, I'll get out of the car.' Lois sighed. She had decided on impulse to telephone Cowgill, and the impulse was fading. Perhaps she was seeing things where there was nothing to see. But no, strange men did not seek to hire private detectives for no reason. And the Mayor? Wasn't he one of the most popular, upright figures Tresham had seen for a long time? Not a whisper of corruption or self-seeking?

'Is that better?' She was relieved to hear him say it was, and now wanted to get the conversation over as quickly as possible. 'Just a call I had. A man asking if I would make some private enquiries. God knows where he got my name. About an old colleague, he said. Somebody "in high office". Ring any bells?'

Same old Lois, thought Cowgill nostalgically. Never wasted time. Straight to the point. 'The name that immediately springs to mind,' he said calmly, 'is Jenkinson. A man of unimpeachable character. Our beloved Mayor.'

'Go on,' said Lois. How Cowgill did love to spin it out. Still, the old thing didn't have much fun, and she'd smiled at the tremor in his voice when he knew it was her.

'Nothing more to tell,' he said lightly. 'Except, perhaps...'

'Oh, come on! I've got work to do,' Lois said, impatient now. 'Except what? Bribery? Double-dealing? Rape and pillage?'

'Close,' said Cowgill.

'I'm switching off in exactly ten seconds,' said Lois. 'One, two, three...'

'Have you noticed a shop opposite your office in Tresham? Name of Rain or Shine?'

'Of course,' Lois said. Then the penny dropped. 'And he's a customer? The chief pillar of the community is into sexy fun with shiny macs and magic moments? So that's why I saw you there ... all part of our brave boys in blue keeping an eye on things, making it safe for the good folk of Tresham?'

'All right, Lois,' Cowgill said, laughing.

'Enough said, I think. Perhaps you'd just watch out for developments? Just in case? And report back, even if you do despise us for wasting time with harmless peccadilloes when we could be solving murders.'

'Peccadilloes?' said Lois. 'Are they the latest in Fergus Forsyth's stocklist? I must tell Derek. Yeah, well,' she added. 'I'll do what you say. Keep an eye, especially as the lovely Lady Mayoress is looking at old Cyril's house in the village. Could be an interesting new customer for our Josie. Mind you, she don't stock no peccadilloes.' She disconnected, glad to have given starchy old Hunter something to laugh at on a dull day.

It was a morning for clandestine telephone conversations, though Daisy's talk with Howard Jenkinson had not been exactly clandestine from her end. Rupert knew she would ring her old partner, but didn't want to be there when she made the call. So as soon as he'd gone off to the shop, she dialled the Town Hall and asked to speak to Mr Jenkinson. To her dismay, a woman's voice answered. 'Mayor's Parlour,' said the cool voice. 'Can I help you?'

'I wanted to speak to Mr Jenkinson,' said Daisy firmly. She was not about to be intimidated by a mere secretary. 'It's personal.'

'May I have your name?' The cool voice was icier. It was Jean Slater, at her efficient best. 'We have to be careful with security, you know,' she added. Who was this woman? One of Howard's many ex-flutters? And why did she want to speak to him now?

'Just tell him I am his old friend Daisy.' That should be enough. And what business was it of this nosy female, anyway? Daisy had long experience of being discreet when needed. 'He'll not be pleased to have missed me, and I haven't got all day, dear.' That should fix Miss Icicle.

It did. Jean decided this would be an entertaining one. 'Call for you, Howard,' she said. 'Your old friend Daisy. Nice to keep in touch with old friends, isn't it?' She put him through before he could reply.

'What a coincidence!' he said heartily, as he heard Daisy's voice. 'I was thinking about you the other day. Remembering the fun we used to have! Ah, those were good old days.'

'Not so much of the old days,' said Daisy. 'You're still looking pretty chipper yourself, Howard. And I'm not looking so bad meself, though I says it as shouldn't. Anyway, plenty of fun to be had, even if we do have a few wrinkles, you and I!'

Howard shifted in his Mayoral chair, a creaking leather-covered seat that looked very like a modest throne. 'Glad to hear it,' he said encouragingly. 'Now, what can I do for an old friend, Daisy?'

'It's more what I can do for you,' she

replied softly. 'Any chance of you popping in here in Farnden one day soon? On your way to somewhere, perhaps? My Rupert's out a lot at the moment, so he'll be sorry to miss you, but I can make you very welcome…'

'Er, hem, yes, Daisy dear, I'm sure you can,' Howard said in a whisper. He could see the door between his parlour and Jean's office was not quite shut. He'd better bring this conversation to a quick close.

But Daisy had not finished. 'Of course,' she said, 'it'd be really nice if you could do me a little favour in return for a warm, very warm, welcome?'

'Certainly. Nothing easier.' So that was it. The Forsyths were hard up and needed money. Business not doing so well? He couldn't believe that. Anyway, better sign off straight away and find a way of calling in on her. Doreen had been keen he should look at the Farnden house, but he obviously couldn't take her to the Forsyths! Maybe it could somehow be arranged. He assured Daisy that anything he could do to help would give him great pleasure. 'For old times' sake,' he said, and as he put down the phone he heard her laugh. 'And new times' sake too, Howard,' she chuckled. Then he heard a click, the unmistakeable click of Jean disconnecting from the same call. Surely not! He knew she was obsessively curious about his private life, of which she had once been a part, but would she stoop to listening in? Yes, she would. Howard resolved that Jean must be moved on as soon as possible.

The door between them opened, and she came in, bearing papers. 'Time to get down to work, Howard,' she said. 'I expect you'll be pleased to be free of all this bureaucracy at the end of your term of office. Give you more time for golf and other pleasures.' She dumped the papers down on the desk in front of him, and departed.

Howard winced as the door slammed. Yes, Jean Slater, he said under his breath. Your days are numbered.

Twenty

Doreen had not told Howard that she and Jean had already seen the Farnden house. She knew he would explode. He took the lead in all things, and would consider it an insult to his head-of-the-family status. The young estate agent had grinned, but promised that he would treat their preliminary visit as a secret. Doreen got the impression that this was not the first time he'd been sworn to secrecy, and she didn't trust him. But it was the best she could do, and had already planned her excuses if Howard should find out.

Now, sitting at the breakfast table, she was surprised when he said, 'Might as well pop over today and see that house. I'll give the agents a ring from the office.'

'Oh, good,' said Doreen, trying not to sound too enthusiastic. Howard always took up a cautious position the minute he suspected she was keen. 'Shall we go this afternoon, then? Will you be free after lunch?'

Howard had his answer ready. 'Well,' he said, as if thinking it out, 'I do have to be in Waltonby at five. School Open Evening and I've promised to look in, informally, so there's no need for you to come. Saves them buying a bouquet, and all that! So maybe the best thing ... yes, that's what we'll do ... we'll go to Farnden separately, in two cars. Then you can come home after we've seen the house, and I can go on to Waltonby. I'll be in my own car, not the limo, so I can meet Ken at the golf club after that. We're hoping for nine holes before supper.' Brilliant, he congratulated himself. That would give him plenty of time to call on Daisy.

What's he up to? thought Doreen. He had that shifty look she knew so well. Still, she didn't much care, as long as they could get an offer in on the house before anyone else. 'So I'll see you there, then,' she said. 'Will you suggest four o'clock?'

'Let's make it two thirty,' said Howard casually. 'I'll see you outside the house. And don't get your hopes up too high,' he could not resist adding. 'It'd be a big change for both of us, living in a village. It'll take a lot of thinking about.'

Not too much, Doreen muttered. She had already made up her mind. The house was full of character and potential, and she wanted it. She wanted to live there, and be a somebody in her own right. Mrs Jenkinson, President of the WI, Parish Councillor, maybe even join the church choir. That'd be one in the eye for Howard!

'Is that okay, Doreen?' Howard stood by the door, briefcase in hand, frowning. Doreen shook herself out of her daydream, and nodded. 'See you later,' she said, and poured herself another cup of tea.

Long Farnden was looking its best. As a conservation village it had the minimum of new building, and what there was had been discreetly placed in a small estate behind the church. The only real eyesore was the new vicarage, which had been rebuilt at the least possible cost to the church, and was just as ugly as the one destroyed in the fire. There had been some problem with insurance, and corners had been cut.

But the rest of the village, its golden stone houses glowing in the sun, seemed welcoming and cheerful as Doreen drove down the long main street, pulling up outside old Cyril's house. It was like coming home, already! She looked into her driving mirror, and saw Howard's sleek car pulling in behind her. He got out swiftly, and tapped on her window. 'Out you get, pet,' he said. 'Nobody here from the agents yet?'

He was in tycoon mode, and pulled out his mobile. 'Hello! Jenkinson here. Where's your chap? I made an appointment, and I expect it to be kept.'

Before there was time for a reply, the Toyota appeared, and the young man was with them. 'Sorry,' he said humbly. 'Got held up in traffic.'

'I came the same way,' Howard said, 'and there were no hold-ups. Anyway, let's get going.' He looked up at the old house, noting the need for re-pointing and the slipping slates. 'Don't suppose it will take us long,' he added, and took Doreen's arm. 'Lead on, then,' he ordered the agent, and they followed him into the house.

It was more of a success than Doreen could have hoped for. Howard was clearly pleasantly surprised. The vicar was out, but the agent had a key and permission to show buyers around. Rev Rollinson was a tidy man, and had loved the old house. He'd re-decorated much of it, and had found a sympathetic home for his lovingly collected antique pieces. 'I bet the vicar doesn't want to move into that dreadful new house,' Doreen said, looking round at vases of flowers and real paintings on the walls. She made a mental note to visit the gallery in the village. Her own reproductions of old masters and scenes of holiday places they had visited would not do for this house. She and Jean could have a lovely time tracking down originals. Mind you, originals cost money.

'Up we go, then,' Howard said. He began to see himself living here, inviting friends from the Club to dinner in the beamed dining room, with its old stone fireplace. A leaping log fire in the winter, some really good wine. Yes, it was looking good.

The bedrooms were pleasant, all white and full of sunlight. 'Not really much to do inside, is there?' he said to Doreen. 'Quite a bit needed on the stonework and roof, I reckon, but we could live in the house more or less straight away.' He looked down into the back garden, and saw an orchard of old trees, a sloping lawn running down to a stream. Oh yes, he could see them in the summer, out on the terrace with tinkling glasses of Pimms, watching the dog playing ball with the grandchildren. They didn't have a dog, of course, but that was easily fixed.

When they were outside on the pavement,

Howard looked at Doreen and nodded. Then he turned to the agent, and said, 'I'll be in touch. Quite a bit to be spent on it, so I'll work out the figures and make an offer. Hold it for us, will you? You know who I am, don't you? Contact me at the Town Hall. Mayor's Parlour. Don't want to bother the little woman with the details, do we, pet?'

Doreen restrained herself with ease this time. She couldn't believe it was all going so well. Maybe Howard wasn't a total philistine, after all.

She watched him drive off, and noticed he had taken the wrong road for Waltonby. A passing suspicion reminded her of his shifty performance at breakfast. He'd probably got another call to make. She looked up and down the street, a villager in spirit if not in fact yet. A familiar car was parked outside the shop, and she saw Bill coming out with a bag of shopping.

'Hi, Bill!' she called. He stopped and stared, then waved, and walked towards her. 'Hello, Mrs Jenkinson,' he said. He noted her car parked outside Cyril's, and added, 'Glad to see you've had a look at the house. What d'you think?'

'I love it!' Doreen's face was alive with enthusiasm. 'And what's more, Howard seemed keen too. We're going to make an offer. It's bigger than I thought, with those bedrooms in the roof, so I'll certainly need you to carry on cleaning for us. I can't tell you how grateful I am for your suggestion.'

'What about the bathroom?' said Bill slyly. 'You'll need to re-do that – install a heart-shaped bath!'

Doreen was ready for him. 'Oh, I dunno,' she said lightly. 'I thought maybe a jacuzzi?'

'Point taken,' said Bill, laughing. 'Well, I must be going. Rebecca'll be home early, and we're going in to Tresham. Shopping, cinema and meal afterwards. High life for us today. Cheers, Mrs Jenkinson.'

'But Bill,' said Doreen, 'isn't Rebecca needed at the Open Evening?' Bill had told her proudly about Rebecca's teaching job in Waltonby. 'Oh, no, that's next week,' said Bill, leaving her speechless on the pavement.

Howard drove around the back streets for a bit, until he was sure Doreen would be on her way home, then he cruised back and parked twenty yards or so on from the Forsyths' house. Daisy opened the door as soon as she saw him at the garden gate. 'Howard! How nice of you to call,' she said in a society lady voice. After the door closed behind him, she became her old self.

'Hey! Watch out,' Howard protested, as she gave him a smacking kiss, leaving lipstick traces that he swiftly rubbed off in front of the hall mirror.

'Just can't believe you're here and all mine

again,' she said, grinning apologetically.

She settled him into a comfortable sofa, and brought in tea. 'You've remembered my favourites,' he said, selecting a chocolate digestive biscuit.

'How could I forget?' she said softly, sitting down beside him.

Later, she told him about the extension and their difficulties with planning permission. As she had hoped, he waved an expansive hand, and said not to worry, he would take care of it. 'Leave it to me, Daisy,' he said, relieved that she had not asked for money.

'We're trying to tidy up the business, you see,' she confided. 'Fergus is fed up, says nobody but his father knows where anything is to be found. Rupert gets cross with him and says he's an idle boy, but he has agreed to sort out everything with Fergus. And so we'll need the extra space for getting records and files in order, Rupert says. He's kept records of every transaction since we started.'

Was there a tiny hint of a threat? Howard said quickly, 'No problem, Daisy dear,' and eased himself out of her front door, looking round furtively to see if anyone was watching. 'And I'll try to call in again soon. Thanks for the tea – the perfect hostess, as always.'

She blew him a kiss, and shut the door behind him. What a dear old plonker, she

126

thought. Pompous as ever, but still lovable. Besides which, she told herself as she stacked the dishwasher, if entertaining Howard was a means to an end, she was not complaining. And when the planning permission was granted, Rupert would be grateful and make a fuss of her again.

Twenty-One

Friday the thirteenth, and Norman Stevenson woke up feeling terrible. He had, as part of his new fitness regime, played golf yesterday evening with three other friends, and had enjoyed himself. His golf was improving, and he certainly felt better for the exercise. They had had a bite to eat in the clubhouse, and then he should have come home. But he didn't. He stayed, playing cards and drinking, until closing time, and his friends had dropped him off outside the house. He'd managed the stairs, and fallen into bed in a more than usually befuddled state.

Now, his head pounding and feeling sick, he made his way gingerly to the bathroom, and then decided to go downstairs and see if a cup of tea would help. He had forgotten it was Friday the thirteenth.

As he approached the bottom stair, he noticed the post had come. It must be late, and he wondered whether to call the office and plead sickness. But one of his fellow golfers was a colleague, and would know the truth. He picked up the letters, and was about to put them aside for later, when he drew in his breath sharply, his head swimming. A square white envelope, with his name and address in blue capitals.

A sudden fierce surge of nausea sent him running to the cloakroom, where he heaved and shuddered for a few agonising minutes. He sank to the floor, his head in his hands, until the cramps ceased. Then he struggled slowly to his feet, picked up the letters from the floor, and tottered into the kitchen. Maybe he would just tear it up and put it straight in the bin. What could Howard do to him now? The threats were empty, surely. He knew as much about Howard as Howard knew about him. He picked up the envelope and twisted it in his hands. On the other hand, Howard had an enormous amount of influence, and he had none. Somehow Howard would be able to wriggle out of any accusations, whereas he would just go under. Old evidence would be resurrected, and he would very likely end up in court – maybe in jail! Serious cases of fraud could end in a jail sentence, couldn't they?

He took a knife and slit open the envelope. The neat blue capitals spelled it out: he was to send money – ways and means detailed – to a box number. It was a large amount, but not so large that he would be unlikely to be able to comply. Once more, the message ended with a threat. DO AS YOU ARE TOLD, NORMAN, OR ELSE. That was all. Or else what? Norman did not need to be told.

He began to shake, and it was not hangover shakes. It was pure fear. The fear of the helpless victim who can only obey. He struggled to his feet again, and went back to bed, pulling the blankets over his head, all thoughts of work gone. He had to think. There *was* something he could do, and there was now no alternative. Blackmailers never gave up. Even though Howard could not possibly need the money, Norman knew that it was a demonstration of power, the power of the strong man over the weak. Yes, he could afford the few hundred in this demand. But how much next time? His resources were not large, and Howard knew that.

Norman reached out for a pill, took a swig of water and swallowed it. When he awoke, he would have a shower, get dressed and pull himself together. He would show Howard Jenkinson just who was the stronger of the two. Then a thought struck him. Was it really

Howard? He couldn't quite square Howard with a demand for money. But who else? An unknown enemy was worse. No, nobody else would know about those business irregularities. It must be Howard.

In the small office in Sebastopol Street, Hazel sorted the post and found no nasty surprises. It was mostly junk mail, with one or two invoices for goods ordered for New Brooms, and a nice letter from a client who was moving away and no longer needed their services. She put that to one side to give to Mrs M, who had telephoned to say she'd be looking in this morning on her way to market. Hazel smiled. Gran was perfectly capable of doing all the shopping required in the Meade household, and loved an expedition on the bus to Tresham on market days. But Lois reserved this for herself. She seemed determined to keep her feet on domestic ground, reflected Hazel. Just like when I first knew her. It was a small outfit, but Lois ran it with a firm hand even then. She knew exactly what she wanted, and worked hard to make sure her children, husband and the business, all received a share of her attention. Of course, it was better when Gran went to live with them. She was a good old thing, and although she and Lois had sparks between them sometimes, mostly because they were so alike, the arrangement worked well. Hazel looked at her watch. Lizzie was next door, and Maureen usually brought her in to have a kiss and cuddle from Hazel for a few minutes. 'Just to remind her I'm not far away,' Hazel had said to Lois, who had nodded and agreed it was a good idea, so long as no clients were in the office. That was Lois all over. First things first. Still, you knew exactly where you were with her.

Hazel's reverie was interrupted by Maureen arriving with the baby, and handing her over with a laugh. 'She knows now when it's time to come,' she said. 'Began ittling a couple of minutes ago. Made it quite plain what she wanted!'

At that moment, Lois's van drew up outside, and she walked briskly into the office. 'Morning all,' she said, and kissed the baby's soft cheek. 'I'll bring her back later,' Maureen said quickly, but Lois said, 'No, don't go for a minute or two. I'd like a chat. Why don't we all sit down and have a coffee? And Lizzie can have some juice, can't she?'

Hazel was puzzled. Lois was not a known fan of small babies, and usually had no time for socialising in the office. An ulterior motive?

'I haven't had much of a chance to get to know you,' Lois said in a friendly fashion to Maureen. 'How's it working out with young Lizzie here? She's certainly growing fast!'

Maureen said all the right things, and then

Lois asked her how long she had lived next door. 'Three years,' she replied. 'My mum lives a couple of doors up. She's a big help when I've got a lot of work on.'

'Work?' said Lois quickly. 'You mean looking after children?'

Maureen shook her head. 'No, I think I told you. I do outwork sewing. Garments and things. The money's quite good, and I do it in my own time.'

'How interesting,' said Lois, although Hazel thought she couldn't imagine anything more boring. She supposed Maureen had to take on anything that supplemented her meagre income.

'Remind me, what kind of garments?' asked Lois, keeping the subject going. 'Designer work, is it? One-offs for the very rich?'

Maureen laughed. 'No, not really. Mind you, some of the clients might be very rich for all I know. They have very squashy cars, some of 'em. I see them coming and going across the road.'

Lois smiled. 'Ah, now I remember. The stuff for Rain or Shine? Shiny macs, frilly aprons, nurses' uniforms, that sort of thing?'

Maureen nodded. 'Very quirky, some of it. Still, there's no accounting for taste, and so long as the money comes in, it's none of my business.' She got up, saying, 'Well, I'd better be taking Miss Lizzie back. Time for her rest.

Come on, sweetheart, come with Auntie Maureen. We'll see Mummy later. Bye, then. Bye, Mrs Meade.'

'Nice to talk to you,' Lois smiled. 'See you again, I expect.'

Hazel narrowed her eyes and looked at Lois. 'What're you after, Mrs M? Don't tell me all that was just polite interest. You got something going with Cowgill again?'

There was a touch of envy in Hazel's voice. She missed her own association with Cowgill, the edge of excitement in providing him with information that only she knew how to find. Still, she had plenty to do at home now, with husband and baby, and her job here in Sebastopol Street. 'Not that you're going to tell me if you have,' she added.

Lois laughed. 'That's right,' she said. 'Now, what've you got in the post?' Hazel showed her the nice letter, and they agreed that it made it all worthwhile. A few minutes later, Lois said she'd better get going, else all the bargains would have gone, and disappeared.

A car went slowly past Rain or Shine, and Hazel got up to look out of the window. It was a large one, and familiar. Yep, it had the town crest on the side, and stopped up the road. It was there for only a few minutes, and when the errand was done it moved off at speed. He's playing with fire, muttered Hazel, and returned to her desk.

★ ★ ★

133

In the stuffy interior of Rain or Shine, Fergus Forsyth opened the note the chauffeur had brought and was puzzled. An invitation to meet the Mayor at a reception for local business people next week. Why on earth should he be invited? Surely His Worship would want to keep him as far away from the Town Hall as possible. Anyway, it should be Dad going along. He's the boss. Fergus scratched his head. Very odd. Oh well, he'd talk to Dad about it. Maybe he'd have a clue what was behind it. He stuck the note in his jacket pocket and got on with sorting a new delivery.

Twenty-Two

Jean Slater walked along the corridors of the stately Victorian Town Hall, carrying a sheaf of papers. It was the second year that Howard had organised a reception for the business worthies of the town. Or rather, thought Jean bitterly, that *she* had organised it. Howard had waved his hands around a lot, issuing ideas and orders and lists of dos and don'ts. It was her job to sort this out, and present him with a plan for the event which appeared to be lavish and generous, but was, in fact, all done on a tight budget.

The guest list this year had increased, and Jean was finding it difficult to keep within the allotted finance. She reached the Mayor's Parlour, and went straight into Howard without knocking. He was on his feet, staring out of the window. He turned rapidly, and seeing that it was her, said, 'Ah, there you are, Jean. I didn't hear you knock. Now, sit down. I have something to tell you.'

He had made up his mind. As he had not long to go in this term of office, he had evolved a plan which he congratulated himself was very cunning.

'You're looking tired, my dear,' he began.

'So would you, Howard, if you had a husband and a job to cope with, and never quite enough money to go round.' She knew immediately what he was about, and decided to forestall him. 'If I didn't have this job – which I hope you'll agree that I do very efficiently – it would be hard for us to make ends meet. I don't suppose Ken ever mentions it. Beneath his dignity! But it's true. I hope you've no fault to find with my work, Howard?'

'Of course not,' he said swiftly. 'But I have been thinking about you. I often do, you know. Think about ways of lightening your load here in the office. Now, what do you think of this? We will get you some help, an assistant. I intend to round off my term with a bevy of engagements and activities for the good people of Tresham to remember me by! So there'll be more for you to do. Too much, I think, to ask of you. I am well aware of how little you are paid. So I have decided to supplement that with a small honorarium from me personally. Then I shall request an assistant for the extra amount of work, and push that through the necessary channels with no difficulty. I have a girl in mind...'

I am sure you have, most of the time, thought Jean sourly. 'Oh yes,' she said. 'Who's that then? Susanna Jacob?'

Howard sniffed, and did not reply. 'All settled then?' he said, after a moment.

'Except for the small honorarium from you personally,' said Jean flatly. 'No thanks. Not in a million years, Howard. Now, if you'll excuse me, I have to make some telephone calls. I'll have a final report on arrangements for this evening's reception for you this afternoon.'

She walked away with a straight, stiff back, and closed the door quietly behind her.

Howard sighed. That had not gone quite as he'd planned, but at least she hadn't turned down the assistant idea. He cheered up. Now, he must get that going as soon as possible. He picked up the telephone.

Rupert Forsyth had been as puzzled as his son over the invitation to the Mayor's reception. He knew such things happened, but never dreamt his business would be included on the list. And why Fergus? He was known to many people in Tresham, being the front man, as it were, for Rain or Shine. Had it anything to do with Daisy's scheme for persuading Howard Jenkinson to help them with planning permission?

'Daisy?' She was ironing in the kitchen, and listening to the radio. It was the afternoon play, and she turned to him, frowning him into silence. He waited until it had finished, then asked her if she had any clues as to why Rain or Shine should be honoured by the Mayor in this way.

She folded a shirt neatly, and shook her head. 'God knows,' she said. 'Doesn't sound like Howard, does it? Anyway, things are different these days. Different attitudes, an' that. Maybe he wants to show how broad-minded and sophisticated he is!'

'Nonsense!' Rupert was irritated by her light-hearted reaction. He smelled a rat, but couldn't place it.

'Oh, don't be silly, Rupert,' Daisy said. 'It'll be nice for Fergus, won't it? He can mix with the high and mighty, and maybe do a bit of business on the side. No doubt that's part of the reason for the whole thing. You know, like Rotary and them.' Rupert had never attempted to join the Rotary Club, though several of its august members were well known to him.

'I suppose so,' he said. It was no good worrying about it. 'I just hope he behaves himself,' he said, and left her to the ironing.

Fergus had taken great trouble with his appearance, and set off for the Town Hall feeling quite pleased with himself. He'd had his hair cut, shaved off his designer stubble, and had his one good grey suit cleaned and pressed. A modest old school tie completed the respectable conservative impression he wished to give, and he walked into Reception with a jaunty air.

'Upstairs, turn right, and you'll see the others,' said the friendly receptionist. Fergus nodded his thanks, winked at her, and set off up the wide stone staircase. An attractive girl with a clipboard stood at the door to the large, oak-panelled room, with its long, velvet-curtained windows looking over Tresham. Standing by one of the windows was Howard, monarch of all he surveyed.

'Fergus Forsyth, Rain or Shine,' he said confidently. The girl looked down the guest list that Jean Slater had given her, and ticked off the name. 'Welcome,' she said brightly. 'Champagne is circulating ... just go on in. You'll find lots of friends, I'm sure,' she added, and turned to the person waiting behind Fergus.

Jean, standing unobtrusively chatting to

Doreen in the corner, watched carefully. 'He's here,' she said, and Doreen nodded. 'Should be interesting,' she said lightly, and walked across to join a group of women from the Soroptomists. These businesswomen would have been the last people Doreen would have sought out, except that she wore her chain of office, and that, for the moment, was her passport to their snooty circle. And, more importantly, from their position in the room, she could keep an eye on Howard.

Jean, too, made sure she had a clear view. Fergus was working his way round the room, and Jean smiled at the startled faces of some of those he passed on the way. He was approaching Howard now, and ... yes, Howard was turning in his direction. She saw Fergus's smile freeze, and then watched with increasing gratification as Howard's colour rose to a vivid purple.

Fergus, on the other hand, was puzzled. Howard Jenkinson hissed at him, 'What the hell are *you* doing here!' Fergus produced his invitation. 'Same as everyone else, I suppose,' he had answered. 'I was invited. Look...' But Howard did not look at it. He glanced swiftly round the room, and took Fergus by the elbow. 'You're leaving,' he said. '*I* did not invite you, and you have to go. Right now.' All this was said in a desperate undertone, as he hustled Fergus through the dense crowd towards the exit.

'Ah, Mr Forsyth, how nice of you to come!'
It was Jean's cool voice, and she placed herself squarely between the pair of them and
their route to the door. 'Let me show you
where refreshments are,' she added sweetly,
without a glance at Howard. 'Just follow me
... Fergus, may I call you?' she said. 'It's a bit
of a scrum!' Finally she turned to look at
Howard. 'So sorry to interrupt, Mr Mayor,'
she said, with a social smile, 'but don't
worry, I'll bring him straight back. How's
your own glass?' she added. 'Shall I get you
a refill? You look as if you need it,' she
whispered, so that only he could hear.

Howard glared at her. There was nothing
he could do without making a scene, and he
turned away in despair. As he did so, he
intercepted a look from his loving wife
across the room to her old friend, Jean
Slater, and did not like it. He did not like it
at all. He returned to the window and made
a great effort to listen to the parking
problems of a transport company director,
but he was uncomfortably aware of the
silence that had fallen, and that only now
was the buzz of conversation resuming. He
was not imagining that voices were lowered,
and heads swivelled between himself and
that interloper now lifting a full glass of
champagne to his lips?

After all the guests had left, Howard went
to find Jean. She was in her office, waiting

140

for him. 'Right!' he said furiously. 'What's the explanation?'

'For what?' she said.

'You know perfectly well,' he said.

She shook her head.

'That Forsyth man!' he shouted at her. 'How did he get an invitation?'

'He was on the list,' said Jean calmly. 'Didn't you notice his name? I did show you the final list this afternoon.'

'No, I bloody well didn't notice!' Howard yelled. 'Of course I didn't! I trust you, you stupid bitch, to do your job properly! I've a good mind to send you packing right now!'

'I shouldn't, if I was you,' said Jean, standing up and reaching for her handbag. 'It wouldn't look good, would it? People might put two and two together, and you know how rumours circulate. Now, I must be going, Howard. Ken and I are off to the pictures tonight. Another re-run of *Brief Encounter* at the Classic Cinema. Quite appropriate, really,' she added with a smile. 'See you tomorrow. Good night, Howard. And don't bother to thank me for all my hard work. I really enjoyed it. G'night!'

Twenty-Three

Rupert Forsyth sat on a rickety chair in the back room of Rain or Shine, and stared angrily at his son. 'Well, what did you expect?' he said. Fergus had told him of his humiliation in the Mayor's Parlour.

'You'd have thought I was a dirty old tramp off the streets!' Fergus said again. 'He was about to turf me out by the scruff of the neck, when that nice Mrs Slater rescued me. I kept on telling him I'd received an invitation and been checked in on the list at the door, but he wouldn't listen. Just kept spluttering and pushing at me to get out. God, what a nasty piece of work!'

Rupert was silent, thinking. If Howard had been as angry as Fergus reported, he'd be unlikely to help them now with the planning permission for the extension. The boy had undone all the good done by his mother. Daisy had been so sure it would all be fine. 'No problem,' Howard had said. And he, Rupert, could not pretend he did not know how she had persuaded him. It rankled still, after all these years, although Daisy

142

protested, now as always, that she regarded the whole thing as a means to an end. 'Nothing serious, dear,' she always said. 'Think of it as a job I quite enjoy. And a little hold on Howard Jenkinson is all to the good, you can't deny that. We'll need a fair bit of influence to get those plans through.' Now he saw his son looking at him as if expecting an answer to some question.

'Are you listening, Dad?' Fergus was still simmering. 'I've a good mind to get my own back on the two-faced old devil!' he added. 'We bloody well know enough about his private life to humiliate *him* in spades!'

'Don't swear in this shop,' Rupert said automatically. 'And anyway, I reckon he was already humiliated,' he added flatly. 'What's more, this business depends on absolute confidentiality. So don't even think of it.' He was silent again, and after a few minutes stood up. 'Well, I must be getting back,' he said. 'There is one thing you can do with your hours of spare time,' he said acidly, 'and that is give some thought to the question of how your name came to be on that invitation list.'

'Does that mean you're not going to do anything about it, then?' asked Fergus angrily.

Rupert's fists were clenched. 'Oh, I promise I'll do something about it, all right,' he said, and added fiercely, 'but it's nothing to do with you, so I'd be glad if you'd just get on with your work and keep your eyes away from that window. The women in New Brooms are also nothing to do with you. I want to see some improvement in our sales figures, otherwise I shall have to come back in the shop myself and keep a check on you.'

Fergus looked at his father, at the veins throbbing in his temples and his high colour, and decided to say no more on the subject of Howard Jenkinson. Dad had said he intended to do something about it, and he seldom broke his promise.

In the kitchen of the Jenkinson house, the atmosphere was heavy with tension. After the reception the previous evening, Howard and Doreen had been driven home in complete silence. Neither said a word. Howard was too furious to speak, and Doreen was waiting patiently until he did, in order to assess the damage. She knew from the way he sat in the back of the big limousine, with a good metre of space between them, that he suspected her involvement in the Forsyth fiasco. She hugged herself with delight when she thought about it. So she had been right, then, about his den and what it contained. Den of iniquity, she reckoned! She'd seen the stack of videos through the keyhole, and the rest was easy, knowing Howard's proclivities.

His reaction to young Fergus Forsyth couldn't have been more revealing. Goodness, in some ways Howard was a complete fool. Anyone with a grain of sense would have welcomed Fergus with a smile, pretended not to know him, asked his name, got away with it smoothly. But then, Howard was in some ways not a sensible man. He always said, at every possible opportunity, that he was a man who called a spade a spade. 'Plain man of the people,' as he had once sickeningly described himself to a local journalist. He never looked beyond the obvious, not even when – as in the case of Ken and herself – it stared him in the face.

Now, the next morning, they studiously ignored each other, and read their separate newspapers. Finally, Doreen decided to push things forward, one way or another. For one thing, she wanted to know how far they'd got with the Farnden house. One or two telephone calls from Howard could usually circumvent the most slow-moving bureaucrats or, come to that, any of the solicitors, agents, surveyors and all the company of hangers-on involved in house purchase.

'It *was* a nice evening, wasn't it?' she said conversationally. 'Successful, would you say?'

He stared at her.

'How dare you!' he spat at her.

'I beg your pardon?' she said politely. There was a strength in Doreen that always prevailed when under attack. Howard knew this, and though he would like to put her over his knee and smack her bottom as hard as he could – well, yes, he would quite like to do that! – he knew that her careful refusal to quarrel, or even raise her voice, always won in the end.

Useless, then, to attempt a confrontation, and ask what the hell she and Jean Slater thought they were up to. He knew, anyway. Jean was angry at him because of her job, and Doreen was angry on Jean's behalf. Funny, that, he thought, as he managed a half-smile and a grudging apology. It was funny that Doreen should be so close to a woman who'd happily tumbled with him in the hay. Well, women were a mystery. A lovely mystery, but very puzzling to a straightforward chap like himself.

'Yes, well,' he said, 'I suppose it was quite a good do. Last one for me, unless I do another Mayoral year sometime. Now, time for a little drinkie before lunch. Your usual, pet?'

After that, Doreen spent the rest of the day in the garden. Jean came round after work and they strolled about the immaculate lawns chortling over the previous evening. Howard was still at home, and looked at them from inside the sitting room, wondering what they were talking about for such a long time. Perhaps he'd ring Ken and fix up a round of golf. It looked like being a fine evening. Yes, that's what he'd do. He always won, and Ken never seemed to mind. He opened the French windows to join the girls and tell them what he planned.

In Long Farnden, Derek walked into the kitchen and pecked Lois on the cheek. 'Hi, love,' she said. 'Good day?'

'Not bad,' he said. 'Traffic was bad in Tresham. I stopped to get an evening paper, and wished I hadn't. Anyway, there's a picture of one of your clients. His Important Worship the Mayor, seen chatting at a champagne reception in the Town Hall. All right for some, I reckon. Especially as my taxes are probably paying for it.' He put the *Tresham Chronicle* down on the table, and washed his hands at the sink. Lois idly took up the paper and looked closely at the photograph.

It was indeed Howard Jenkinson, towering over a familiar figure. Howard was not smiling. In fact he looked frighteningly angry. Somebody had mischievously chosen an unflattering aspect of Tresham's Mayor.

'I reckon a few harsh words are being said,' Lois laughed. 'Here, Derek. Isn't that young Forsyth? Our Rupert's son? Hazel and her pal are chums with him, seeing as his shop's opposite ours. A surprise guest, from the look of it. What a joke!'

'Wheels within wheels, if you ask me,' said Derek. 'Corruption in high places. You stay well clear of it, me duck,' he added, seeing Lois's expression. 'Nothing to do with us.'

But Lois remembered the anonymous telephone call. She looked again at the photograph, and decided she'd not want to meet Howard Jenkinson in a narrow passage on a dark night. Especially if she'd somehow got on the wrong side of him. Whoever made an enemy of Howard Jenkinson would have cause to regret it. She was sure of that.

Twenty-Four

A month or so later, Howard had, as Doreen anticipated, pulled out all the stops. He'd arranged to buy the Farnden house, had put their own on the market, sold it within a week, and got builders working on old Cyril's roof and windows. A moving date was fixed, and the removal vans ordered from a local company who owed Howard one or two favours.

'They're doing all the packing, pet,' he said to a dutifully impressed Doreen. 'And all at a very good rate. I've got some chaps from the yard coming to help sort it all out at the weekend, and we should be straight by Monday.'

'I might go up to London tomorrow,' Doreen said lightly. 'Get new curtain fabric and one or two other things. Probably go to Harrods.'

'You'll be too busy see your sister, then?' Howard dreaded Doreen's visits to her sister. She always returned with stories of how emancipated and successful the wretched woman was. Unmarried, she had made a brilliant career in banking, and Doreen was exceedingly proud of her. And, thought Howard, more than a little envious.

'Of course I shall. It's only a step away from Harrods. I'll probably be fairly late back. She likes me to have supper with her.'

'You'll need some extra cash, I suppose,' said Howard grudgingly.

'That's nice of you, dear,' she said. 'My account's healthy, but curtains and things aren't personal, are they? Don't worry, Howard, I'll go easy.'

Privately, Doreen had no qualms about the spending spree she intended to have. They'd sold the Tresham house for well over a million, and Howard had beaten down the Farnden price. The work being done was all in the trade that Howard knew so well. It would be cost price for everything at old Cyril's. She always thought of it as old

Cyril's. Maybe she'd have a house nameplate engraved 'Old Cyril's'. That would annoy His Worship!

She was a wonder, this wife of his, Howard thought. He congratulated himself on choosing her from all the others. And now, as the move drew closer, she was unflustered, and seemed to think the whole thing was a great adventure.

The week before the move saw a great deal of activity in Farnden. The village knew all the details, of course, and was looking forward with eager anticipation to having such a rich source of gossip living amongst them.

In the shop, Gran and Josie were laughing at Derek's suggestion that they should put a welcome card through the Jenkinsons' door, with a list of specialities available. 'Fat chance,' Bill had said. 'Mrs Jenkinson has shopped at Waitrose since time began. She ain't likely to change her ways now.'

Lois propped herself on a stool by the post office window and said she thought it was an extremely good idea. The Jenkinsons already employed a Farnden cleaner, so why shouldn't they patronise the village shop? Josie agreed to think about it, and Gran disappeared to the store room to check supplies. 'Looks like they're just about finished across the road,' Lois said. 'The big day is almost here. Bill says Mrs J is very organised.

Everything labelled and sorted. He's been helping her, as there's not much cleaning to do now. Mayor's useless, apparently. Just walks about giving orders, which Mrs J ignores. The only thing old Jenkinson has done is pack up his mysterious den himself. Bill offered to help, but no, it was to be left to him.'

'Well, we all know now what he's got in there, grubby old sod,' said Gran, coming in with a pile of boxes. 'Anyway, who cares? Probably keeps the likes of Rupert Forsyth in business, from what I hear.'

'Is there anything you don't hear, Mum?' said Lois, laughing. 'Now, what did I come in for? Oh yes, Josie, have you got any more of that cheese your dad likes?'

Next morning, Doreen left Tresham on an early train. She parked at the station, and bought a return ticket to Euston. Once on the train, she felt all the heavy weight of being Howard's wife, Mayoress of Tresham, mother and grandmother, gradually slipping away. Now she was just Doreen, on her own with a pleasant day ahead. She had one duty job to do, and then she could relax in Harrods, meet her sister and talk about a different world altogether.

'You look good, for a woman about to move house,' her sister said. They were sipping martinis before supper, and Doreen looked around approvingly at her sister's cool, elegant flat.

'I'm looking forward to it. Chose some gorgeous stuff for new curtains, and ordered a new suite for the lounge. Howard will be furious, but he'll get over it.' She settled comfortably in her chair.

'Here,' said her sister, 'you've dropped a letter.' She looked at it idly. *'Is* it yours?' she added. 'It's addressed to a PO Box.'

Doreen took it swiftly and put it in her handbag. 'I just collected it for a friend,' she said. 'Now, how d'you make this martini? It's really delicious! I think I could be persuaded to have another.'

And so they moved on to other topics, were relaxed and happy with each other, and consumed a supper of salmon and strawberries with relish.

It was late by the time Doreen collected her car from Tresham station, and set off for home. She was pleasantly tired, but alert enough, she told herself. How had Howard managed? she wondered. Probably spent the evening at the Club with Ken Slater. She hoped all had gone well. So far, her plans for the day had been trouble free. She turned into the drive and saw the house in darkness. Fair enough, she said to herself, it is very late.

She walked through to the sitting room and put on a low lamp. There were newspapers on the floor where Howard had dropped them, and a whisky glass left on the table by his chair. All perfectly normal. She tidied the papers, stretched out a hand to pick up the glass, but then left it where it was. Then she walked over to the French windows, opened them wide, and walked out into the starry night.

'How lovely!' she murmured to herself. 'A perfect end to a perfect day.'

She walked through the shrubbery that Howard claimed was his idea, though in fact she had selected the plants and overseen the planting. Strolling out on to the lawns that swept up towards the pond, she smiled to herself. One day away from Tresham made her see things in perspective. Could I have lived my life differently? she wondered. Set out on a different course right from the beginning, more like my sister?

Now she was by the big pond, and a full moon shone down, its reflection shimmering in the water. By its light, Doreen could see the water lilies and the shadows of somnolent fish.

And something else.

Doreen peered down, and saw a long, dark shape floating on the surface, half covered by the wide leaves of the lily plants. It was the shape of a man, and she recognised the back of his head. She drew in her breath sharply, and then, looking round and seeing lights still on in the neighbouring house, she opened her mouth and screamed at the top of her voice.

She went on screaming, until her neighbour came running round and took her back into the house. He then took over, making the necessary telephone calls, and left his wife to sit with Doreen, who sat perfectly still and quiet, staring straight ahead, apparently oblivious of everything around her. Shock, thought her neighbour, and took Doreen's small, cold hand.

Twenty-Five

'Lois?'

'Oh, it's you. What d'you want at this hour of the morning?'

'Have you heard? About Jenkinson?'

'No, what about him? Bill's due there today to help with the packing up.'

'Ah,' said Cowgill. 'I think not necessary today. Howard Jenkinson has been found floating face down in his ornamental pond. Dead, of course. We'll be there today, checking everything over. You know the form. No,' he continued, 'it's not your Bill I want to see, though I will be speaking to him. I need to speak to you, privately as usual.'

'Oh, bloody hell,' said Lois, stunned at Cowgill's news. 'Was it an accident?' Even as she said it, she knew that it was exceedingly unlikely that a grown man would drown in his fish pond, provided that he was alive and well when he went in, and alone.

'That remains to be seen, at this stage,' replied the ever-cautious Cowgill. 'Now,' he continued, 'I want you to be at a new meeting place at two thirty tomorrow.'

'Hey, hey, wait a minute,' said Lois sharply. 'Let's have less of this "I want", if you don't mind! If I am free, I will certainly try to be there, wherever it is, but I do have a business and family to run, in case you've forgotten.'

There was a slight pause, and then Cowgill said, in a softer tone, 'Sorry, Lois. I'll re-phrase my request. Could you possibly be at your usual supermarket, by the bread counter, at two thirty on Saturday?'

'You're joking!' said Lois. 'In the super-market? How private is that?'

'Let me finish,' said Cowgill patiently. He had to get her to agree. Not only was one of her cleaners working for the Jenkinsons, but the Mayor had been moving to Long Farn-den, Lois's daughter ran the village shop, Jenkinson was now known to patronise Rain or Shine, and Lois's town office was right opposite in Sebastopol Street. He needed

Lois now, more than ever.

'I have an arrangement with the manager,' he continued. 'There is a small room behind the staff toilets that is not used. Except by me. You will see me waiting by the bread, then just follow me, not too closely. You'll see the door. And,' he said, anticipating her reaction, 'can you think of a better place than a supermarket for you to be seen without arousing suspicion?'

Clever bugger! thought Lois. Very proud of himself, our Hunter Cowgill. Ah well, she supposed it would be okay. She could always say she was taken short if anybody questioned her. Permission to use the staff toilets. 'Not a bad idea,' she said grudgingly. Then the overwhelming idea of Howard Jenkinson, Mayor of Tresham, dead in his own fish pond, drove everything else from her mind. She said a quick farewell and dialled Bill's number.

The news spread quickly. 'It was on the telly news,' said Josie in the shop. 'The whole village is in a state of shock, I reckon. What with him moving here, and everything. Everybody's very sorry for his wife. Seems she's been coming here on and off, measuring up and seeing to things, and people have liked her. No side, they say. A really nice woman, poor soul. What did you say you wanted, Mum?'

156

'Can't remember,' said Lois. 'It'll come back in a minute, but I'm just as shocked as the rest. Poor old Bill was speechless. I've told him to take the morning off, then he's at the vets this afternoon, so he'll be fine. Nothing like having your hand up a cow's arse to take your mind off murder.'

'Murder! Mum, d'you know something?' Josie's eyes widened, and Lois hastily backtracked.

'No, no, Josie. Of course I don't. Just a figure of speech. For God's sake don't spread that around, else I'll be in trouble.'

'Oh, so you're in touch with your copper again, are you?' Josie was not pleased, not just for herself and worrying about her mother's safety, but for her father's sake. She knew how much he hated Lois's involvement with Cowgill.

'I've just remembered!' Lois said quickly. 'We're out of Dad's chocolate ice-cream. Have you got one of those big tubs? And some digestive biscuits, too, please.'

Josie was well aware that Lois had changed the subject, and sighed. 'Do be careful, Mum,' she said. 'Old Jenkinson has an evil reputation in some circles. Made one or two enemies, apparently, and close to home. There'll be a lot of muck-raking, and you'd be well advised to stay out of it.'

'Yes, dear,' said Lois, smiling. 'And the ice-cream?'

Jean Slater was woken by Ken, who had got up early to make their usual cup of tea.

'Jean! Jean! Wake up! Something terrible has happened to Howard!'

Jean jerked up in bed and stared at him. 'Howard who?' she said stupidly.

'Howard Jenkinson, of course! Are you awake?'

She nodded, and rubbed her eyes. 'Has there been an accident?' she said.

Ken nodded. 'He's been found dead in that pond in his garden. You know, the one he boasts about.' Ken sat down heavily on a chair by the bed. 'Doreen found him,' he continued, 'and the police have been on the phone, wanting you to go round to the house. Seems Doreen is asking for you. Doesn't want to see her family. Just you. So you'd better get up and get round there.'

Jean put down her mug of tea untouched, and got out of bed. 'Right,' she said briskly. 'Ring back and say I'll be there in half an hour ... no, make it an hour. I've got arrange-ments to make.'

'I expect you have,' said Ken dully. 'And so have I. Howard ... we were going to have a round of golf this afternoon...'

Jean snorted. 'Golf? Again? You'll be wanted for questioning about a lot of things besides golf, Ken dear. Now go and make that call, and I'll get dressed.'

Sebastopol Street was deserted, and the door of Rain or Shine firmly locked. A furtive-looking man tried several times to alert Fergus, clearly visible speaking on the telephone inside, but had no luck. He went away, hurriedly glancing up and down the street as he went.

Fergus had heard the news and immediately telephoned his father, who had scarcely been able to speak. Rupert had finally managed to instruct him to keep the shop closed all day, and to talk to nobody. Nobody at all. 'Not until I get over there,' Rupert had said. Fergus had started to argue, saying they'd already lost a potential customer, but Rupert had interrupted, 'Do as you're bloody told, boy!' Fergus had put down the phone without replying.

Rupert had turned from the telephone to find Daisy beside him, looking puzzled. Now she followed him out of the hall, and said, 'What's going on?'

'Disaster,' Rupert replied in a choked voice, and brushed past her to go into the sitting room. He gave her a quick account of what Fergus had told him, and was shocked to see the pallor of her face. She raised her hands in horror, shook her head, and then slid gently to the floor in a faint. A glass of cold water and gentle coaxing from Rupert brought her round, and he lifted her bodily and set her down on the sofa.

He stroked her face, and eventually she opened her eyes and said, 'Sorry.' Tears splashed out on to his hands, and she tried ineffectually to rub them away. 'How...?' she said.

'Drowned,' said Rupert. 'At least, he was found by his wife in their fish pond. Apparently she'd been in London all day, and got back late.'

'Oh, poor Howard,' Daisy said shakily. 'He was so proud of that pond. Told me all about it when we...'

'Yes, well,' said Rupert, his jaw set. 'The less we say about that, the better. I expect we'll get a visit from the police. Howard's shopping chauffeur is bound to be questioned. Don't forget he was always nipping round to Rain or Shine in the Mayor's car. *And* they'll be wanting to talk to us about Jenkinson's Town Hall do, where Fergus represented the business. The whole town saw that picture in the paper – remember Howard glaring angrily at Fergus? What on earth made the little fool decide to go?' he added furiously.

Daisy turned her face away from him, and began to cry again, softly and quietly. 'Poor Howard,' she murmured, and Rupert walked away, his face thunderous.

In his dusty flat in the Manchester suburb,

Norman Stevenson sat listening to the local radio station. He had heard an early news item about Howard's death, and was now rooted to his chair in a state of shock. He had listened to every bulletin after the first, until the story slipped out of the headlines and was finally superseded by more recent items. But Norman remained in his chair, ignoring the telephone which had been ringing repeatedly all day. Finally, after listening blankly to persistent knocking on his door, he got unsteadily to his feet and looked out to see his secretary, a worried frown on her face, standing there.

'Norman!' she said, as he opened the door. 'Are you all right? We were worried in the office. You never said anything about not coming in, or...' Her voice tailed off as she saw that he was unshaven, fully dressed in a rumpled suit, and stared vacantly at her as if he had no idea who she was.

'And it's Friday again,' was all he said.

Twenty-Six

Saturday, and Lois sat at the lunch table with Gran and Derek, reading the Tresham paper. The front page was edged in black. A large portrait of Howard Jenkinson in full Mayoral rig occupied most of the page, and a single line of text expressed the town's feelings exactly. It was all-embracing, and Lois nodded approval. '"Tresham Mourns a Legend",' she read. 'Read on for details of the legend,' she continued, handing the paper to Derek. 'Mayor found dead in eighteen inches of water,' she improvised. 'Floating bum up. Wife distraught. Questions asked. What d'you think, Derek?'

'Lois,' interrupted Gran sharply, 'I do think you should show more respect for the dead. The poor man did a lot of good in the town, you know. Helped a lot of people, and worked very hard. Harder than most mayors we've had in Tresham. I don't know what you've got against him.'

Lois shook her head. 'Nothing at all, Mum. You are quite right.'

'And so are you, Lois,' Derek said, head

down and reading avidly. 'There's a lot of stuff in the inside pages about suspected corruption and waste of money, as well as the usual guff about being kind to old ladies and dogs.'

'And talking to every student as if he was actually interested,' added Hazel, coming into the kitchen. 'Kids I know think he was wonderful.' The Tresham office was closed on Saturdays, and she had the week's report for Lois. 'Hope you didn't mind my coming in – couldn't make anyone hear. Everybody's in a state of shock in the village and your Josie's been rushed off her feet with everybody coming in for news.'

Lois looked at the clock. 'Blimey,' she said, 'it's time I was moving. I'm going shopping this afternoon.'

'I might come with you,' Derek said. 'I need a few bits and pieces from the supermarket. And I can keep an eye on your trolley,' he added with a grin. Lois was known for sudden bursts of shopping fever, and Derek still paid the housekeeping bills.

Her reaction surprised him. 'No need,' she said quickly. 'Give me a list, and I'll get them for you. I can do without you chivvying at my elbow. I'll be off in ten minutes, so get writing.' She stood up and left the kitchen, leaving Derek and Gran looking at each other.

Hazel filled in the silence. 'What's Mrs M

got in mind, d'you think?' she said lightly. 'A secret assignation?'

Derek did not laugh, but made an effort. 'What? At the second checkout from the right? You'll have to do better than that, Hazel.'

Gran said nothing, but knew her daughter too well to doubt that she was up to something again.

Lois spotted Cowgill's tall, upright figure above the heads of the shopping crowd, and waited until he disappeared before making for the bread counter. She put a bag of doughnuts into her basket, and walked slowly towards the door he had described. A young assistant stopped her. 'Excuse me,' she said. 'This is private through here.'

Lois smiled at her, and made her prepared excuse. 'My friend works here,' she said, 'and I know there's a staff toilet. I've got this cystitis bug, and need to go badly.' She made a convincingly agonised face.

The girl stood aside. 'Right, then,' she said. 'But we can't have just anyone...'

Lois walked quickly through and located the room where Cowgill stood waiting for her. He closed the door, and said, 'We shan't be disturbed. Sit down, Lois, and listen for a bit. Then you can have your say.'

'Have a doughnut,' Lois said, offering him the bag.

'This is extremely serious,' he said firmly. Then he gave her an admirably succinct account of the story so far. Howard Jenkinson had been found by his wife, and was taken from the pond to be subjected to a series of tests. These had shown that he was drowned, had been alive before going into the water and, in spite of first suspicions, had not suffered a heart attack. He must have been mildly drunk, judging by the level of alcohol in his blood. A whisky glass had been found by his armchair, and bore his prints only. At this last detail, Lois raised her eyebrows, but said nothing.

'What I want from you, Lois,' Cowgill said, 'is all the information you and your family and cleaners can supply, as quickly as possible, on the Jenkinsons. We shall, of course, be questioning all the known contacts, but there are some who'll tell you things they won't tell us. Not straight away, anyway. Just do your usual ferreting, and keep in touch. This is going to be a nasty case, I'm afraid, so be careful.'

'What *are* you talking about?' Lois said. 'It looks pretty straightforward to me. Old Jenkinson is left on his own. Little wifey living it up in London. He sits down with the telly and the whisky bottle, until he feels a bit sick. Goes out into the garden to clear his head, trips on a stone and falls headlong into the pond. Fish scarper and are fine, but old

165

Howard is so befuddled he can't get out, and drowns. Simple?'

Cowgill shook his head. 'You know perfectly well it isn't,' he said, moving towards the door. 'Howard Jenkinson was a fit, strong man. Even a stomach full of whisky – and there's still half a bottle left in the cupboard – wouldn't have stopped him crawling out. The instinct to survive is very strong. And Howard Jenkinson was a great survivor,' he added, as he opened the door. 'Keep in touch, Lois. And thanks for coming.' He touched her arm as she passed by him, and she gave him a smile that made him dizzy.

In the neat and tidy sitting room of a pretty stone cottage on the outskirts of Round Ringford, only a few miles from Long Farnden, the television was on with the sound turned down. Hunched on the sofa, Susanna Jacob was also reading the local paper.

Her long blonde hair had fallen over her face, but she didn't flick it back behind her ears as usual. She stared at the portrait of Howard Jenkinson and the short caption beneath. Her father, a Tresham solicitor who knew more than most about the late Mayor, entered the room, but did not see the tears splashing down until he noticed wet spots on the newspaper.

'Susanna! What on earth's the matter?'

'Nothing,' she muttered, and rushed from

166

the room, leaving Howard Jenkinson staring confidently up from the sofa. Her father retrieved the paper, and studied the strong, handsome face. 'Come here, dear!' he called loudly to his wife. She would know what to do. His only daughter was very dear to him, but he had long ago acknowledged that he needed her mother to interpret what went on in her lovely head.

Twenty-Seven

The funeral of Howard Jenkinson would be a grand affair, according to gossip. 'Pity he couldn't have been here to see it,' Lois said to Gran, as they stood in the crowd, waiting for the procession to approach.

They had come into town, claiming they had to do market shopping, but both were keen to see the spectacle. Gran because she was a Royal watcher, and, for her, the Tresham Mayor came a close second; and Lois because she hoped to pick up some clues. They had immediately noticed flags flying at half-mast on all the public buildings.

'Anybody'd think he'd done some really good things,' Lois said, and Gran said how did Lois know he hadn't? He might have hidden his light under a bushel. 'What? Howard Jenkinson? Not likely!' Lois had laughed, and been reprimanded once more for speaking ill of the dead.

'Here they come, Lois!' The crowd had become thicker outside the Victorian red-brick parish church, built optimistically large for congregations who never came. But now, when municipal power and glory were on show, it came into its own. Gran had to stand on tiptoe in order not to miss anything. First came the Mace-Bearer, with black tie and solemn tread, his Mace draped below the coronet. Then the Mayor's large coffin, highly polished and with ornate silver handles. 'Look, Lois – oh, isn't that sad? There's his Mayor's robe and hat on the coffin, and them red ribbons.'

'I wonder if it all gets buried with him?' Lois said. 'I mean, suppose the next mayor was a little short, fat man?'

Gran didn't answer. She would just ignore Lois and her flippant remarks. The Leader of the Council followed, bearing the Chain of Office on a black cushion, and Gran whispered to Lois that she remembered that Martin Briggs from when he was a pimply youth causing mayhem on the estate.

Then came the family, and a respectful hush fell upon the watchers. At the head of the group was Doreen, immaculate, very upright and dignified. Her face was blank, expressionless. With her the next two generations, some dabbing their eyes. 'But who's that next to her?' said Lois curiously.

Gran shook her head. 'Don't know – maybe her sister?'

Lois looked closer as the group passed by, and recognised Jean Slater, the mayor's secretary, who'd once called in at the office to rearrange dates for Bill, when Howard and Doreen were away on holiday. Must be very close to Doreen, then. There had been rumours about Howard and his secretary some while ago, but it looked as if they were false.

'That's the mayor's Deputy, young John Middleton,' said Gran, fount of all knowledge. 'He'll take over, I expect.'

'Little short, fat bloke.' Lois could not resist. 'He'll need a new robe, then.'

Gran bit back a reply, and concentrated on the procession of Councillors, their local MP, and other worthies, all wearing black rosettes according to the rules laid down. It was a very splendid, solemn occasion, and Gran fumbled for her handkerchief.

'Mum!' said Lois, 'what're you doing? You didn't know him, never even met him! And from what we hear, he wasn't worth shedding a tear over.'

'Sshh, Lois! That's really enough,' Gran said, and turned away, to push her way back to the market place. She stumbled, and accidentally pushed the tall man in front of her off the pavement into the gutter. He had a hat pulled down over his face, and looked a bit like a tramp in his long, shabby coat. 'Oh, goodness,' Gran said, 'so sorry! I overbalanced ... I'm really sorry...'

The man turned around and smiled briefly. 'No problem,' he said. 'Just take it steady.'

Gran muttered her thanks, adding, 'We've got some shopping to do.' But the man had slipped quickly away into the crowds.

As they walked through to the market, Lois frowned. 'Mum,' she said, 'have you seen that man before? He was familiar, some-how...'

Her mother shook her head. 'Nope,' she said. 'Nobody I know.'

Then it dawned on Lois. It was his voice. Though he hadn't said much, she knew the voice. And the last time she had heard it, it had been on the telephone, asking her if she would take on a snooping job. Her heart skipped a beat, and she felt a stab of alarm.

'Come on, then, Lois,' Gran said, quite restored. 'Step out. I'm in the shop this afternoon, while Josie goes to the whole-saler.' Lois quickened her pace, following her mother into the crowded Market Square. Who *was* that man? How far had he come for the funeral, if it was the same man? An old friend of the family, now out of favour? Bill might have an idea, maybe had heard something. Bill had got quite close to Mrs Jenkinson, supporting her in all kinds of ways, as well as keeping her house clean. And then there was that dirty den of Howard's. Yes, Bill might well have a suggestion who might want to see without being seen.

Norman Stevenson was too hot in the coat, but kept it on. He'd been careful to look as uninteresting and insignificant as possible. The sun shone cheerfully, and Norman reflected that funerals should have rain, and a cold wind that would carry off aged relatives. Norman had not shed a tear, and nor, he'd noticed, did any of the watchers. Except that little woman who shoved him into the gutter. She was the only person he spoke to, and he returned to the station and caught the next train home. He was not at all sure why he had been there. It was a long journey for the sake of fifteen minutes staring at the long procession. Just to make sure, he supposed. Doreen had impressed him. No veiled, sorrowing face for her. She had been dry-eyed, and had no doubt sanctioned all the trappings of the ceremony. She would have known without question that Howard would have wanted as much pomp and circumstance as possible. Good old Doreen.

Norman went to sleep on the train, and awoke just in time to alight. He felt light-headed with relief, now that no more of those letters would land on his doormat. Not even Howard could send blackmailing messages from the other side.

Twenty-Eight

A few weeks later, but not for the first time, Norman woke up sweating and shaking. He had dreamt that Howard had appeared at the foot of his bed, smiling that mirthless smile of his, and holding out his hand. In it, a white envelope with blue capitals gleamed in a ghostly, sunless light. He had screamed, and then awoke. Now he lay looking at the comforting reality of sunbeams penetrating the gap in his curtains and calmed down, reassured once again by the memory of that long coffin with its lifeless occupant. One who could threaten him no more.

It was time he got up. He switched on his bedside radio and listened to jaunty voices conveying disaster and a leaven of feel-good stories. Nothing could depress him now. Howard was gone, gone for good.

Only one more day at work, and then the weekend. Norman had his eye on a new girl he had met in the pub, and meant to her give a ring. If he read the signs right, she might well be willing to come to the golf club dinner dance with him. Just as a friend, to give him the status of a couple, instead of a deserted husband. And then who knew what might develop? He pulled on his dressing-gown and fumbled in last night's jacket pocket, pulling out the scrap of paper where the girl had written her telephone number. What was her name? Heather? Hannah? Something like that. He set off down the stairs, laughing at his faulty memory. Half-way down, his laughter dried up. He swayed, and clutched the banister with both hands. It couldn't be ... It was not possible.

Galvanised by fear, he ran down the last few steps and stared at the door mat, where a scattering of letters waited for him. As if a spotlight had been trained on it, Norman's horrified eyes saw a square, white envelope with blue capitals. 'No, God, *no!*' he yelled, and sank to his knees, picking up the envelope and tearing it unopened into half a dozen small pieces.

The telephone rang. Norman rose up unsteadily and staggered towards it. He caught his slipper in the edge of the mat, and fell heavily, descending into blessed blackness as his head slammed against his pottery

173

umbrella stand. The little figures sculpted on the sides of the heavy stand, each carrying an umbrella and sheltering from a downpour, stared at him with eternal smiles, uncaring and dry as a bone.

'Hello? Hello?' The busty blonde, who had kept Norman company the evening before, shrugged and muttered, 'Oh, well, tick that one off, Hattie dear,' and put down the phone.

It was Friday, of course.

Twenty-Nine

Doreen and Jean stood in the bare sitting room of the now nearly empty Jenkinson house and stared out of the windows into the garden. It looked exactly the same as always, now that the police had finished and gone away. 'That pond,' Doreen said. 'I never liked it. He loved those enormous great fish. I thought they were sinister.'

'I expect they'd have eaten him, if he'd been in there much longer,' said Jean reflectively. An eavesdropper would have been aghast at her lack of sensitivity.

Doreen just shrugged. 'Fair enough, really, Jean,' she said. 'We eat fish, so why shouldn't they eat us?'

They turned away from the window and walked together out of the room.

'What did you do with all that stuff in his den?' Jean was curious. That young bloke who cleaned for the Jenkinsons had helped Doreen with boxes and boxes of very dubious videos and photographs. Jean had been amazed at how sanguine Doreen had seemed, when the whole distasteful truth had come out about Howard's liking for the merchandise offered by Rain or Shine. The family had agreed to keep it as quiet as possible, and hoped that nothing would become public. It had been a while since the photograph of Howard and Fergus Forsyth had appeared in the newspaper.

'Bill offered to take it away. Said he could destroy the whole lot for me, so I let him. I was glad to see the back of it.'

'And of Howard?' said Jean.

'Don't know what you mean,' said Doreen, meeting Jean's eye with a straight look. 'Fancy a glass of wine before you go? Might help us to keep our eyes on the ball.' Jean had spent as much time as possible since the funeral with Doreen, and their leisurely games of golf gave an opportunity for Doreen to talk and Jean to listen. They both had a lot to talk about, of course.

The move to Long Farnden had been postponed, and many of her friends had advised Doreen to back out of the whole thing. 'Stay where you are, dear,' they said, 'until you have time to decide what you really want to do.' Doreen was quite certain what she wanted to do. She wanted to leave this too-large house, with all its associations, and start a new life. That is what she had planned from the beginning, and Howard's death had not changed her mind. As soon as it was decently possible, she had set in motion once more the half-finished arrangements.

Now she and Jean linked arms and set off for the remaining few bottles of wine that Doreen had reserved. The rest of the stuff had been loaded on to removal lorries and was due in Long Farnden next day.

'It'll be a long day tomorrow,' Doreen said, pouring out two generous slugs of wine into plastic tooth mugs.

'Don't worry,' said Jean. 'Ken and me'll be there to help you. You can get it all just as you like it.'

'I hope so,' said Doreen, and the ghost of a smile crossed her face.

'So you'll be busy with the Jenkinson move all day tomorrow,' said Lois, sitting opposite Bill in her office in Long Farnden. He nodded, and there was a pause. 'So why did you want to see me, Mrs M?' he said.

'Well, it's not much really,' Lois said. 'I've

just got this feeling...'

Bill sat up straighter. 'Ah,' he said. 'A feeling that something's wrong? Police still investigating? Mrs M not far behind?' Lois did not smile, and Bill wondered if he had gone too far. You never knew with Mrs M. She took her cleaning business very seriously, and it followed that her longstanding association with old Cowgill was serious, too.

'I'm worried, Bill,' she said finally. 'I had an anonymous call just before our late Mayor snuffed it, asking if I could do some private-eye stuff on him. I sent him packing and then forgot about it.' This was not strictly true, but it was near enough. She then told him about the funeral procession and the man whose voice she had recognised. And then, this morning, a very groggy sounding voice, but the same, she was sure, had called and asked if New Brooms was a detective agency. 'When I snapped back that it certainly wasn't, he sort of groaned and put down the phone. What the hell's going on, Bill? If it was the one who wanted me to snoop on Howard Jenkinson, what did he want this time, now Howard's dead?'

'An old enemy, maybe,' said Bill. 'Scores to settle – money owing – something like that?' Lois stared at him, and he realised that this was indeed serious. 'So what do you want from me?' he said.

'Just to know if you've spotted anything in the Jenkinsons' house, anything that Doreen has said, to give us a clue about this man. Any letters left lying about that you have accidentally run your eye over before replacing.'

'Mrs M!' said Bill, in mock affront.

'Yes, well,' said Lois. 'Think back, Bill. Can you remember anything?'

'Not really,' he said slowly. 'It was all porno stuff in the den. All pretty mild, really, but not the sort of thing the Mayor of Tresham would want revealed to his adoring public. Or have his wife know about, come to that.' He thought for a moment, and then added, 'It was a surprise, you know, how well Doreen took it. I was there when we opened up the room, and she seemed almost amused. Strange, when you think what kind of woman she is. Respectable grandmother, pillar of the golf club, charity coffee mornings, all that.'

'Women are full of surprises,' said Lois, smiling suddenly at stocky, straightforward Bill sitting across from her. 'Well, anyway, if you remember anything, let me know. And keep your eyes and ears open, won't you?'

Bill got up, relieved to be dismissed. He was more at ease with a sick sheep than this kind of thing. But he had a great respect for Lois, and would do, more or less, anything legal to help her.

'Cheerio, then,' he said. 'And watch your back.'

Norman Stevenson walked shakily back and forth in his sitting room, fortified by a couple of glasses of wine, trying to think. He had a fleeting cautionary thought that perhaps he should have tried something to eat as well, but his stomach turned at this, and he promised himself a good meal this evening. His head hurt, and he could feel a bump like an egg. If sleep would come, he would rest until lunchtime, and then force himself to get up and make a couple more calls. He needed more information, and Ken Slater would be the one to supply it. Good old Ken. And Jean, too, of course.

It had been Howard who had introduced Ken to him on the golf course, and they'd met a number of times after that. Several rounds of golf, when Ken had been up in the area. Funny that, he remembered, as he climbed back into bed. Old Ken had seemed such a dry sort, but he'd surprised the chaps with a few jars inside him! Brilliant shot, apparently, and had got into a long, incomprehensible conversation with a couple of fellow shooters at the bar. He picked up the pieces of the envelope and put them on the kitchen table, then went slowly upstairs.

His troubled sleep was broken by a sharp knocking. He looked at the bedside clock.

Oh damn! It was two o'clock, and he remembered an appointment he'd made at the office for two thirty. He scrambled out of bed, legs trembling, and made his way downstairs. It was his loyal secretary once more, her face anxious and concerned.

'Come in, dear,' he said. 'Sit yourself down, and I'll get dressed quickly. I can move when I want to!'

His bravado did not deceive his secretary, but she nodded. 'I'll drive you back to the office,' she said. 'You don't look in a fit state to be in charge of a pram, let alone a car. Are you sure you want to come? I can make some excuse...'

'Wait there,' said Norman. 'Or go into the kitchen and make yourself a cup of tea.'

He disappeared upstairs, and she went through to the kitchen. The torn up envelope lay like jigsaw pieces on the table, and she idly pieced them together. Then she saw that the letter had not been taken out, and extracted the small squares, assembling them. It took only seconds, and she read the message. THIS IS THE LAST YOU'LL HEAR FROM ME. IT'S BEEN NICE KNOWING YOU. That was all. Nothing urgent there, then. Norman had not even bothered to open the envelope, so he must have known the contents already.

She heard his footsteps descending, and quickly scrambled the pieces all together in a heap. 'I've made us both a quick cup,' she said. 'And phoned the office to tell them we'll be late. The client hasn't arrived yet, so we're okay. Oh, and do you want these scraps? I've muddled them up, I'm afraid.'

Norman looked at them sideways, and said firmly, 'No, chuck them in the bin. And thanks, dear. What would I do without you?'

'God knows,' said the secretary, and threw the torn letter in with the remains of several of Norman's disgusting instant meals.

Thirty

Moving day dawned. The removal vans were already packed, but a final, smaller one, arrived to pick up the last bits and pieces. They came early, and Doreen was ready for them. She had hardly slept, but had spent most of the night walking around the house, grappling with haunting memories and trying to imagine what it would be like living on her own in the old house in Long Farnden. She had finally collapsed on to an old sofa that was destined for the dump, and had dozed fitfully until pigeons tuning up outside had intruded into a near-nightmare involving Howard and water and fish. She was relieved not to see it out to its grisly end, and made herself a cup of strong tea with lots of sugar.

'Ugh!' she said to Jean, who, with Ken, arrived on the back doorstep at the exact time they had arranged.

Jean laughed. 'Tip it out, and I'll make some coffee. Ken, you can—' But Ken was already carrying boxes and garden tools to the van, chatting with the driver and generally making a gallant effort to brighten the day for Doreen.

After the first half hour, he realised there was no need. Doreen was excited, rushing around checking that nothing had been forgotten, and then, at last, closing up the house, locking the doors, and jumping into her car as if off on a luxury cruise.

'She didn't look back at all,' said Jean, who had turned round to check that Doreen was following them. 'Not at all.'

'No,' said Ken. 'Well, would you?'

'There they are,' said Josie to her mother. They were standing inside the shop, but with a good vantage point for watching the arrival of the widow Jenkinson and her friends.

'There's three of them,' Lois said. 'I think that's the secretary, Jean Slater, and the bloke must be her husband. Bill's in the house already, waiting for them. Mrs Jenkinson is relying on him quite a bit at present.'

'So does that make things awkward for New Brooms?' Josie said.

Lois shook her head. 'Not now that Susanna is with us,' she said. 'She's doing well, so I can use her a lot. There was some problem when she left the Town Hall – some kind of illness. But she's fine now. I'm keeping an eye on her, though.'

'Bit snotty, isn't she?' Josie said, moving away from the window, and busying herself behind the counter. 'She came in for some stamps, and Gran said she was a bit buttoned up.'

Lois laughed. 'Just because she didn't join in the gossip club, I expect. She's had the warning, like all the team. Not that they all take much notice, but Susanna's new and keen.' She too turned away from the scene of activity, and picked up her bag. 'Better be off on my rounds,' she said.

'First stop Cyril's old house?' Josie said with a sly look.

'Well, naturally,' Lois said. 'It's only polite to pop in and see how they're getting on, isn't it?'

Josie just looked at her, and Lois left, grinning broadly.

She walked briskly across the road, and encountered Doreen. 'Be with you in a minute!' she said to Lois. 'Do go in, Mrs Meade. You'll find Bill in there somewhere!'

Lois hovered for a moment, then walked into the crowded front hall. It was the usual scene of house-moving: boxes everywhere, carefully labelled, some half-empty, with piles of newspaper and bubble-wrap cluttering up every space.

'Sorry about that,' said Doreen, following close behind. 'So much to do, Mrs Meade.' But she sounded cheerful and competent.

Well, thought Lois, hardly the grieving widow. 'You seem to be managing very well, Mrs Jenkinson,' she said. 'I just called to see if you needed any help – not just from New Brooms, but from the village in general. We like to make newcomers welcome.'

This was a lie, of course. Newcomers were regarded with deep suspicion by most in the village, especially the old guard, the families who had been in Farnden for generations. Still, Lois had every reason to be different. She had a natural gift for good public relations. Then there was the village shop, desperately in need of custom, and just keeping its head above water. If Mrs Jenkinson could be snared, if only for one or two of the specialities that Josie now stocked, then it might encourage others.

'That's really kind of you,' Doreen said. 'But so far, my friends, Jean and Ken, have been great, and your Bill is a tower of strength. Ah, Jean, there you are, come and meet Mrs Meade.'

'My daughter runs the shop over the way,' Lois persisted, 'and she has various services, as well as the post office. Clothes cleaned, shoes mended. You name it, Josie's got it. I heard that even the police are setting up mini-stations in village post offices. Mind you, I hope you won't need that! Crime in Long Farnden is not exactly rife...'

Another lie. Lois had been involved over the years in no less than four serious cases in the area, and was beginning to think that fate sent them her way, knowing her fondness for amateur sleuthing. But the latest, Howard Jenkinson, had died in Tresham, and she'd not heard from Cowgill for sure that anything sinister had plunged him head first into the fish pond. So that didn't count.

Bill came from the depths of the crowded house, and looked anxiously at Lois. 'Did you want me, Mrs M?'

'Nothing urgent, Bill,' she said. 'Just wishing Mrs Jenkinson well. But if you could look in on your way home, there are a couple of things I need to tell you.' Bill nodded, and disappeared again. 'So I'll be off now, Mrs Jenkinson,' Lois continued. 'Goodbye for now, and don't forget, I'm just up the street, and Josie's in the shop.' She smiled at Jean Slater and the man who stood at her elbow, and made her way out and up the street.

As she opened her gate and walked up to collect her car, she pondered on the odd fact that neither Mrs Slater nor her husband had reciprocated her smile.

Rupert and Daisy Forsyth had certainly not turned up to welcome Doreen Jenkinson to Long Farnden. Both were very aware of her presence, and intended to steer well clear of her. Howard's association with Rain or Shine was now more or less common knowledge, and the general opinion seemed to be that Fergus and his shop had led the Mayor astray. Daisy privately wondered what Doreen herself thought. There was not much chance that she would get to ask her.

'I wonder if she'll join the WI?' Daisy said fearfully. She herself was a new and not very keen member, and wondered if she should retire gracefully in case Doreen joined. 'She's just the sort,' she continued. 'Bossy and confident. Good at making jam, turning the heel of a sock, conducting a meeting, arranging flowers.' She broke into a hearty, throaty chuckle. 'All the things I loathe! No, I shouldn't miss it if I never went again.'

'I don't know why you joined in the first place,' Rupert said.

'Because that Mrs Weedon in the shop asked me so nicely, I couldn't refuse,' Daisy replied. 'And anyway, I'm being a bit unfair. They do have more interesting things these days, some of the time. Like playing Scrabble, and learning how to gift-wrap presents, and watching holiday slides...' She was off again.

Rupert shrugged. 'You're hopeless, Daisy,' he said. 'How are we ever going to be accepted as a respectable couple here?'

'That's your problem,' Daisy said. 'I shan't change. And Fergus takes after me, luckily for you. Now, isn't it time you got going on answering letters? Looks like there's one from the council in that lot. Might be some news on our extension.'

Bill tapped on Lois's front door, and went in. He found Lois in her office, and she told him to sit down. 'All going well?' she said. He said it was, and could she make it snappy as he had to be at the vets in half an hour.

'Right,' Lois said. 'Anything to report? Any clues about that stranger who makes anonymous telephone calls and turned up at Howard's funeral?'

Bill hesitated. 'Yes?' Lois said.

'Well, there *was* a call came into the house this morning. I answered it, and a man's voice with a really phony Welsh accent asked for Mrs Slater. I asked his name, and he didn't answer at first. Then he said "Jones". So I fetched her, and she rushed to the phone. Shut the door in my face, and was in there, talking, for quite a while. Could be nothing but it was a bit strange. If he was a

Welshman, I'm Irish. Must've known Mrs Slater would be there, and on the very morning Mrs Jenkinson moved in. I saw Mrs J looking several times towards the telephone room, but Mrs Slater didn't say anything when she emerged. Just glowered at her husband. Anyway, as I say, it was probably something personal. But I thought I'd mention—'

'Quite right,' Lois said. 'Anything more?' Bill shook his head.

'Fine,' she said. 'Off you go then, Bill. And let me know if there's anything else.'

Dismissed, thought Bill, and grinned. 'Probably see you tomorrow, then,' he said. 'I'll be back at the house in the morning. Should get it all sorted for her then.'

Lois watched him get into his car and speed away. It had indeed been a strange story. Perhaps time to put in a call to Cowgill. She turned and picked up her phone.

Thirty-One

'Thanks for telling me. So now we know,' said Lois. 'His Worship the Mayor was done to death by persons or fish unknown.'

Hunter Cowgill's voice on the other end of the line was stern. 'It is no laughing matter, Lois,' he said. 'And we are well on with our investigations.'

'So you don't need me?'

'Of course I – we – need you, Lois. There are a number of areas where we need to fill in gaps.'

'Like what?'

'Oh, all right, Lois. Like who killed him.'

'Ah.' Lois smiled to herself. 'Right then. Listen to this and see if it helps at all.' She filled him in on the latest on the mystery caller. 'I'm sure it was the same man. It can't be beyond the wit of your lads to find out where the call came from?'

'Do you have an idea, Lois?' Cowgill was suspicious. 'Are you keeping something from me ... some hunch, maybe?'

Lois was silent for a few seconds. Then she said, 'Well, since you ask, there is something

189

else, something to do with Jean Slater and her husband – Ken, I think he's called. She was Jenkinson's secretary, wasn't she? If she had a long conversation with this phony Welshman, what was it all about? And why were she and her Ken plainly not pleased to see me?'

'Odd,' said Cowgill. 'We questioned both of them thoroughly, of course. They couldn't have been more helpful. Jean Slater was very upset, and her husband too, since he was a very old friend of Jenkinson. Schoolboys together, apparently.'

'Yes, well,' said Lois. 'I think there's more for me to do there. I might just pop in again tomorrow. A message for Bill. Aren't you lucky to have an informant with such easy access?'

'I know when I'm lucky, Lois,' said Cowgill quietly. Just to speak to her on the telephone made him feel it was his lucky day. He sighed. 'How's Derek?' he said politely.

'As if you care,' said Lois, and signed off.

Norman Stevenson was not much reassured after his call to Jean Slater. She had been incommunicative and said it was difficult to talk properly. She'd whispered that she didn't want Doreen to hear. 'She's got enough to worry about without you and your troubles. We never talk about you. No fond memories of Norman Stevenson for

190

her, I'm afraid, after that business with Howard ... and the rest.' He could hardly hear her but he'd managed to keep her answering his questions for quite a while, then she'd slammed down the phone. But the big question, the explanation for the blackmailing messages, especially the last, had been unanswered.

Jean had said she had no idea, but was sure that Howard would never have sent them at all. Norman had repeated that his ex-boss and adversary had had a long-standing hold over him, and was quite capable of torturing him for fun. Jean had snorted, and said he was talking rubbish. She had been Howard's secretary for a very long time, and knew him better than anybody. Better than Doreen, probably. And blackmail was not his style. Shiny macs with naked blondes inside them, yes. But white envelopes and blue capitals, no.

Norman had said he knew all about the shiny macs. Howard had got him in on all that, and he couldn't deny that it had been fun. 'But it wasn't *that* he threatened me with,' he had said to Jean. 'It was the business scandal, all those years ago.' At this point Jean had snapped, 'Well, why don't you call the police?' He had replied that she knew very well why, and then she'd hung up on him.

Now Norman sat dejectedly in his grubby

kitchen and tried to think. If those letters were going to continue, he'd soon be bankrupt. He had been so sure it was Howard. The man was a ruthless bully and always had been, even at school. He'd got his fun from tormenting the weakest. And then he'd succeeded in everything, got all that he wanted, including Doreen, who'd been one of the nicest and prettiest girls around town. Howard had beaten him in that race, too. And then she'd stuck to him, though there must have been times...

But now he was faced with an even more fearful thought. Somebody else knew about the scandal, and hated him enough to put him through hell. It was before Jean Slater's time, but of course Howard could have told her about it. Did she and Ken need money? No, surely not. He had a good, steady job, and they had had no children. She was earning, and they had few expenses, as far as he knew. So it was another, unknown person. Somehow the thought was more frightening than anything. At least he knew where Howard was. Or used to be. Now he hoped the Mayor had gone to his own version of Hell. The bugger deserved it. No, an unknown person could be anywhere. Could turn up at the door, pushing his way in, threatening God knows what.

Norman's heart began to pound, and he stood up, looking out into the back garden, as if the bushes might conceal a lurking stranger, bristling with gun and knife.

Suddenly a sharp knocking on his front door caused him to sway in terror. He wouldn't answer. He hid in a corner where he could not be seen through the window and prayed for the caller to go away. But the knocking was repeated, more insistently this time. Norman groaned, and went through to the hall. Through the glass door, he could see the outline of a man ... a policeman. Oh my God, what had they found out? He opened the door and stood speechless in front of a fresh-faced young cop.

'Mr Stevenson?'

'Yes.'

'May I have a word, sir?'

'What about?'

'We have found an abandoned car, wrecked I'm afraid, on the waste ground up by the cinema. Joy riders again. All the hallmarks. A lot of it about, sir. We've traced the number, and it looks like it's yours?'

When Norman looked past him, out into the drive where his car should have been, he saw it was not there. It was the final straw, and, much to the embarrassment of the young policeman, he burst into tears.

Thirty-Two

Hazel and Maureen stood by the window of New Brooms' office, idly talking, and watching the comings and goings across the road. 'Looks as if young Fergus has done well out of Jenkinson turning up his toes,' Hazel said. 'Free publicity, and all that.'

Maureen laughed. 'I reckon all them closet weirdos reckon what's good enough for the Mayor of Tresham is good enough for them,' she said. 'And, hey, look, there's a woman going in, bold as brass!'

'Well, why not? I suppose we can indulge our fantasies just as well as the blokes. But wait a minute, Maureen ... don't we know that smart lady?'

Both peered across, as a tall, neatly dressed woman disappeared inside Rain or Shine. 'I know who that is,' Hazel said. 'Seen her in Long Farnden, helping the widow move into Cyril's old house. It's Mrs Slater, her that was secretary to the Mayor. Doreen Jenkinson's bosom pal.'

'Maybe it's bosoms she's after,' Maureen said, and they both hooted with laughter.

'Morning, girls, what's the joke?' It was Lois, who'd parked round the corner and crept up on them. Maureen smiled nervously and left, saying she must go and relieve her mother, who was looking after the babies.

'That was a sneaky entrance, Mrs M,' said Hazel, not in the least put out. 'There we were, wasting time, watching the passing entertainment in Sebastopol Street, and laughing our heads off. How are you this morning?'

'Just watch it, young Hazel,' Lois said pleasantly. 'What's been going on then, across the road?' The street was empty now, and Lois sat down behind the desk, establishing her authority.

'It's not just this morning,' Hazel replied, 'but these days there's a fairly steady stream of customers for Fergus Forsyth. Rain or Shine is the "in" place to go. By Appointment to His Worship the Mayor. Anyway, it was something Maureen said about bosoms. Belonging to that Mrs Slater, the Mayor's secretary and one or two other things, according to gossip. She just went in. I expect we'll see her come out again, if we keep our eyes open.'

Unaware of the watchers, Jean Slater followed Fergus into the back room of the shop, and sat down on a stool among piled-up boxes of goodies. 'He's about to crack, Fergus,' she said. 'He sounded terrible on the phone. Who the hell has been sending those letters? I think we have to find out, and soon. The poor sod needs some help.'

'Yes, well, if he gets carted off to some clinic, who knows what he might say about Howard? Could be difficult for you.' Fergus frowned. 'Where can we start?' he added. 'Haven't you got any ideas? You were closest to the old bugger. Was it him?'

Jean shook her head. 'No,' she said firmly. 'Not in a million years. Howard would not have stooped that low. For all his faults – which were many – he was not a blackmailer. No, it's someone very clever. Someone who knows Norman Stevenson would never go to the police. Ever since his brush with the law over that embezzlement charge, he's kept his head down. And needs to keep it down.'

'So it's somebody who needs money?'

'Not necessarily,' Jean said, and got to her feet. 'I must be going. Doreen needs my help still, so I'm off to Long Farnden. Is your mother at home? I might call in and say hello.'

'Mum's mostly there,' Fergus said. 'And Dad. Mind you, he's not the most cheery of men at the moment. Still, Mum'll be glad to see you.'

Jean came out of Rain or Shine, and paused, looking over at New Brooms. She took a step into the road, as if to approach the office where Lois and Hazel sat watching, but then apparently changed her mind and went back up the street at a smart pace.

'Well,' said Lois, 'that was a turn up. What did *she* want with Fergus Forsyth?'

'Unfinished business, maybe,' Hazel suggested. She thought it wiser not mention bosoms.

Daisy and Rupert Forsyth were in the garden, inspecting a new rose bush that looked more dead than alive, when Jean Slater stopped her car and came over to greet them. 'Morning!' she said.

Daisy looked delighted, and opened the gate. 'Come in, Jean, come and have a coffee.' Rupert barely managed a smile, but followed them into the house.

'How's Doreen getting on?' Daisy said.

'Pretty well, considering. We should finish the sorting this morning. She's got all sorts of different plans for conservatories and patios and—'

'Fish ponds?' suggested Daisy maliciously.

'Daisy!' Rupert was furious. 'For God's sake, woman, have you no respect?'

Jean looked from one to the other and said, in an attempt to cool the air, 'Doreen is bearing up very well, actually. We're all so glad she decided to go ahead with the move. It has given her something else to think about, and – as she says herself – an opportunity to start a new life. She's even intending to join the WI.'

'Ah,' said Daisy. 'I thought as much.'

Rupert drained his coffee, and said, 'I've got work to do. And so have you, Daisy, so don't keep Mrs Slater gossiping. Bye,' he added perfunctorily, not looking Jean in the eye, and disappeared.

'Don't take any notice of him,' Daisy whispered. 'Bear with a sore head, and all that. Been like this ever since the council turned down our extension plan again. I suppose Howard didn't have time to push it through before?'

Jean shrugged. 'Don't know, I'm afraid. Anyway, he didn't have as much influence as he claimed. I think he deluded himself sometimes. He was prone to fantasize about things.'

'You don't have to tell me that,' said Daisy, and they both chuckled.

'D'you remember Norman Stevenson?' Jean said, preparing to leave. 'Used to be around, working for Howard?'

'Course I do,' Daisy said. 'Still a customer, you know. But not lately. Mostly by post, anyway, since he moved away. Why?'

Jean sighed. 'It's a bit of a mystery,' she said. 'He's got an enemy somewhere. Anonymous, but persistent. Threats ... you know the kind of thing. It's got to be sorted.'

'Something to do with Howard?' Daisy asked.

'Isn't everything?' Jean said, and went out to her car.

Thirty-Three

Norman Stevenson looked at himself in the hall mirror and made a disgusted face. Ugh! What a wreck.

The police constable had been kind, and stayed with him for ten minutes to give him time to recover himself. He'd reassured him that there'd be no problem in getting his insurance company to replace the car, though Norman privately doubted this. Then, in accordance with his views on how to treat victims of crime, the policeman changed the subject. In an inspired moment, though not exactly changing the subject, he had begun to talk about his passion, Formula One car racing. Norman had once worked in administration at the Silverstone circuit, and his eyes had brightened. The young constable had regarded him with awe and envy, which was an unfamiliar experience for the hounded Norman. He'd begun to cheer up, and grew visibly taller. A sudden, wonderful thought struck him. Now that Howard was dead, he had no need to stay in this alien northern suburb, but could chuck in the job and move back to his beloved Midlands. Maybe even get a job back at the track. And, best of all, with any luck, escape from the fearful white envelopes. He would move quietly, tell no one where he had gone. Perhaps even change his name.

This encouraging daydream had been broken by the policeman saying he must be going, and would Norman be OK now?

'Yes, indeed, I'll be fine,' he'd said. 'And I'm eternally grateful to you, lad. Good luck, and good racing!'

Pleased with himself, the well-trained young lad had driven off with renewed zeal.

Now, Norman said to himself, taking his eyes off his empty driveway, first I need a wash and brush-up. He must see about hiring a car. He'd get a hair cut, collect a suit from the cleaners, and then write a letter of resignation.

The plans he now had to make, including contacts to renew at Silverstone, but above all the prospect of escape, filled him with optimism. He felt years younger, and noted with pleasure that the sun had come out from behind dark clouds and lit up his garden. No assassins lurked behind the bushes, nobody would knife him from behind. He was free – or would be, in no time at all.

'Yippee!' he yelled, and took the stairs two at a time.

This was not a good idea. He had forgotten just how bad a shape he was in, and halfway up he clutched his chest, blacked out and tumbled higgledy-piggledy backwards, ending up in an awkward heap at the foot of the stairs.

Monday morning, and in Norman's office, his secretary looked at her watch. 'Oh, God,' she said to her friend. 'He's late again. Better give him a ring.'

There was no reply from Norman's number, nor from his mobile. 'Must be on his way,' she said. But an hour later, he had not turned up, and she tried again. No reply. 'I suppose I'll have to go and find him,' she said. 'If this goes on, both him and me'll be out of a job. Hold the fort for me, will you?'

She walked up Norman's garden path, and banged hard on the door. Then she peered through the frosted glass and gasped. She could see him now, lying where he had fallen, and she yelled at the top of her voice. He didn't move.

'Norman! For God's sake, Norman, wake up!' There was no stirring. He was so still, and rising panic made his secretary delve in her bag for her mobile. 'Police? I'm not sure, but I think this is an emergency.' She gave the details and renewed her efforts to attract Norman's attention. But after a while she gave up and went wearily to sit in her car and wait for the police.

The ambulance arrived first, and with no trouble forced a way in. Norman's secretary watched as the paramedic knelt down by his side. She held her breath, willing the still figure to move. Or groan. Or *anything* to show that he was not...

'I'm afraid he's dead,' the paramedic said gently. 'Looks like he fell down these stairs. So sorry, Miss.' He put his arm around her shoulders, and she said in a muffled voice, 'Poor old Norman. I wish I'd been nicer to him and now it's too late.'

Thirty-Four

'Oh no, Monday again,' said Lois, reluctantly opening her eyes and slapping the alarm clock firmly to stop its insistent ringing.

'So why aren't you leaping up and making me a cup of tea?' said Derek, putting his arms around her, knowing exactly how to cheer her up.

'Mmmm, don't,' murmured Lois, turning

to kiss him sleepily. But he did, and so they were late up.

Gran had breakfast keeping hot on the Rayburn when they arrived down into the warm kitchen. 'Morning,' she said, without further comment.

'Morning, Gran,' Derek said. 'Good smells ... sausages?'

'And bacon, tomatoes and fried bread,' said Gran. 'Should set you up for a day's work. Are you having some, Lois?'

Lois frequently settled for a plate of muesli and an apple, but this morning she nodded. 'Team meeting at twelve,' she said. 'I need fuelling up, too.'

Gran raised her eyebrows, but dished up platefuls of her undoubtedly unhealthy fry-up to each.

Derek left for work whistling, and Lois disappeared into her office, where she stayed, making notes and telephone calls, but mainly thinking. She had called at Cyril's old house, now rechristened Hornton House. 'Why Hornton?' Lois had asked Doreen.

'It's built of Hornton stone, of course,' Doreen had replied.

'Well, fancy me not knowing that,' Lois had replied drily. Jean Slater had been there again, and was marginally more polite. But the atmosphere was cool and unwelcoming, causing Lois her to wonder afresh what was going on, and she had left promptly.

Now she took a pen and a clean sheet of paper, and began a list of people involved. At the top, she put 'Howard Jenkinson', underlined in red, to indicate he was dead. Then she added 'Doreen', 'Jean Slater', 'Ken Slater', and after a pause for thought, she wrote 'Rupert, Daisy and Fergus Forsyth'. Under all that, she drew a line with a question mark. This was the anonymous caller, the man in the crowd at the funeral, the mystery man.

She turned over the events of the murder – it was now certain to be that – in her mind once more. Someone knew Doreen was to be in London that day. Doreen herself had the perfect alibi. The Slaters had everything to lose by Howard's death – she her job, and he a good and helpful friend. She could not believe the Forsyths would have had any reason to want Howard out of the way, unless it was revenge. One of the most compelling reasons for murder, wasn't it? But revenge for what? Surely not that rumpus at the Town Hall reception. Rupert had a bad temper, but so had lots of men, and Fergus was, according to Hazel, a bit of a wimp. And the story had apparently done nothing but good to their business. Free advertisement, and all that.

So she was left with a blank space. The mystery man. Cowgill had said they were on his track, but she knew from his tone of voice that they hadn't got far along the track.

'Lois! There's somebody at the door, and I can't leave this saucepan,' yelled Gran.

Lois looked at her watch and was surprised to see it was midday. She opened the door and let in Bill and Hazel, and the rest arrived minutes after. Enid Abraham, from the mill, Sheila Stratford from Waltonby, Hazel's mum, Bridie, and last of all, Susanna Jacob.

'Morning everyone,' said Lois, sitting at her desk. 'Schedules first, as usual, then we can have reports and a chat about the week.'

All went smoothly, with nothing alarming to report, until it was Susanna's turn. 'Um, well everything's fine,' she said, 'except for this week's jobs.' She hesitated, and Lois waited. 'I see you've put me down for working at Mrs Jenkinson's,' Susanna continued.

'Well?' Lois frowned, suddenly alert. What was this?

'Um ... I wonder if you could send someone else?'

'Why?'

'It's a bit awkward for me,' Susanna blurted out. 'I was working in the Mayor's office now and then, just before he ... um ... well, you know...'

'*Died*, do you mean?'

Susanna nodded dumbly.

'So what?' said Lois. 'You might be able to help the poor widow. Seeing as you knew the late Howard. Listen to her if she wants to talk. I don't see your problem?' Lois asked herself why she was being so unrelenting. It would have been relatively easy to switch Susanna with one of the others. She knew why, of course. A spy in the camp, one who had been close to Howard, would be very useful. She'd have to tread carefully with the girl, who'd obviously taken the no-gossip rule to heart.

Bill stared at Lois. What was she up to? He'd expected to continue at Cyril's old house indefinitely. 'Isn't Mrs Jenkinson satisfied with me?' he said. The others sat motionless, feeling a ripple of trouble.

'Of course she is,' Lois said positively. 'But I need you to start on a job over at Ringford next week. Miss Beasley has had a fall and broken her hip. She's chairbound at the moment, so needs help.'

'Ah,' said Sheila Stratford, a long-time member of the WI, and well acquainted with Miss Ivy Beasley, 'so that's it. Susanna lives in Round Ringford, and could go there easily. But you'll need to send Bill!' she added, laughing. 'Nobody else could handle the old battle-axe.'

The atmosphere warmed up, and Lois sighed with relief. Thank you, Sheila!

'So will you give it a try, Susanna?' Lois said more kindly. 'We can always switch things around if there's a good reason.' Susanna nodded miserably, and was the first to leave at the end of the meeting.

When the others had gone, Bill lingered. 'Something else, Bill?' Lois said.

'Any further forward with the mystery caller?' he asked casually.

Lois shook her head. 'Keep your ears open,' she said. 'Miss Beasley is reckoned to be the fount of all local knowledge. She might remember something. Introduce the subject of our ex-and-not-much-missed mayor, and see what comes up. Now, I must get going. Cheers, Bill.'

Ivy Beasley was furious, and when furious she was formidable. She had been walking along a narrow lane with her two friends when she'd caught her foot in a snaking bramble and fallen heavily. For once, she was helpless and had had to rely on others for assistance in getting her home and calling the doctor. A spell in hospital had not sweetened her one jot, and now she was back home, still relying on friends and social services, and having to agree against her will to hiring help from New Brooms. This morning, the new cleaner was coming to see her and had been told to collect a key from the shop next door, making sure she presented her credentials.

Miss Beasley waited, arms metaphorically akimbo. She heard a knock, and called 'Come in.' On seeing Bill, she had a moment's fear of an intruder, and said sternly, 'And who might you be, young man?'

Bill introduced himself, and presented his authorisation. He was used to seeing suspicion and surprise in clients' eyes at first. 'I've worked for New Brooms for ages,' he said. 'You'll get used to me.'

'I doubt it,' Ivy said firmly. 'Still, now you're here, you'd better start work. Can't waste money on gossiping. And,' she added with emphasis, 'I'll be watching what you do, and if it's not up to my standards, out you go!'

Bill smiled disarmingly at her, and set to work. Old spins were always the worst. But quite often, they warmed up quicker than you'd think. This one was going to be tough, but Bill was not a Yorkshireman for nothing. Not been beaten yet, he said to himself, and polished and dusted with extreme thoroughness.

At eleven o'clock exactly, Ivy Beasley called him into the kitchen. 'Put the kettle on,' she ordered. 'I've no doubt you'll be expecting a cup of tea.'

Bill shook his head. 'I don't drink tea,' he said, 'and anyway, I prefer to continue working.' He thought this would please her, but Ivy Beasley was as unpredictable as ever.

'You'll do as you're told, while I'm paying you,' Miss Beasley replied. 'There's Nescafé in the cupboard. You can have that. I like a good strong cup of tea. Milk in the fridge. There's the kettle.' She pointed towards the kitchen worktop.

Bill shrugged. 'Right,' he said. 'I'll happily make you a cup, Miss Beasley. And where d'you keep the sugar?'

'I'm plenty sweet enough already,' she answered. 'Can't speak for you. Sugar's in that top cupboard.'

He made the drinks and set a little table by her chair. 'Anything else I can get you?' he asked.

'There's home-made buns in the tin,' she said shortly. 'My friend Doris. Help yourself and give me one. And you can sit down for a couple of minutes. Don't like to see food taken round the house, dropping crumbs and sloshing coffee about.'

Bill was beginning to appreciate Sheila's warning, and he perched on the edge of a stool and sipped his hot coffee. Conversation did not exactly flow, but he persisted, asking her about her life in Ringford, and how long she'd been there.

'All me life,' she said proudly. 'Born and bred. My father came from Tresham, and my grandfather. Grandad was a fishmonger and poulterer in the High Street. Important man. They made him Mayor several times.'

'Oh, really?' Bill pounced. 'They were real mayors in those days. Pillars of society, weren't they?'

Ivy fell straight into the trap. 'Unlike the present no-goods,' she said, getting into her stride. 'It's who you know, these days, that gets you into high office. Take that Jenkinson, him that ended up in a fish pond. I remember him as a snotty kid at the Grammar School. Always was a twister. They said he cheated in his exams. Him and his friend, that Slater who works at the Tourist Office now. No, if you ask me, there's more to his demise than meets the eye.'

'Had enemies, did he?' Bill said.

'More enemies than friends. One of 'em's just passed away up north. In the local paper this morning.' She indicated a folded newspaper on the kitchen table, and Bill picked it up. A small photograph, and a couple of paragraphs announced that former Tresham man, Norman Stevenson, had been found dead at his house in a suburb of Manchester. He'd once worked at Jenkinson's timber yard in town, but had been gone from the district for some while. That was all. But Bill read it several times, committing it to memory. It just might be of interest to Mrs M. He tried asking Miss Beasley more about the man, but she clammed up, and told him it was time to get on with his work.

At the end of the morning, Bill packed up his things and said, 'Now, before I go, is there anything more I can do for you, Miss Beasley?'

'Yes,' she said. 'You can shut all those windows you've opened. I'll be dead from pneumonia, let alone a broken leg. And don't forget to shut the front door quietly and take the key back to the shop. You can drop the snib. Doris is here next, and she's got a key.'

'Right,' said Bill. 'See you next week, then.'

Miss Beasley nodded without looking up from her magazine, and Bill tiptoed out.

Thirty-Five

Bill called in to see Lois on his way home. No sooner had he told her about the man called Norman Stevenson than she pulled on her jacket and said she would give him a ring later. She disappeared down the street faster than he could reply.

'Josie! Have you got last night's *Gazette*? *Please* say yes!' Lois was breathing hard.

'Good heavens, Mum, what can possibly be urgent in the local?' said Josie.

'Just look, there's a good girl,' Lois said, collapsing on the old person's stool.

'Hang on ... yep, here's one. They usually take the unsold ones away, but he's not been yet. Here you are.' She handed the paper to her mother, and watched her turn the pages feverishly. Then she stopped turning, and Josie saw the colour drain away from her face.

'That's him,' she said. 'That's the man.'

'What man? Really, Mum, could you be a bit less mysterious? Gran says you're working with that Cowgill policeman again. Is it something to do with that?'

'Sort of,' Lois said, and explained about the anonymous calls and the man at the funeral. 'It's the same,' she said. 'I'm sure of it, but I'll take this and check with Gran. She was there, and has a good memory for faces.'

Gran was certain. 'Yes, that's definitely him,' she said. 'Oh dear, what a shame, he seemed a nice sort of man, though a bit shy. Does it say how he died?'

'No, it doesn't say much at all. Except...'

'Except what, Lois?'

'It does say he used to work at the timber yard in Tresham. You know, Howard Jenkinson's place...'

'Blimey,' said Gran, 'hope he didn't end up face down in a fish pond.'

'Don't be ridiculous,' Lois said, but felt a cold shiver down her spine. She clipped out the photograph and paragraphs, and took the cutting through to her study. 'Just got a call to make,' she shouted back to her mother.

'And I know who to,' muttered Gran disapprovingly.

'Is that you?' Lois said.

'Of course it's me, Lois. Who else would it be? And how are you today?' Cowgill could not keep the delight out of his voice.

'Never mind about that,' Lois said. 'Just listen. I don't suppose you've noticed it in yesterday's evening paper.' She read it out to him, and said that the photograph was definitely the man she'd seen at the funeral, and whose voice she had recognised. 'And it says he was living in a Manchester suburb,' she added.

'Right,' Cowgill said briskly. 'Leave it with me, Lois. I'll get back to you. We were nearly there, hot on his trail.'

'Liar,' said Lois, 'but never mind. Have a good day.'

Bill left Farnden, and drove back to his cottage in Waltonby thinking hard. He had an uncomfortable feeling that Mrs M was on the edge of some murky goings-on that could get dangerous. If only she'd left him working at Hornton House. He could have tactfully asked questions and maybe discovered something more about this Norman Stevenson chap. What was it Miss Beasley had said about Mayor Jenkinson? More enemies than friends. And she'd seemed to include Stevenson among the enemies. He had forgotten to tell Mrs M that. He stopped the car and dialled her on his mobile. 'Yes?' Lois said. Bill filled her in on what he'd just remembered, and she sounded excited. 'Thanks, Bill. I might just pay a call on old Ivy. Just to see that she's satisfied with everything. You know, like I usually do.'

'Good luck!' said Bill. 'She'll have you for breakfast if you're not careful.'

'I'm a match for her,' said Lois confidently.

'Fine,' said Bill. But he privately doubted it. Miss Ivy Beasley had perfected stubborn unpleasantness over more years than Lois had been alive. Should be an interesting confrontation, he thought, as he drove on.

The *Tresham Gazette* lay unopened on the highly-polished table in the hall of Hornton House. Doreen had combed through it for so many years, looking for news reports that would interest Howard. Now, though she continued to take the paper, she scarcely ever looked at it. She was no longer interested in Tresham. Long Farnden was her home, and she intended to make it a happy one. She had been to her first WI meeting and had thoroughly enjoyed it. They had been so welcoming, such a pleasant lot of women. They came from several villages around, and were a mixed bunch. It would all be a wonderful change from the would-be friends she'd met in Tresham when Howard was Mayor. She'd never been sure if they were genuine, or just sucking up to her for what could be got out of Howard. Jean was the only one she could trust, and, thank goodness, now that she'd retired they could meet often on and off the golf course.

Doreen ran her finger along the shining surface, and looked forward to Bill coming this afternoon. Her house had never looked so good, and it was a bonus that he was such a nice young chap. She picked up the local paper and went through to the kitchen to make a coffee. The phone rang, and she picked it up, hoping Jean wasn't going to cancel their game this morning. 'Mrs Jenkinson? Mrs Meade here. I'm just letting you know that a different cleaner will be coming to you this afternoon. I've had to redirect Bill to Ringford. An emergency job for Miss Beasley – do you know her?'

Doreen frowned. 'No I don't, and what's so special about her that she has to have Bill and not one of your other cleaners?'

'Ah,' said Lois firmly, 'she is a very difficult old lady, and Bill is the only one who can handle her. I did explain, if you remember, that you would not necessarily have the same cleaner each time. *All* my team are excellent workers.'

'I suppose so,' said Doreen grudgingly. 'So who am I getting this afternoon?'

'A very nice girl. I'll bring her along and introduce her. And I know you will be satisfied, Mrs Jenkinson. See you later!' Lois's breezy, cheerful voice left Doreen no room to complain further, and she went back to her coffee.

She flipped over the pages, not really concentrating, still irritated at having her day spoilt. She looked at her watch. Jean would be picking her up in ten minutes, but all her golf things were ready and she could sit and finish her coffee. Try to relax, she said to herself. Just as she heard the doorbell, her eye was caught by a familiar face on the page. Surely not? She began to read the text quickly, on her way to open the door. 'Oh, my God!' she said aloud, and stopped.

'Doreen?' shouted Jean from outside the door. She had heard her friend's footsteps in the tiled hall. What was she up to? 'Doreen! It's me ... Jean!'

The door opened slowly, and Jean was shocked at the sight of Doreen's pale face. 'What on earth's the matter with you?' she said, pushing her way in. Doreen seemed to have gone into a trance, but managed to hand the paper to Jean and point to the photograph with a trembling finger. 'It's Norman,' she said in a hoarse voice, and then sat down suddenly on the hard, wooden hall chair that was not designed for sitting.

'The poor old sod!' said Jean. 'Doesn't say what killed him?'

'Or who,' said Doreen flatly.

'Don't be stupid, Doreen,' Jean said quickly. 'There's no mention of foul play, or whatever it is they always say. Probably his heart. He wasn't in the best of health when I last spoke to him. Anyway, there's no need for you to be so upset,' she continued. 'I seem to remember you never liked him much when he lived around here.'

Doreen took a deep breath, and with a big effort got up and led the way into the kitchen. 'I'll just finish this coffee,' she said. 'And no, I didn't like Norman Stevenson much. He caused Howard a lot of trouble. A slimy toad, most of the time. But that doesn't mean I wish him dead.'

Jean thought it best to change the subject, and asked Doreen if she'd got her waterproofs. 'Looks like rain over Waltonby way,' she said. 'Now, come on, girl. Buck up and let's go. Your turn to beat me.' She shepherded Doreen out of the house and into her car, and they drove off.

Josie Meade watched them go. She noticed that the Slater woman helped Mrs Jenkinson into her car as if she was an invalid. Funny, she thought to herself. Mrs J is usually a nimble old duck, rushing around the place, busying herself at this and that. Then Rupert Forsyth came up the steps, and she retreated from the shop window, bracing herself against the latest complaints about the inefficiency of the Post Office.

Thirty-Six

Lois's euphoric mood changed rapidly when, just before lunch, she received a call from Susanna Jacob.

'I'm very sorry, Mrs M, I won't be able to make it today. I'm sick, I am afraid.'

'Sick? How sick?' said Lois. 'And why couldn't you let me know before this? How am I to find someone else at this late stage? Have you been to the doctor?'

There was a stifled sob, and Susanna said that yes, she'd had to wait for hours in the surgery, and that's why she couldn't let Mrs M know earlier. It was a flu bug going around, and she was definitely out of action for a few days. She was very, very sorry.

'Not as sorry as I am,' Lois muttered, as she put down the phone. Well, there was nothing for it. She would have to do the job herself. Gran had planned to go shopping in Tresham, and Lois was driving her in, but now that would have to be postponed.

'Never mind,' Gran said obligingly, 'we can go tomorrow. It might be nice for you to get to know Mrs Jenkinson better. She seemed a good sort of woman at the WI.'

This cheered Lois, who had been so irritated with Susanna that her first thought had not been that cleaning at Hornton House would indeed be a good opportunity to get to know Mrs Jenkinson better.

Doreen was surprised, but quite glad that Mrs Meade had come herself. A strange girl, taking over from the experienced Bill, would need licking into shape, but Mrs Meade was the boss, and would no doubt set standards for the others. Doreen welcomed her, and showed her around the house.

'No rooms we mustn't disturb?' said Lois lightly.

Doreen looked at her sharply. 'No, no,' she said. 'That was my late husband's room, if you remember, for private study.'

Ah, but study of what? Lois thought with a suppressed smile. 'Fine,' she said. 'I'll get on, then.'

'Cup of tea about half past three?' Doreen said. Lois nodded. 'Thanks, that would be nice. I'll start upstairs, then. Just forget I'm here.'

She had hoovered the bedrooms, and was just starting on the master bathroom when the telephone rang. She tiptoed out on to the landing, duster at the ready, and listened. Doreen picked it up after a couple of rings, as if expecting the call. 'Yes? Oh, it's you,

Jean,' she said. Lois realised she was muffling her voice, obviously suspecting Lois might be eavesdropping.

Lois leaned over the banisters a little, and could hear quite well. 'Well, I don't know.' Doreen sounded reticent. 'Much the best thing would be to do nothing. After all, nobody knows you and Norman had talked recently. What was that? No, of course not! I haven't spoken to him for years. Now listen, Jean. I'm a bit busy just now. New cleaning woman arrived ... so I'll call you back. Bye for now.'

Norman? Lois quickly added 'Stevenson', and realised they could have been talking about the mystery man who had tumbled downstairs to his death. Why was Doreen so anxious to keep quiet? And why had Jean Slater been talking to Norman? Lois heard Doreen's steps coming along the hallway, and scuttled back into the bathroom, where, by the time her employer had reached her, she was energetically scrubbing the big bath.

'Lovely taps, Mrs Jenkinson,' Lois said. 'I expect you must have done a lot inside the house. I came in here a couple of times when old Cyril was sick, but it was a gloomy old place then. Quite a transformation!' She smiled innocently, and Doreen visibly relaxed.

'Poor old man,' she said. 'He died in this house, didn't he? But there's no bad feelings anywhere. I'm quite sensitive to atmospheres in houses, and I felt nothing like that when I first looked at it.'

'No, well, there was nothing criminal about his death,' Lois said quickly. 'And he was a nice old man,' she lied. Her memories of Cyril were of an interfering old busybody, but Mrs Jenkinson did not need to know that.

'*Your* house belonged to a doctor, I believe?' Doreen said. 'And wasn't there a scandal some years ago, about him and—'

'I worked for him,' Lois interrupted firmly. 'He was a good man, and an honest one. Now, if you'll excuse me, I'll get on.'

Doreen said she'd put the kettle on in ten minutes, and disappeared downstairs, feeling snubbed. Not a very good afternoon so far. First Jean, with her stupid suggestions, and then Mrs Meade putting her in her place. She picked up a photograph of Howard, placed strategically by the telephone to remind her of all the reasons she had decided to move to Farnden. 'You stupid bugger,' she said under her breath. 'I wonder whether you went Up or, more likely, Down? Not Up, I'm sure. I doubt if even He could be that forgiving.'

Lois came downstairs when called, and sat at the kitchen table, as instructed. 'How are you getting on, then?' Doreen said pleasantly.

'Fine,' Lois said. 'This a lovely house, and everything so neat and tidy, it is a joy to work here. No wonder Bill was reluctant to be moved! Miss Ivy Beasley keeps an immaculate house, of course, but she's an impossible old bird. Only Bill could put up with her.'

'But she won't be needing him once she's up and about?' Doreen realised how much she missed Bill's cheerful confidence.

'No, no, he'll be coming back in a few weeks. But meanwhile, I'm sure you'll like Susanna, once she's feeling better.'

'Susanna?' Doreen said quickly. 'Susanna who?'

'Jacob. Used to work in the Town Hall. Really loves the cleaning job.' Lois looked curiously at Doreen, whose hand holding her mug suddenly shook, and she slopped tea on to the table.

'Yes, well,' Doreen said, mopping up the puddle. 'I expect she'll need at least a couple of weeks off. Flu, didn't you say? I wouldn't want her coming here until she's completely free of infection.'

'I wouldn't dream of allowing her back too soon,' Lois said. 'No, I'll come along myself, if that's all right with you.'

'Much better idea,' Doreen said. 'Then we can talk again about this ... this Susanna girl.'

Later, when Lois walked over the street to the shop, she said to Josie, 'I need to talk privately to you. And Gran. Little job for you both. I'll come back after you're closed, if you're not going to the wholesaler's.'

Josie shook her head. 'Nope, come and have a cup of tea. I've got some new expensive biscuits we can try. See you later then, Mum.'

Now what's she cooking up, she thought, as she watched her mother hurry out of the shop and disappear up the street.

Thirty-Seven

Gran agreed reluctantly to ask around her friends in Tresham. 'It's very unlikely they'd know Susanna Jacob,' she said. 'Her family are nobs. The likes of my lot are not in the same social whirl.' She added sourly that Lois should have found out all she needed to know before hiring the girl.

'She had very good references,' Lois snapped. 'I just need to know a bit more about her background. But don't trouble yourself.'

Gran bridled. 'Of course I'll ask,' she said. 'If it's a help to whatever it is you're doing.' Lois didn't react, but changed the subject. 'Josie's got some new biscuits we're trying out after closing time. Why don't you come down?'

Gran shook her head. 'I'll be cooking our tea. Derek'll be hungry – he was having a sandwich for lunch. Working miles from anywhere on a barn conversion. No, you go, and sound out Josie on your own.'

Lois sighed. Not much got past her mother. She went through to her office and shut the door. 'Hello? Is that you? Oh, good.' Lois put the phone to her other ear and picked up a pencil. 'So how much have you found out about Norman Stevenson? What do mean, "not much"? I thought you were well on his track? Anyway, I know from your voice that you're lying again. So just listen. If you're not straight with me, that's it. Do your own investigations.' She slammed down the receiver and glowered at it. A minute passed, and then, as she expected, it rang.

'Lois, for God's sake don't be so touchy,' Cowgill said. 'And okay, you're right, we've been in contact with the locals up there, and they've found something interesting. Stevenson was being blackmailed. During the search of his flat, one of our boys found a bundle of letters. Threats of exposing something or other, and demanding money. We're doing tests, of course, and following that up.'

'Blimey,' said Lois, perking up. 'What did the letters look like?'

'Why?'

'Never mind why! Aren't I allowed to ask a question?'

'Of course you are, Lois. I haven't seen them, but our boys describe them as in square white envelopes, addressed in blue ballpoint capitals. That's all I know at present.'

'Right,' said Lois. 'No wonder poor old Norman wanted me to snoop on His Worship. Probably thought the letters had something to do with Jenkinson. So how did Norman die? Not natural causes, then?'

Cowgill sounded disappointed. 'Well, yes, actually the doctor said it was his heart. Probably went upstairs too quickly. He was pretty unhealthy, apparently. So yes, death due to natural causes. No suspicious circumstances. Sorry, Lois.'

Lois said she had quite enough to do to turn up dark and dirty facts about one murder, thanks very much. Norman Stevenson was a sad character, from the sound of it. But yes, she would bear in mind the blackmailing letters.

'Good afternoon, Miss Beasley.' Lois had knocked and the door was opened by a neat little woman with a friendly smile, who announced herself as Doris Ashbourne, Miss Beasley's oldest friend. She had led Lois through to the kitchen, where Ivy Beasley sat by the range, comfortably settled with a cup of tea and slice of cake at her elbow.

'Oh, it's you, Mrs Meade,' said Ivy. 'Not coming to tell me your cleaner's gone back to Yorkshire, back to farming where he belongs?' There was a gleam in Miss Beasley's eye.

Doris turned apologetically to Lois. 'Ivy's feeling a lot better,' she said. 'Your lad has done her good, I reckon.'

'Rubbish!' said Ivy.

Lois laughed. 'He's a good sort,' she said.

'It's a good worker I want, never mind a good sort,' snapped Ivy.

'Something you're not satisfied with?' said Lois with assumed concern. She'd handled all sorts in her time, and this one was easy. Besides, she wanted something from Miss Ivy Beasley. 'That's why I'm here,' she continued. 'To make sure everything's going well with you and Bill.'

Miss Beasley stared at her. 'Of course it is,' she said. 'So don't you go changing him around with some useless young girl.'

'Ivy, no need to be...' muttered an embarrassed Doris.

Ivy rounded on her. 'Well, Doris,' she said firmly, 'you remember that young slip of a thing – her that was a home help from Social Services? Came to you when you were poorly? More trouble than she was worth!' Doris agreed meekly, and Lois stepped in.

'All my cleaners are experienced and well-trained,' she said. 'Been with me for years. Except for Susanna, and she's new. But a very nice girl, and turning out well. Cleaning is a bit of change for her, of course. She used to work at the Town Hall, in the Mayor's office. Wanted a complete change, she said, and so far she's shaping up satisfactorily.' Lois sat back, and was rewarded by a quick exchange of glances between the two elderly women.

'Susanna who?' said Doris Ashbourne casually. It was a poor attempt to disguise the obvious sudden interest of both of them.

'Jacob,' said Lois. 'Father's a solicitor. I expect you've heard of the family, being real locals, apparently. Him and his father before him with offices in Tresham.'

'He's our solicitor,' said Doris, after a pause. 'My late husband had all the dealings with him, of course. Wills and things. But I remember the old man. Very kind and nice, he was. Thrilled with his grandchildren. A real family man. Such a shame,' she added thoughtlessly.

'Doris!' said Ivy swiftly. 'How many times do I have to tell you? No gossip in this house.'

That's a laugh, thought Doris, but looked suitably chastened.

'What was a shame?' said Lois quietly.

'Shouldn't be allowed,' said Ivy, enigmatic

227

as ever. 'In my day, once you were in the club...'

'Ivy!' said Doris. 'How can you, after what you just said to me?'

'Time you went, Mrs Meade,' Ivy said firmly, turning to Lois. 'Everything's fine here. And don't bother coming again. I'll let you know if there's anything wrong.'

I bet you will, Lois said to herself, as Doris ushered her out. 'Don't take any notice of Ivy,' the little woman whispered. 'Her bark's worse than her bite.' She grinned. 'Though they say a barking terrier is the best deterrent to unwelcome callers,' she chuckled, and shut the door.

In the club? Lois sat in her car, pondering, Up the spout? A bun in the oven? She turned the key, and drove off slowly, deep in thought.

Thirty-Eight

Josie Meade had an idea. If her mother wanted to know more about Susanna Jacob, there was one person who might well know her. The local lady of the manor, Mrs Tollervey-Jones, had a niece who had spent some time in the village and was one of the yah set who hunted and played polo, and talked very loudly in pubs. Susanna, daughter of a solicitor, was very likely one of them.

What was that girl's name? It was on the tip of Josie's tongue. Arabella? No, that wasn't it. Josie remembered her brother Jamie having a fling with Miss Tollervey-Jones, so she could ask him. She picked up her mobile and was about to call when the shop door opened and Daisy Forsyth walked in, grinning as always.

'Hello, dear. How are you today?' she greeted Josie.

Anyone would think they'd lived here for years, Josie thought. These newcomers – and there were more and more of them buying up the old houses – they moved in and took over, or tried to. But Josie smiled back, telling herself she was not really being fair. Daisy was a nice woman, unlike her tetchy husband. She seemed to be quite happy with her garden and gossiping in the shop. She'd been once to the WI, but Gran said she hadn't come back. Never been to church, either, apparently, but that applied to most of the villagers, old and new.

'What can I get for you today, Mrs Forsyth?' Josie asked politely.

'Call me Daisy, dear. I'm not used to formality.' Daisy giggled. 'All these years I've been married,' she said, 'and I still can't get used to being Mrs Forsyth.'

'Well, Daisy's a very pretty name,' Josie said diplomatically, wishing the woman would get on with whatever she wanted. Jamie might have his phone switched off, and she'd have to think again.

But Daisy was in a mood for conversation. 'Are they settled in now, over the road?' she said. Josie assured her that Mrs Jenkinson seemed very happy in the old house.

'A bit too happy, don't you think?' Daisy asked. 'For a woman not long widowed?'

'Perhaps she's just being brave,' Josie said, and sighed. 'Was there anything else?' But Daisy was not to be got rid of that easily. She looked around the shop, as if checking nobody was listening. 'I knew her husband, you know,' she said, leaning over the counter. She winked. 'Knew him quite well,' she added. 'We went back a long way, Howard and me.'

Oh, please, Josie thought. Not the old nostalgia trip. I don't care what you got up to with our late Mayor. Please just go away and let me ring my brother.

By the time Daisy had collected up a basketful of groceries, there were several customers waiting, and it was not until lunchtime that Josie was able to dial Jamie's number and hear his familiar voice.

'*Annabelle*, you twit,' he said cheerfully. 'Blimey, are you getting old and losing your marbles, or something?' Josie retorted that she hadn't known the girl as well as Jamie had. 'I'd forgotten all about her,' he said laughing. 'There's bin a few on the list since Annabelle.'

'Yes, well, thanks. And yes, we're all fine at home, in case you were wondering. I don't suppose you've still got Annabelle's number?' There was a pause, then Jamie rattled off a London number. 'Cheers, then,' she said, 'talk again soon.'

Josie looked at the old wall clock, which had ticked its way through a number of shopkeepers in Long Farnden, and went to get herself a quick sandwich. She had thought of closing the shop at lunchtimes, but it was surprising how many people came in during that hour.

So now she had Annabelle's number. But what could she say to her? Did she know Susanna Jacob? And if so, what salacious secrets did she know about her? Josie bit into a succulant piece of ham, and wondered what exactly her mother wanted to know. Perhaps the best thing would be to ring Annabelle and say someone – an old school friend? – had come into the shop asking for details of her whereabouts. Annabelle hadn't been seen in Long Farnden for a long while now, and maybe wouldn't know that Susanna was working for New Brooms. It was worth the risk.

Josie washed her hands, and took out her

mobile again. She dialled the London number, and after a few rings, a bright voice answered, 'Yes, hallo?'

Josie explained, and there was a short pause. 'Are you Josie Meade?' said Annabelle. 'Yes, that's right,' Josie answered.

'Um, how's Jamie?' Annabelle's voice was light and casual.

'Fine, he's up North now. We don't hear a lot from him ... you know what lads are like.' Josie wondered what was coming next, but Annabelle just coughed, and said, 'Okay, fine. Now, it's Susanna Jacob you wanted – let me think.'

After a pause long enough for Josie to take another bite, Annabelle said slowly, 'Yes, she was at the school I went to for a while. I went to a good few, one way and another. I do remember her. Blonde, good shape. We were all a bit envious, being on the puppy plump side ourselves. And she had boyfriends long before the rest of us. I'm afraid I lost touch after ... well, after I was asked not too politely to leave!' There was a fruity chuckle, and then Annabelle added, 'But I know who her best friend was – she might be able to help. A Tresham girl, not exactly top drawer, if you know what I mean, and a bit older than Susanna. Maureen something-or-other – Smith, it was. That's right. I knew it was an unusual name.' Annabelle hooted loudly, and Josie held the phone away from her ear.

'You don't remember if she got married, or where she lived?' A bit of a blind alley, this, thought Josie.

'Sorry, that's all I can dredge up, I'm afraid. Maybe you could ask Tresham Comprehensive? I'm sure she went there. Anyway, I must dash. Love to Jamie, next time you speak to him. Tell him I haven't forgotten him, dear thing. Byeee!'

Lois listened carefully that evening to what Josie reported. 'That was very clever of you,' she said. 'I'd never've thought of asking Annabelle.'

'Not much help, though, is it?' Josie sounded disappointed, but Lois gave her a hug, and said it was very useful indeed. 'One of my old mates is a dinner lady at Tresham Comp, been there for years,' she said. 'Dinner ladies know everything about everybody. I'll give her a buzz tomorrow. Now,' she said, catching Derek's eye, 'who's for a delicious Sleepytime tea bag?'

Thirty-Nine

Doreen and Jean were out on the golf course, on the first tee. The sun shone down warmly, the fairway was a long, green-striped ribbon stretching ahead, until it turned out of sight around a small spinney of conifers. It was quite early, and few people were out on the course.

'I don't know what I'd do if I couldn't play golf,' Doreen said. 'It's a wonderful feeling of freedom, out here in the sun, walking through a lovely landscape, and nobody to warn us off or tell us to put that bloody dog on a lead.'

'We haven't got a dog,' Jean said, looking sideways at her friend. 'And what about when we get in the rough, and can't find the ball, and some ruddy men are behind us shouting "Fore!" at the tops of their voices?'

'Oh, Jean,' Doreen said, smiling, 'you've got no soul. *Sometimes* it's like what I said. Anyway, it's your turn to go first.'

Jean took a swipe at the ball with her driver, and the ball soared into the air, sliced off to the right and landed in a patch of thorny bushes. 'And *sometimes* it's like what *I* said,' she muttered drily. 'Your turn, Doreen. Do your worst.'

Doreen squared up to the ball, wiggled her bottom to settle into a good position, tucked her head down firmly, and brought her club down powerfully. The ball rolled gently off the tee peg, and stopped less than a metre in front of them.

There was a short silence, and then Doreen looked up at Jean. 'Shitty buggers!' she said, and collapsed into hysterical laughter.

Jean joined in, and finally had to cross her legs to stop an even worse disaster. 'Oh, go on,' she said, when they had both sobered up. 'Have another shot. I'm not counting.'

This time, Doreen's drive was respectable enough, and the two set off side by side down the fairway, pulling their trolleys behind them and talking amiably. 'Everything going all right in Farnden?' Jean said. 'Your nice Bill back with you yet?'

Doreen shook her head. 'No, still on the emergency job over at Ringford. Mrs Meade's coming herself at the moment, though she's threatening me with young Susanna Jacob. Seems she works for New Brooms now.' Doreen's head was down, her voice almost inaudible.

Jean stopped dead. She stared at Doreen. 'You're joking,' she said in a choked voice.

Doreen shook her head and shrugged. 'She's not been yet. Ill, apparently. But I've got a couple of weeks to think about it. Mrs Meade's said it'll take that long for her to recover from flu.'

'Like last time?' Jean said.

'I don't think so,' Doreen said flatly. 'But who knows?'

Susanna Jacob was fed up and scared. She had been keeping to her bedroom for a couple of days now, pretending to be ill and feigning sleep whenever her mother came in with a cup of tea. 'No point in calling the doctor,' she had said firmly, when her mother suggested it. 'With flu, it's just a matter of time and painkillers.' She was bored, but too apprehensive to move from her room. Perhaps she would not shake off the flu until she heard Bill was back at Hornton House. Meanwhile, she thought, looking at the sunlit garden, I could go for a gentle walk across the meadow and look at the river. The thought of water and fish brought back memories of Howard Jenkinson, and she had no difficulty in shedding real tears.

Downstairs, her mother and father were in conference. 'I don't think she's ill,' her mother said baldly.

'Why else would she condemn herself to solitary confinement?' said lawyer Jacob.

'Something's frightening her,' her mother

said. 'Mothers know these things.' She went to the window and looked out at the bright morning. 'Don't you remember when she was at school?' she continued. 'Always a mysterious illness just before exams.'

'But she managed to take them, and did reasonably well.'

'Yes, but maybe this time the escape route is easier.'

'What do you mean?' Sometimes Susanna's father wished his wife would not be so elliptical. 'Speak plainly, woman, do.'

'You're not in court now,' his wife retorted. 'I am speaking plainly. Susanna does not want to work for Mrs Jenkinson, and knows that she can give up the cleaning job to get out of it. If Mrs Meade gets fed up with her, she'll get the push – and her escape.'

Susanna's father shrugged. 'A very good thing, too. Then she can get herself a proper job,' he said. 'And we certainly don't want that Meade woman asking unnecessary questions and upsetting Susanna.'

'*Oh, what a tangled web we weave, when first we practise to deceive,*' said Mrs Jacob sadly, and left her irritated husband wondering why a woman couldn't be more like a man.

Lois let herself into Hornton House with a key Doreen Jenkinson had given her. Doreen had told her she was off golfing with Mrs Slater very early in the morning. 'Early bird hits a straight ball,' Doreen had said, not very wittily. Lois had no idea what she was talking about, but said it would be fine. She would carry on with the routine, and if there was anything special Doreen needed doing, to leave a note on the kitchen table.

The house, as usual, was immaculate, and Lois reflected that if she whipped round with a duster and the vacuum, she could finish in half an hour, and nobody would be the wiser. She scolded herself; if she suspected one of her team had the same subversive thought, they'd be out on their ear. She glanced at the kitchen table, and saw there was a note for her. It reminded her that the silver candlesticks in the dining room could do with a polish. 'Right,' Lois said, 'message received.' She crumpled up the paper and threw it into the bin.

She switched on the portable radio, turned down to a respectful level, and set off upstairs to start on the bathroom as usual. Without interruptions, Lois found a kind of rhythm in the work, and hummed along to the thudding beat. Mrs Jenkinson had said she would not be back before lunch, and as Lois moved into the kitchen, the last room on her list, she noticed she still had half an hour to spare. Cupboards? She opened several doors in the units, and every cupboard was tidy and regimented. Copper saucepans, ornamental only, hanging on the clean white wall? She took them down to clean. Fumes from cooking discoloured them quickly, so it would be a job well done. Finally it was time to go, and she remembered the rubbish had not been emptied. She took it out to the wheelie-bin, catching sight of Doreen's screwed-up note as it fell.

Something clicked in Lois's mind as she slowly picked the paper out of the messy rubbish. CANDLESTICKS IN DINING ROOM NEED A SHINE-UP! – D.J. Why was that familiar? Lois gazed out at the garden, tamed and conquered since poor old Cyril's day. Blue capitals? Oh, my God! Cowgill ... the mystery man...

She put the paper in an unused Dogpoo bag in her pocket. Setting the elaborate burglar alarm, she locked the door and headed up the street, reminding herself that anybody could write with blue pen in neat capitals. Even so, she went straight into her office, shut the door, and lifted the telephone.

Forty

The supermarket was crowded. Mothers and small children cluttered the aisles, and as Lois walked casually down towards the bread counter, a toddler suddenly changed direction and walked uncertainly across her path. 'Oops!' she said, and then noticed the red-faced mother was Hazel's friend, Maureen, apologising profusely. 'So sorry! Oh, it's you, Mrs M. Well, I'm even more sorry. I'm afraid Robert's not too steady on his pins yet. Oops! Must go...' There was another flurry of anxiety as the toddler crashed into a shelf full of herb jars, which wobbled and then cascaded to the floor, rolling under shoppers' feet.

Smiling to herself, Lois resumed her zig-zag approach to the room where she was to meet Hunter Cowgill. Toddlers were so lovable! She wondered when Josie would get going. What was it like to be a grandmother? Josie was a warm-hearted girl, and would make a good mother.

Lois idled by the counter, then asked for an oatie loaf and four chocolate muffins, and smiled as she heard a loud childish wail. She was a nice girl, Hazel's friend. Maureen ... Maureen what? Lois suddenly turned around and retraced her steps. But she saw only the girl, her toddler now in his pushchair, and festoons of shopping bags, heading for the car park. A shout from the bread counter called her back, and she collected her purchases. 'Just going to use your loo,' she said, and in a stage whisper. 'Got permission ... bladder weakness, you know.' The salesgirl raised her eyebrows, but turned to the next customer and forgot Lois.

Cowgill was sitting at a small table, reading a newspaper, but stood up as Lois came in. Her colour was high from chasing uselessly after Maureen, and tendrils of dark, silky hair had slipped their moorings. She had changed from working clothes, and was smartly dressed for once. He took in her easy grace, comfortable in black jacket, shortish skirt and – as always, his heart skipped a beat – her long, slender legs in schoolmarm black tights.

'Seen enough?' said Lois, reverting to the playground. 'Now then,' she added, softening her voice, 'see what I've got for you.' She reached into her bag and extracted the Dogpoo carrier.

'Lois! Is this a joke?' Cowgill retreated in horror.

'No, o' course not. This is all I had in my

241

pocket at Hornton House. It's a clean one!' She pulled out the crumpled note, and handed it to him. He got out an ice-white handkerchief and carefully took the paper from her. 'Bit pointless, that,' said Lois. 'It's been in the rubbish bin, and got my prints all over it.' 'No matter,' Cowgill said. 'Does no harm to follow the proper routines.'

Lois sighed. 'Have a chocolate muffin,' she said, handing him the paper bag.

'Lois! You've tried that one before, and the answer's still no thanks. Now, this is very useful indeed, and a smart piece of work on your part. Leave it with me, and I'll report back when we've done the tests.'

'Have you got those letters – the blackmailing ones? I wouldn't mind seeing one.' Lois was furious. Just handing over the note wasn't enough. This was clearly a breakthrough, and she intended to be part of it.

'Not a chance, I'm afraid,' Cowgill said. 'But I'll keep you informed. Anything else for me?'

'Wait a minute!' Lois said. 'Let's at least talk about Doreen Jenkinson, and what she was doing blackmailing Norman Stevenson. If you add this to him asking me to snoop on Howard, doesn't that add up to something interesting?'

'*If* is the important word,' Cowgill answered placatingly. 'First our experts must compare this note with the letters. We shall know for certain then. I agree with you that it is probably the most important lead we've had so far, but it never does to get too excited too soon.'

Lois groaned. 'Thank God your lot never took me on as a Special,' she said. 'I don't think plodding is in my line.'

Cowgill laughed. 'No,' he agreed. 'You're more useful as you are.'

'Huh! Well, I'm off now,' she replied. She had thought of telling him about Susanna Jacob, but decided to say nothing. Still some work to do there.

He came towards her and put his hand gently on her arm. 'I am grateful, you know,' he said. 'You are much appreciated.'

'Oh, my Gawd,' said Lois, and went swiftly out of the room.

Next stop, the New Brooms office in Sebastopol Street. Lois was calling there, anyway, but now she wanted to check up on Maureen. She parked outside the office, and noticed a familiar car outside Rain or Shine. Where had she seen that before? It was a dark green, anonymous-looking Audi, but with one distinctive feature. Discreetly stuck on to the rear window was the legend: 'Stop Prejudice, Fight Ban'. Hunting, of course. Lois laughed to herself. Outside that particular shop, it could have a very different meaning. Not that there was a ban on Fergus

Forsyth's goods for sale – quite the reverse. Even Boots Chemists were reportedly thinking about planning a sex toys counter, and poor old Fergus would soon be out of business, what with Ann Summers and other like-minded shops everywhere and pictures in the papers of girls brandishing shiny, plastic vibrators! Lois was not easily shocked, but she was the first to admit she was conditioned by generations of her family who firmly believed that sex was what went on behind closed curtains, at night, and in bed, and was a private business between two – what was it? Consenting adults?

But the green car. She had seen it parked often outside Hornton House. It was the Slaters' car. What did the Slaters want with Fergus Forsyth? Maybe what all his customers wanted, but Lois doubted this. She reckoned they would balk at calling, when a phone call would order what they fancied to be posted or delivered anonymously. No, she'd place a bet that it was Jean Slater, and would give a lot to be a fly on the wall in Fergus's back parlour.

'Morning, Hazel,' she said.

'It's really afternoon,' Hazel replied, glancing at her watch. 'Shall I get us some sandwiches from round the corner?' A new takeaway shop had opened, its owners presumably convinced by the Council's projected plans.

'Good idea,' said Lois. 'I'll hold the fort. Chicken for me.'

When Hazel had gone, Lois sat down facing the window, waiting to see who emerged from across the road. It was quiet. Very few cars passed, and Lois glanced down at Hazel's diary of appointments. One at three and another at three thirty. Both were new names, and she thought again of Susanna. When was she coming back? Lois decided to call without warning at the Jacobs' house on her way home.

Nothing happened outside Rain or Shine, and Hazel returned with sandwiches, full of a story she'd heard in the queue. Work was due to start on the leisure centre in three weeks time. 'Might save old Fergus's bacon,' she said. 'His business has taken a dip lately. The upsurge after old Jenkinson's death has fizzled out, and he was moaning the other day that the postal orders had fallen off too. Seems sex is coming out of the closet!'

'When were you talking to him?' Lois said quickly.

Hazel laughed. 'Don't worry, Mrs M,' she said. 'I haven't taken to patronising Rain or Shine. Don't need any o' that yet. No, he comes over sometimes if no clients are here. Doesn't stay long, but I reckon the poor bloke gets bored. He's quite nice, really. Tells me things that he should probably keep to himself. But he says he gets desperate for the sound of a human voice sometimes.'

'What things does he tell you?'

'Oh, you know, famous customers, marriages he claims to have saved, that sort of thing.'

'Has he ever talked about Howard Jenkinson?'

Hazel shook her head. 'Never,' she said. 'I asked him something once, and he clammed up and scooted back across the road.'

Lois was silent for a few minutes, and Hazel opened the sandwiches. 'Is this just a social call, Mrs M? Or did you have a special reason for dropping in?' Hazel was no fool.

'Not really,' Lois said. 'Just passing. I'd been to the supermarket. Oh, and I saw your friend Maureen there, with a wandering Robert causing chaos around the aisles! He's a nice little chap. What does his father do? I've never heard you girls talk about him.'

'That's because he's vamoosed,' Hazel said cheerfully. 'Did a runner before Robert was born. Little lad has never seen his father.'

'Are they divorced, then?'

'No, never married. Maureen Smith is still Maureen Smith, and says she intends to remain that way!'

'What a shame, though, that Robert's got no father,' said Lois, trying not to show mounting excitement. Maureen Smith. Best friend of Susanna Jacob at school? They would be about the same age. But it was probably a coincidence. Smiths were not exactly uncommon! 'Is Elizabeth with her today?' she said. 'Or is Grannie on duty?'

'No, she's next door with Maureen. I expect she'll bring her in any minute. She usually does, after she's had her lunch. We have a little game and a cuddle. It's really working out well.'

'That's good,' Lois said. 'Well, now I'm here I'd quite like to check through the records for a while. Past clients and so on. Shan't get in your way.'

'You're the boss,' Hazel said. 'And I'm always pleased to see you, as you know.' She smiled warmly at Lois, and they settled down happily until the door opened and Maureen came in with Elizabeth, just as Lois had hoped.

They played with the baby and chatted generally, and then Lois said casually, 'I was talking to an old friend of yours, Maureen. At least, I think you were at school with her. Susanna Jacob? Ring any bells?'

'Susanna? Yes, of course it rings bells! Haven't seen her for ages though. What's she doing these days?'

'Working for us,' Hazel said, and frowned. What was Mrs M up to? Not like her to waste time on trivial conversation. 'She's our latest recruit. Not that she's much help at the moment, is she Mrs. M? Off sick. I think she's a bit of a wimp, personally.'

'Hazel...' Lois warned her with a sharp look.

'Goodness, that's a bit of a come-down for our Susanna, isn't it?' Maureen looked quite pleased. 'What's the story?'

'It's not that unusual,' Lois said, a little stiffly. 'We've had all sorts on the team. Like young Gary, and Bill Stockbridge.'

'And Enid,' said Hazel loyally. 'She was a piano teacher, and well educated and that.'

'Okay, okay,' Maureen backtracked. 'Just that our Susanna, well ... Anyway, she always was unreliable. Spoilt rotten at home. Daddy's little darling. Got away with murder! And she had all the boys drooling after her. Still, we got on all right. Didn't see much of her after I left school and my Robert came along. Then I heard she had that business with—' She stopped short, and bent down to pick up Elizabeth, who had begun to grizzle.

'What business?' Lois said, willing Maureen to continue.

Maureen shook her head. 'All in the past now. Gone and forgotten. Now, must go, Hazel. See you later. Byee, Mrs M. Nice to see you.' And she was gone.

Neither Hazel nor Lois spoke for a while. Then Hazel said, 'You'd like to know what the business with Susanna was, I suppose?'

Lois nodded.

'Leave it to me,' Hazel said.

As Lois came out of the office and went towards her car, she saw the door of Rain or Shine open, and a man emerged. He looked across the road, and stared at her. Then he jumped in the green Audi, and drove off quickly. Lois would've lost her bet. It was Ken Slater.

Forty-One

The Jacobs' house was set back from the road, on the edge of the village. A high beech hedge gave it privacy, and as Lois turned into the curving drive she saw well-maintained gardens and an elderly man in blue overalls working in a flower bed. All this was so different from Bridie's semi-detatched and Sheila's farm cottage, that Lois wondered if, after all, hiring Susanna had been a mistake from the first. Mrs Jacob was apparently Sheila's sister, the one who'd married above her station. Lois chuckled.

She parked round the back, and knocked at the kitchen door. She could see a middle-aged woman, who bore a close resemblance to Sheila, busy with a mixing bowl on the table, and when she saw Lois, an odd look crossed her face. She came to the door at once, and apologised for floury hands.

'Susanna? Oh, she's still in bed, I'm afraid, Mrs Meade. I don't advise seeing her, as the doctor said this flu bug is very infectious.'

'I'll risk it,' Lois said bluntly.

'Oh, well ... Well, if you'll just come through and wait in the sitting room, I'll pop up and see if she's awake.'

'Thank you,' said Lois, and followed her through to the front of the house. She noticed that Mrs Jacob shut the door of the sitting room behind her, and when she heard footsteps going upstairs, she quickly and silently opened it again. Standing very still, she heard voices, one of them Susanna's, sounding alarmed. Then there was scuffling and the thud of shoes being dropped on the floor above.

'I think she's just waking up,' said Mrs Jacob, reappearing. 'If you're sure you want to...?'

'Quite sure,' Lois said, and followed her to a long landing, thickly carpeted, and with several bedroom doors firmly shut. Mrs Jacob paused at one standing ajar, and said softly, 'Are you awake, darling? Mrs Meade is here to see you.'

'Thanks,' said Lois, and walked firmly past her and into the room.

It was a little girl's room, all frills and flowers, with photographs of Susanna at all stages of her girlhood. Very sporty, Lois

250

noted. Hockey, tennis, swimming – all were fully represented, with Susanna holding trophies and shields and always with a glowing smile at the camera. A big strong girl, then.

In the bed, duvet pulled up halfway across her face, was Susanna. She looked flushed, and peered through half-closed eyes at Lois. 'Mrs M, you shouldn't have, it's a rotten bug.'

'So your mother said,' Lois replied. 'But you should be on the mend by now. We're very pushed for staff, and I'd like some idea of when you're coming back. Have you seen a doctor?'

Susanna shook her head, and Lois wondered when, in that case, a doctor had told Mrs Jacob the bug was very infectious.

'I'm very sorry,' Susanna muttered. 'How's Mrs Jenkinson getting on? Is Bill back with her?'

Lois shook her head. 'I'm filling in at the moment. But I can't do that for long. Anyway, I'd like you to see a doctor, and let me know a date when you'll be back on duty. I'll leave you to sleep now.'

She walked to the door, and then turned back suddenly. Susanna had moved in the bed, and the duvet slipped to one side. Lois saw she was wearing jeans and a cotton sweater. Anger flooded in, and she snapped, 'No wonder you look hot! You'd better carry

251

on with what you were doing, and we'll talk again later.'

She marched past Mrs Jacob, and through to her car, slamming the kitchen door behind her. 'That's it, then!' she muttered as she drove off. 'No more Susanna Jacob.' Then it occurred to her that this might well be exactly what Susanna wanted, and she thought again.

There was a message waiting for her at home. It was from Miss Beasley at Ringford. 'This is Miss Ivy Beasley here. Your Bill has said you're thinking of sending that Susanna Jacob instead of him. I won't have that. It's either your Bill, or nobody, and I'll manage with Doris's help.'

Poor Doris! Lois thought. But she was puzzled. She had not mentioned sending Susanna to Miss Beasley, nor had thought of doing so. What made Bill say that? She would have to have a word. But first to answer Miss Beasley. She dialled the number and steeled herself for a barrage of complaint.

'Ah, Mrs Meade. What have you got to say?'

'Bill was wrong,' Lois said firmly. 'He will continue to help you until you don't need him any more.'

'Right!' That was all. The phone went dead, and Lois stared at the receiver with eyebrows raised. 'Well, Miss Beasley, that was easy,' she said, and prepared to get hold of Bill.

There was no reply from his home, and his mobile was on answerphone. 'Give me a call, please, Bill,' Lois said, and rang off.

She went through to the kitchen, where Gran was cooking. 'Good smells,' Lois said.

'You hungry?' Gran asked. Her daughter was often an enigma to her, but she stoically carried on holding the family together, providing for their material needs with good home cooking, immaculate ironing, and a plentiful supply of homespun philosophy.

'Mmm.' Lois smiled ingratiatingly at her mother.

Gran cut a large piece of the cake cooling on a rack, and made a cup of milky coffee. 'Here,' she said, 'this'll keep you going – whatever it is you're doing.'

'Running a cleaning business, of course,' Lois said, with wide, innocent eyes.

'And some,' Gran said. 'Well, you can't put a quart into a pint pot, so just remember not to overload your plate.'

'Blimey,' Lois said. 'Our minds are on food and drink this afternoon, I can see. Mmm, this cake is gorgeous!' She bit into the light chocolate sponge, and wondered how she would cope without her mother. She'd have to give up something but no need to think about that yet.

'Did you find out anything about Susanna

Jacob?' she said, knowing that Gran would never bring up the subject without being asked.

'Not much. I did speak to my old friend Olive in Tresham. Biggest gossip under the sun.'

'So what did she say?'

'She knew more'n she said. Looked at me a bit sideways, and then tut-tutted, and said some people who had more money than sense wasted it on giving girls a posh up-bringing an' all that, and then look what happened! In her day, she said, girls were taught how to cook and sew, and catch a husband.'

'What else?' Lois held her breath, hoping her mother wouldn't remember that she never gossiped.

'Nothing ... well, she did add that at least Susanna had had the right idea about catching a husband, but she didn't even make a good job of that.'

'Meaning?'

Gran shrugged. 'Anything you'd like it to mean, I suppose. Now, I must get on. I expect you've got work to do.'

End of conversation. Lois retired to her office to think. Her concentration was broken after a few minutes by the sight of a green Audi driving slowly along the High Street, and pulling up outside Hornton House. Lois moved to the window and shielded herself from view behind the curtain. Talk about lace curtains! she said to herself. Must be a real busybody villager at last. But she stayed still and watched. The car door opened, and once more Lois had guessed wrongly. It was not Jean, but Ken Slater. He was soberly dressed in a good grey suit, his thinning hair brushed neatly back, and a document case under his arm. An anonymous, perfectly respectable caller for Doreen Jenkinson. Could have been the tax man or a Jehovah's Witness. But it was Ken Slater, and he looked up and down the street before darting into the front garden of Hornton House and ringing the bell. In seconds, he had vanished inside, leaving Lois to speculate what he could be doing, calling on his wife's best friend in the middle of the afternoon, when he should be hard at work in the Tourist Office.

Doreen was wearing high heels, Ken noted happily as he followed her through to the kitchen. She trailed expensive perfume as she walked, and he sniffed appreciatively.

'Your usual?' Doreen said, turning to smile at him warmly. He nodded, and moved towards her. 'How's my girl today?' he said. 'Still sad?' As he put his arms around her plump waist, he felt her laughter bubbling up.

'Oh, yes,' she said, 'still heartbroken!'

Forty-Two

Lois finally had a call from Bill, who apologised for being out of touch. 'Tricky job with an old Labrador at the surgery,' he said.

'All right, was it?' Lois was sympathetic.

Bill coughed, and said, ''Fraid not. Poor old fella snuffed it. He was a good age, but his owner went to pieces. She was a good age herself. Sometimes it's very sad, Lois.'

But Bill would be a good strong shoulder to cry on, Lois was sure. 'Can you spare a moment for me to ask a question?' she said kindly. He sounded upset himself, and her irritation with him had quickly evaporated. 'Sure,' he said. 'What is it?'

Lois explained about the call from Miss Beasley, and asked why he'd said she was considering sending Susanna. 'Wh-at?!' he said. 'Nothing like that came from me.' Then he paused. 'Wait a minute,' he said. 'I did mention that she would be back on duty soon. That was all. The old thing must have put two and two together and made five. Did you sort her out?'

'Yes, that was easy enough. I do want you

to stay there until Miss Beasley is able to cope. I just wonder now why she reacted so strongly? I remember she and her friend Doris knew the Jacob family – weren't they Doris's solicitors?'

'Don't know, I'm afraid, Mrs M. Ivy asked me who the other cleaners were, and I mentioned Susanna.'

'Well, bring the subject up next time you go. Miss Beasley made one of her remarks when I saw her – hinting at something, but nothing definite. You might coax some more out of her.'

'Why are you so interested in Susanna, Mrs M?' Bill knew he wouldn't get much of an answer, but it was worth a try. Lois hesitated, then said, 'Because there is something lurking about in her past, and I need to know what it is. There's some connection with the Jenkinsons, and I intend to ferret it out. For the good of New Brooms, of course. I'll need your help, Bill, so do your best. Now, must go. Why don't you have a couple of pints at the pub tonight to cheer you up? Derek will be there, so I'll tell him to watch out for a gloomy-looking young vet. Bye.'

Perhaps I should go over and see Miss Beasley again myself, Lois thought. But then she knew she would not be welcome. No, Bill was well in there. He would be the one to winkle salty titbits out of Ivy, if anyone could. Well, what about Doris Ashbourne?

She seemed pleasant enough. Yes, she would see if she could have a casual word with Doris next time she passed through Ringford.

Meanwhile, what was Ken Slater up to? Lois had kept an eye on his car, and it had been outside Hornton House for at least a couple of hours. The school bus had been and gone. Josie had telephoned to ask if Gran could hold the fort while she went round to the village hall for a quick look at the WI Bring and Buy Sale. Derek, too, had rung and said he'd be a bit late, as he wanted to put the finishing touches to a job. And still the green Audi stood silently outside Hornton House. But when Lois closed her computer and stood up to have a last look out of the window, it was gone. Ah well, what was she expecting to see? Ken Slater being thrown out with his trousers round his ankles? Lois chuckled, and went through to the kitchen to put the kettle on.

The Audi did not go far. After a few hundred yards, down a side road, it came to a halt again, this time outside the Forsyths, and Ken went in, once more looking carefully to right and left.

'Hello, stranger!' Daisy said. 'Mind you, Fergus has told us you've been into the shop and had a couple of chats with him.'

Ken frowned. 'Is that lad as discreet as his

father? I've always known Rupert could be trusted, but Fergus ... and anyway, is Rupert at home?'

Daisy nodded. 'He's upstairs, working on accounts. We've had the planning application turned down again, and our new extension seems as far away as ever. As for Fergus,' she added defensively, 'he knows when to keep his mouth shut, never fear.'

'Glad to hear it,' said Ken, unsmiling. 'Now, why don't you put the kettle on, Daisy, and give Rupert a call. I have some urgent business to discuss with him.'

Rupert was halfway down the stairs, having heard Ken's voice, and walked into the sitting room with outstretched hand. 'Good afternoon, Ken,' he said formally. 'How are you, and how is Jean these days? Enjoying her retirement?'

'Plays a lot of golf,' said Ken, and smiled now, remembering his afternoon's visit to Jean's golfing partner. 'Still, keeps her out of mischief.' He reflected that there seemed to be no mischief in Jean's life now, unlike those early days when she first worked for Howard, the randy sod. But it had all been a lot of silly fun and no harm done.

'Was there something particular you wanted to talk about?' Rupert said, polite as ever. He and Ken were settled with cups of tea and biscuits, and Daisy had taken herself tactfully off to the kitchen, muttering about

259

ironing.

'Yep,' Ken said. 'It's about Norman Stevenson. You knew that he...?'

Rupert nodded. 'Nasty one, that,' he said, giving nothing away. 'Has there been a final verdict on what killed him?'

'His heart, apparently,' Ken said. 'No foul play suspected.'

They were silent for a few seconds. Then Ken began again. 'But there were letters, I have been told.'

'Who told you?' Rupert frowned.

'A little bird,' answered Ken. 'But the important thing is, they were blackmailing letters. And it puts a whole new complexion on Norman's death. We both know there were things in his past that made him vulnerable. And that he was not a particularly attractive character. There was that financial scandal, duly smothered by Howard but known about by most of us.'

'And his patronage of Rain or Shine,' Rupert said. 'And more than our usual straightforward blow-up dolls and saucy videos. Oh dear, yes, we knew far too much about Norman Stevenson, Daisy and me. And he was married. Less permissive days then, of course. But confidentiality is the life-blood of our business, Ken.'

'And Fergus?' Ken's voice was sharp.

Rupert stared at him.

'What are you suggesting, Ken?' he said.

260

'I'm suggesting that any one of us would have plenty of ammunition for successfully blackmailing Norman Stevenson. You, Daisy, Fergus, Howard, me, Jean ... and it wasn't either Jean or me. And it's the last thing Howard would have done.'

Rupert stood up. 'I think you've gone too far, Ken Slater,' he said. 'What you are insinuating is a slur on the honour of my business and my family.' He looked like an offended cockerel, with his chest puffed out and his face suffused with colour.

Ken guffawed. '*Honour?*' he said. 'The honour of Rain or Shine? Don't make me laugh, Rupert Forsyth. Now I'm going,' he added, 'but if you think of anybody else who would have had reasons to blackmail Norman, let me know. Whoever it was, he could well know more uncomfortable facts ... uncomfortable for the rest of us.'

Daisy appeared suspiciously quickly – had she been eavesdropping? 'Thanks for the tea. See you soon,' Ken said, and Daisy thought it sounded like a threat. Ken left then, and directed the green Audi home.

The pub was full by the time Bill took Lois's advice and went in for a pint or two. He had persuaded Rebecca to come too, and the warmth and chatter lifted Bill's spirits. He spotted Derek by the bar, and waved. 'Got one set up for you, lad,' Derek yelled above the noise. 'What'll you have, Rebecca?'

Time passed, and conversation had quietened to a mellow buzz. Bill and Rebecca sat with Derek and one or two of his friends at a table by the fire, and a needle dominoes match was going on at the next table. Old Fred won again, and there was cheering as he made his way reluctantly to the bar to buy his round.

'So how's New Brooms goin'?' Derek said. 'Lois never tells me nothing about it. Says it would bore me stiff, just like me going on about electrics gives her the yawns!'

'It's fine,' Bill said. 'Never a dull moment. My favourite client at present is Miss Ivy Beasley at Ringford. Quite a challenge, that one! But we're hitting it off well now. I wouldn't say she was exactly fond of me, but at least she doesn't give me the evil eye so often.' Rebecca laughed, and said it would teach Bill to be nice to old ladies, which could only stand him in good stead. That reminded him of the old lady who'd sobbed over her dead Labrador, and he fell silent.

'Ivy Beasley?' said Fred, returning with the pints, and listening in to others' conversations as usual. 'She were a holy terror when she were young. One or two o' the lads fancied her, but she frightened 'em off afore they had a chance!' He laughed throatily, and went into a spasm of coughing.

Derek saw Bill's face, and tried to cheer

him up. 'Still, you got that young Susanna Jacob on the team now,' he said. 'Best pair o' legs for miles around.'

'Huh!' interrupted Fred. 'No better than she should be, that one. You should tell your Lois to get shot of her quick. My granddaughter's a nurse up at the 'ospital, and she could tell you a thing or two about Susanna Jacob.' And then he was off again, bent double with a coughing fit.

The conversation wandered off to the comforting subject of farming, and how awful the weather had been and what a rotten harvest it was again. 'Who'd be a farmer?' Derek said.

'I would,' Bill said. 'But I'd rather be a vet.'

'And a cleaner?' one of the others chipped in maliciously.

Bill nodded. 'As I said,' he replied, 'never a dull moment, and girls with the best pairs of legs for miles around.'

And one, he added to himself, with a past that grew more mysterious by the minute.

Forty-Three

'Are you shooting this weekend?' Jean Slater was washing up the supper dishes, resentment in every word. They had a dishwasher, but Ken said it was a waste of money for only two people. She was idly speculating why Ken was in such an unusually good mood this evening. At home with her, he lapsed into a grumpy silence most of the time. Perhaps the prospect of firing at targets and hitting as many as possible had put him in a pleasant humour. It could be that. She had wondered more than once whether her own face had been superimposed by Ken on the target, as he lined up his sights.

'Yep. I shall be there. I mean to win a competition tonight.' He was almost conversational, adding, 'Golf tomorrow?' His voice was casual, but his question was not. He never quite trusted Doreen and Jean together. He suspected they confided most things to each other. But he had no option but to hope that both were loyal girls, and that Doreen's affection was strong enough to prevent betrayal.

264

'Certainly,' Jean replied. 'It's a regular fixture. Nine o'clock on the tee. Rain or shine...' Ken stared at her. 'What did you say?'

'"Nine o'clock on the tee". Why? What's wrong with that?'

'No, after that.' Ken shrugged. 'Doesn't matter. Anyway, it's golf on the telly, so hurry up with that.'

'You could dry up the dishes,' Jean said acidly. But Ken had disappeared. Jean finished at the sink, and went through to join him. She knew perfectly well what she had said that startled him. Rain or shine. Those letters to Norman Stevenson – had they been something to do with the Forsyths? Surely Ken himself wouldn't have sent them? He had absolutely no reason to do so. She dismissed the thought, but a nagging doubt stayed in her mind.

While Doreen and Jean stood on the tee next morning, flexing their muscles and looking forward to a morning's gentle exercise, followed by a slap-up lunch in the clubhouse and a game of bridge after that, Lois set off on her rounds. Today she planned to go via Round Ringford, and see if she could find Doris Ashbourne. She would have to think of a convincing reason, other than the real one, and decided to invent a mythical old friend of her mother, one who had lived in

Ringford many years ago. Doris would be flattered to be asked, she hoped.

First shop in Ringford. Lois drew up outside, and went in. A pleasant-faced woman behind the counter asked if she could help. 'Some of those tomatoes on the vine, please,' Lois said. They were Derek's favourite, and she'd got some of Josie's best ham for tea. 'A kilo?' the woman said. 'Goodness, I don't know,' Lois said. 'Whatever a couple of pounds is now will do.'

The woman smiled. 'I'm only just used to the new system myself,' she said. 'Some of my elderly customers have real trouble with it. And one or two still think in shillings!'

'Like your neighbour, Miss Beasley?' Lois said with a laugh. 'And her friend ... Doris Ashbourne is it?' She explained how she knew about them.

The woman confirmed that Miss Beasley had washed her hands of the whole metric system. 'Though Doris is quite up with it all,' she added. 'Up there in her bungalow in Macmillan Gardens she has plenty of young neighbours to keep her up to date. Very popular, is our Doris, though mostly I think it's her baking the kids are after!'

Lois thanked her kindly, and set off for Macmillan Gardens. This was a small development of old folks' bungalows and semi-detached council houses, now mostly privately owned. She cruised round the central square of grass, and pulled up. A bulging lady with a white terrier looked at her enquiringly. 'Which one is Mrs Ashbourne's, please?' Lois said, looking reassuringly at the woman.

'What was it you wanted?' the woman said suspiciously. There had been frightening visits from men disguised as electricity inspectors and water company operatives, and money had been taken fraudulently.

'Just to chat about a mutual friend,' Lois said. 'She will remember me.'

'Up there, number four,' the woman said. 'I shall be in my front garden, in case you want to know anything,' she added, in a threatening rather than helpful voice.

'Thanks very much,' Lois said, sighing for the untrusting world around her, and went to ring the doorbell of number four.

The door was opened, but the inside chain left on while Doris peered through at Lois. 'Oh, it's you, Mrs Meade,' she said, and released the chain. 'Come in, do. Is it about Ivy? I saw her this morning early, and she seemed fine.'

'No, no. Nothing to do with Miss Beasley. She's very lucky to have such a good friend. No, Bill's getting on fine, and she seems pleased with him.'

'And that's quite an achievement with our Ivy!' Doris laughed.

'I was passing by, and remembered my

mother – she lives with us in Farnden – talking about an old friend who'd lived in Ringford years ago. They've lost touch, and I wondered if you might remember her and what became of her. She was Mabel Richards. I *think* that's right.'

To her amazement, Doris's face brightened. 'Mabel Richards! Goodness, that was a long time ago.' Just as Lois was beginning to think she had conjured up a ghost from the past, Doris added, 'But it wasn't Mabel, was it? I think her name was Mavis. Yes, I'm sure it was Mavis.'

They talked about Mavis for a while, and Lois promised to pass on the details to her mother. Fortunately – though not for Mavis – she had emigrated to New Zealand, and had been killed soon after in a road accident. 'What a shame,' she said hypocritically, wondering how she could get the conversation round to Susanna Jacob.

But Lois's luck was in. Doris herself introduced the subject. 'Did you sort out Ivy on changing her cleaner?' she said. 'Got it into her head that Bill was leaving, and you were sending Susanna Jacob instead.'

Lois said that had been straightened out, but asked Doris why Ivy had been so against the idea?

'Oh, that's Ivy all over,' Doris said. 'Most particular who she has in her house. She's a very churchy person, you know, and everybody has to be as blameless as she is. Well, chance would be a fine thing, I often think. Who would want to lead Ivy Beasley astray?'

'Was that what happened to Susanna?' Lois tried to sound casual.

'Well, I shouldn't really tell you,' Doris answered, 'what with her being your employee, an' that. The truth is, Susanna was working in the Town Hall. Not much of a job for a girl with her education, but apparently she wasn't all that bright. What she lacked in brains, though, she made up for in looks. Really lovely, she was and is. Heads turned, all that. Loads of boyfriends and men friends, too. Then it happened.' Doris paused and looked out of her window at the starlings fighting on the bird-table.

'Shall I guess?' Lois said finally. 'Like Ivy said? Susanna got pregnant?'

Doris nodded. 'She did. And got rid of it. Her father organised all that.'

'And who was Dad? The baby's Dad, I mean.'

Doris shook her head. 'There were rumours flying everywhere, but nobody really knew. There were so many possibles! No, it was all hushed up, and she went away for a bit. When she came back, she returned to the Town Hall, and people forgot. Except Ivy! So now you know, Mrs Meade, and I hope you'll keep it to yourself.'

Lois assured her that her lips were sealed,

and left shortly after, wishing Doris well and telling her not to exhaust herself looking after Ivy.

'Tell that to Ivy!' Doris shouted after her, and waved.

What a nice person, thought Lois, as she drove off with a wave at the fat lady and her dog.

Forty-Four

Time for an update, Lois decided, as she went into her office, her mind turning over all the possibilities that Susanna's pregnancy had opened up. She picked up a pen and a blank sheet of paper. Write it down, Cowgill had suggested years ago. A good way of organising your thoughts. She began by making a sort of family tree, with Howard Jenkinson at the top. Dead, and not by accident.

Next, she added a line of possible culprits' names. Fergus Forsyth (revenge – or fear?), Norman Stevenson (desperation in face of blackmail), Rupert Forsyth, Daisy Forsyth (a mysterious couple with secrets), Ken Slater (lifetime of being patronised by rich

270

friend), Jean Slater (ex-employee with a grudge?) ... Who else? Doreen? Well, from all that Lois now knew about Mayor Jenkinson, she would have had every reason. But she was miles from home, and had a perfect alibi. Besides, Doreen Jenkinson was the very model of a middle-class, cosseted housewife. Bill had never hinted at any trouble there. Ah, but wait a minute – what about Howard's den? But then, Bill had said Doreen had seemed not to mind at all – had even found it amusing. Who else?

Lois drew a long line beneath the list. Then she added in large letters: A Burglar (nothing taken), An Old Flame, or An Old Flame's Husband (too many to mention), and Norman Stevenson. His anxious voice came back to her over and over again. The look on his face as he watched the funeral procession. A mystery man indeed. How close had he been to colleagues in Tresham timber works? *Somebody* must have known him well.

Another blank sheet of paper. This time she put a list of all the characters, including Howard, at the top, and drew lines connecting them. Howard knew them all. The Forsyths knew Howard, Ken, Jean, Doreen, possibly Norman. The Slaters knew Howard and Doreen, probably Norman, and the Forsyths. No, this would not do. Everybody knew everybody. Lois screwed up the paper and threw it in the bin. She stared again at the family tree. Her thoughts roamed, and she was back with Doris Ashbourne, and the morning's revelation. She had left off one name: Susanna. Was it possible? Doris Ashbourne had said boyfriends and *men friends*. Her first job had been at the Town Hall. Could Howard have spotted her, and if so...?

A furious, vengeful Mr Jacob, in the heat of the moment? Lois's head spun. That kind of thing only happened in films, surely. Not in *Tresham*, small market town in the Midlands? But Lois knew only too well that crime did not restrict itself to big cities, and added Susanna's father to the list. She thought about it, and decided that if he had given Howard a push on a supremely angry impulse, it would have been at the time the girl was pregnant, not months afterwards. She crossed him off. Although it was not as simple as that, Lois had a strong feeling that she was on the right track.

Next: how well did *she* know the names on the list? Another sheet of paper. The Jenkinsons – not very well personally, but with plenty of information from Bill, and from her recent cleaning job at Hornton House, she probably knew them best of all the others. The Slaters – hardly at all, except that they obviously disliked her. Or distrusted her? Did they think she knew something they were anxious to hide? But why should they suspect her of anything? Ah yes, because of the office in Sebastopol Street. Ken Slater had seen her there, knew it was her business, and expected her to share in the confidences Fergus Forsyth frequently exchanged with Hazel and Maureen.

Lois felt a sudden chilly shiver down her spine. Ken Slater had an icy stare, and his wife's dark eyes had looked at her malevolently. Rubbish! She was imagining it. Still, she put a big question mark by the Slaters, and carried on. The Forsyths – Rupert and Daisy. Sounded like an old music-hall act. The Flying Forsyths. *Let the Forsyths Help You to Fly!* Well, they had the merchandise. Lois was pleased with that, and smiled. But how well did she know them? There were two people she could consult: Gran, who knew Daisy from her brief membership of the WI, and Josie, who saw them regularly in the village shop.

Of course, the whole village knew what Rupert's shop in Tresham supplied. It had all come out at the time of the Mayor's funeral. Rupert and Daisy had kept their heads down for a while, and Fergus had hardly been seen in Farnden. But when the fun had died down – and it had been great new material for the pub's wags – the Forsyths slowly emerged. It was indeed a permissive age, and one which, Rupert was coming to realise, would eventually render their confidential services unnecessary.

Norman Stevenson – Lois grimaced. She knew his voice, and what he looked like from the funeral day and a smudgy photograph in the local paper. She knew he received blackmailing letters, and suspected he had telephoned Jean Slater at Hornton House. So he knew the Slaters well? And there was a possibility his frightening letters had been written in Doreen Jenkinson's hand. This last was difficult to swallow. Why on earth should the very well-heeled Doreen blackmail a former employee of her husband, probably fallen on hard times, for money which she could not need? Lois shook her head. She would have to wait for the results of Cowgill's investigations.

That left her with the Jacob family. Mrs Jacob she had met only once, and in not very friendly circumstances. As for Susanna, although she worked for Lois, and they had had a number of conversations, she was well aware that she had failed to get close to her in even a preliminary way. She knew quite a lot *about* the family, from Doris Ashbourne and even the formidable Miss Beasley. Not much chance of gleaning anything more from them. But Maureen Smith? She had clammed up quickly, but another approach might work. Perhaps that would be the best place to start.

The telephone rang; it was Hazel. 'Mrs M?

I've got a lady here who would like us to clean for her, but I'm wondering whether you want to travel that far. She's a few miles this side of Birmingham, and I'm not sure what our radius is.'

'That's too far for us at the moment,' Lois said. 'Too much time spent travelling. Maybe in a year or two, when we're operating worldwide, but make our apologies nicely and send her on her way. Oh, and Hazel, I'll be dropping in this afternoon – around three. See you later.'

Hazel and Maureen were chatting at the door when Lois arrived. 'Well, I'll love you and leave you,' Maureen said, turning away with the pushchair. She was out for a stroll with her toddler, and said she'd be going to the park for an hour or so.

'Just a minute, Maureen,' Lois said. 'We mentioned Susanna Jacob last time we met, and now I'd really like to ask you some questions. It won't prejudice her job with New Brooms—' Here Hazel interrupted with a *sotto voce* 'Pity!'

'It is just that something has come up, and you're the most likely person to be able to help me. Of course, if you'd rather not, I shall respect that...' Hazel's eyes widened. This was a new, tactful Mrs M.

'Well, all right, then,' Maureen said. 'But if there's something I don't think it's right for me to tell you, I shan't.'

And that will probably tell me more than what you do say, Lois thought, and smiled encouragingly. 'You'd better take Robert now, and perhaps we could have a quick word when you get back. Is your Mum at home? Perhaps she could have him for a few minutes?'

It was arranged, and Lois said Hazel could go early, as *her* mother was looking after Elizabeth. Hazel knew this was because Lois wanted private words with Maureen, but accepted gratefully. It did occur to her to wonder what Mrs M would do if Josie had a baby. How much time would she be willing to give to liberate her daughter? It would be interesting to see.

Maureen came back into the office in due course, and Lois asked her to sit down. 'I do appreciate this,' she said, 'and I certainly won't keep you long. It's just a small point.'

'Right,' Maureen said. 'Let's have it, then. Mum wants to change her books at the library.'

'I'll say straight out,' began Lois, 'that I know about Susanna's pregnancy. So that's out of the way. Now, I need to know who the father was.'

'Why don't you ask her?' Maureen said belligerently.

Lois paused, then said quietly, 'You know the answer to that.' Then she was silent for a few seconds.

Maureen shifted in her seat. 'Could've been one of several,' she said finally.

'But you know which one,' Lois said.

Maureen chewed the corner of her lip. 'Mmm,' she said. 'But I promised Susanna I'd never tell anybody.'

'Okay,' Lois said. 'Now, if I make a guess, and it's right, will you tell me?'

Maureen shook her head. 'That's as good as breaking the promise, isn't it.' She looked at her watch. 'I must get back,' she said, beginning to rise from her seat.

'Howard Jenkinson?' Lois's tone was conversational, but her eyes were fixed intently on Maureen's face. It was enough. 'Fine,' Lois said. 'No broken promises, Maureen, and I've got my answer. I shan't mention it again.'

After Maureen had gone, Lois tidied the office, put out the lights, and locked up. She drove off in her van, and on the way home, going slowly through the twisting lanes, she began to see why Mayor Jenkinson had ended up in close watery association with his beloved fish.

Forty-Five

'Mum,' Lois said, sticking her finger in the raw cake mixture and licking it appreciatively.

'Yes,' Gran said patiently, moving the bowl out of Lois's reach.

'You know Daisy Forsyth. She joined the WI, didn't she? What's she like?'

'What d'you mean? She's a middle-aged woman, mutton-dressed-as-lamb, but nice and cheerful. What else?'

'Well, did you chat to her? Has she mentioned the old days or anything?' Lois knew how her mother loved to talk about the past. She supposed all old people did. After all, the past was a lot more interesting than the present or future to them.

'Um, let me think.' Gran did not approve of Lois's sudden interest in Daisy Forsyth, and knew quite well there was a reason behind her curiosity, a reason to do with that Cowgill policeman. On the other hand, Gran could not resist passing on interesting tit-bits, and thought hard. 'She hasn't been to the WI more'n a couple of times,' she said, 'but I did sit next to her when we had our cups of tea, and we chatted. She said she found Farnden very quiet, and I asked her what she was used to. She roared with laughter – she's got a nice laugh – and said most of it wasn't a suitable subject for the WI. Well, I knew about the shop'n that, so I didn't think much of it. Then I had a good look at her when she wasn't noticing, and you know, Lois, she must have been a really fine girl when she was young. Good features, pretty hair, even now, and a good pair of legs. She shows a bit more of 'em than she should at her age, but at least they're still in good shape.'

'I suppose you're right,' Lois said. 'But what were the things unsuitable for the WI? Was she a model – you know the sort – for some of those weird things they sell?'

Gran paused, and hatched a wicked plan to stop Lois asking questions. 'Adult posters,' she said, 'late-night videos, all kinds of stuff. You know the sort of thing. Lodger's Voluptuous Dominant Landlady...' Gran chuckled.

'Mum! How do you know all this?'

'Blimey, you've only got to look at the back of the *Exchange & Mart*! *On Her Knees in the Dungeon, Naughty Nurse Natasha* – there's hundreds of 'em. And there's a lot worse than that. A really good read, those pages!' Gran laughed again, but mostly at the expression on Lois's face.

Lois was speechless. She thought she was unshockable, but the sight of her old mum beating the cake mixture with a wooden spoon, coming out with all that, was too much. 'Well, I don't know, I'm sure,' she said, unaware that she was echoing her mother's favourite phrase. 'I think I need a coffee. D'you want one?'

'Tea for me, please,' Gran said demurely, scooping the mixture into a baking tin and shunting it into the oven. 'Now, what else can I tell you about Daisy Forsyth?'

'That's plenty to be going on with,' Lois said, filling the kettle. 'So you reckon she's led a colourful life?' she added, collecting her thoughts.

Gran nodded. 'Though how she came to marry that old misery is a mystery. Old Rupert is a real grouch at home, and she's a girl used to lots of fun ... No wonder.'

Gran paused, and Lois said, 'No wonder what?'

'No wonder she gets dressed up and disappears off up to London now and then,' Gran said.

'Does she do that?' Lois wondered how much more her mother was likely to dredge up from only a couple of conversations with Daisy. But then, of course, the WI was the swap-shop for gossip. Daisy did not have to be at the meeting for her life to be chewed over by the girls.

'Yep,' Gran said. 'Rupert takes her to the station, but doesn't wait to see her on to a train. Goes off with a face like thunder.'

Lois sat down heavily. 'Mother,' she said. 'Is there anything you *don't* know about Daisy Forsyth?'

'Yes,' Gran said, looking straight at Lois. 'I don't know why you are so interested in her. And I don't suppose you are going to tell me.'

'No, I'm not,' said Lois. She made for the door, anxious to consider all that she had heard.

Gran hadn't finished yet. 'Oh yes, and before he snuffed it, his late Worship's car was seen parked outside Forsyths' house once or twice. Stayed there quite a while, and those that saw it knew for sure Rupert wasn't there. What d'you think, Lois?'

'Josie,' Lois said. She sat in Josie's little sitting room, sampling some disgusting new herb tea that Josie had got in specially for Mrs Tollervey-Jones up at the Hall. 'Ugh,' she said. 'Don't ask me to try any more of this.'

'Okay,' Josie said. 'But what did you want to ask me? There was something?'

'Yes.' Lois hesitated. She didn't much like questioning her much-loved daughter like this, but her session with Gran had been so

281

fruitful, and she wouldn't press Josie too hard. 'I was wondering,' she said, and then stopped. 'No, I'll come straight to it. I need to know more about the Forsyths. Daisy and Rupert, and Fergus too, if you've heard anything about him.'

'For Cowgill?' Josie said, as straightforward as her mother.

Lois nodded, and waited.

'Well, as you know, I hear a lot of stuff in here, and I decided right from the start that I wouldn't gossip. Not pass on anything I heard in here in confidence.'

'Quite right too,' Lois nodded.

'But,' Josie added with a grin, 'if I hear the old tabs gossiping away about stuff that's general knowledge, then that's different.'

'So?' Lois said.

'Well, this comes under that heading, I reckon. Daisy and Rupert started the Rain or Shine business, but most of their sales are by post. Tailed off a bit recently, after a bumper lot when the Mayor snuffed it. More people are quite open about it all. But not everyone, and Rupert still gets lots of orders by post. Oops!' she said. 'Forget I said that.'

'Forgotten already,' Lois said.

'And anyway,' Josie continued, 'Their only son Fergus runs the shop, with his father in strict control.'

'And Daisy?'

'She's a live wire! Not really cut out for

282

village life, if you ask me.'

'You sound like Ivy Beasley,' Lois laughed. 'What else?'

'Well, it was quiet in here one day, and she came in and started talking. I didn't encourage her, because I had work to do. But she ignored my hints, and spilled out a lot of stuff about being a model, and making little films with other girls and blokes, all in the altogether, and getting up to all kinds of tricks. Enjoyed it, she said. It was a bit of a laugh. That's her favourite phrase! She met Rupert in some dodgy bar, and was curious about him. He was certainly out of the usual run of customers. But then, she said, he turned out to be a great surprise, and worth making a fuss of. Is that enough, Mum?'

Lois chortled. 'She's a great girl, our Daisy,' she said. 'Who'd've thought it of old Rupert? No, there's only one more thing, love. It is serious, of course, not just curiosity. Do you know of any connection between Daisy and Howard Jenkinson?'

'Oh, yes – he was one of her regulars, from years back. She was quite open about it. Said it made it difficult for her when the Jenkinsons moved to Farnden. Well, only Mrs J moved in the end.'

'Nothing startling about Fergus?'

'A dark horse, I reckon. Never heard much about him, but he's very much his mother's boy, according to report. Now that's it,

Mum! How about another lovely cup of this gnat's pee? No? Well, I'll make us a nice, strong cup of Sergeant Major's.'

Forty-Six

Miss Beasley had sent for Lois. It was a Royal Command, and Lois would not dream of ignoring it. As she drove through the twisting lanes, she saw green fields stretching out as far as she could see, bordered by neatly cut hedges and spinneys of tall ash and beech. Circling black crows intimidated her with raucous cries as she accelerated up a steep hill where the overhanging branches made a dark tunnel. I wonder if I'd qualify as a country person now, she thought. Derek might. He spent hours in the garden, and had lately taken on an allotment to grow even more vegetables. Josie sold the surplus in the shop, and said customers had begun asking which were Derek's. Lois knew she could not go back now and live on a housing estate. But after a morning in Tresham, trawling the charity shops and market stalls, she felt refreshed. A foot in both camps, she reckoned, and smiled. She knew one person who would not accept her as a country girl! Ivy Beasley, born and bred in Ringford, narrow-minded, bigoted and censorious. But, so Doris Ashbourne had confided to Lois, with a heart of gold. 'Hides it well,' Lois had said, and now approached Ivy's front door with trepidation.

The door was opened by Ivy herself, walking with a stick. 'Ha! That surprised you, didn't it, Mrs Meade?' she said. 'Didn't expect to see me up and about ... well, come on in. Don't stand there letting in the draughts.'

Would she offer Lois a cup of coffee? Not likely. Ivy sat down in her seat by the range, and with her stick motioned Lois to a kitchen chair that wobbled on the uneven floor. 'What can I do for you, Miss Beasley?' Lois realised there was no point in pleasantries, such as asking how the old girl was, and how nice it was to see her on her feet.

'It's your young Bill,' Ivy said. Lois could not believe Bill had put a foot wrong, and prepared to defend him. But Ivy said, 'He's a very good lad. Can't say I gave him much of a chance when he first came, but he's done a good job. And Doris'll tell you I'm very particular.'

I don't need telling, Lois said to herself. What was the old thing leading up to?

'I'll come straight to the point,' Ivy said. 'I've decided I'm too old to be doing all the work myself, and I'd like to keep him on

285

permanently.'

Lois smiled in surprise. 'Well, of course—'

'*But*,' said Ivy, 'when I say "him", I mean Bill and nobody else. I don't want no flibbertigibbets coming here and making more mess than they clear up. So what have you to say?'

Lois took a deep breath, forced another smile, and said, 'That will be fine, Miss Beasley. I will make sure Bill comes to you regularly, and I'll only send a substitute if he's ill.'

Ivy Beasley shook her head. 'No substitutes. If Bill is sick, I'll do it myself. I doubt he's sick very often, anyway.'

'Not once, in all the time he's worked for me.'

'Mind you, I'd let him have time off for honeymoon.' Ivy Beasley was delighted to see the surprise on Lois's face.

'What do you mean? Has he said something to you?' Lois couldn't believe Bill wouldn't tell her first.

'I never repeat what's said to me, and others would do well to do the same.' Miss Beasley looked at the old clock on the mantelshelf. 'I expect you've got other calls to make,' she said, and as Lois got to her feet, she added, 'And if you want to know who pushed the Mayor into the fish pond, as I know you do, you'd better ask those Slaters. Never were any good. I knew his

286

mother, and you couldn't trust her with a sixpence.'

Lois was stunned. How could the housebound Miss Beasley possibly know she was after Howard Jenkinson's killer? She shivered. There was something very creepy about the old woman and her cat curled up in her lap. Then she thought of Bill. But he would not have even hinted. She was quite sure of that.

What was it Doris Ashbourne said? Ivy Beasley had a sixth sense, and used to tell fortunes at the village fête? Oh my God, let me out of here. Lois was still muttering to herself as she got into her van. 'Ken Slater's mother. "Couldn't trust her with a sixpence". Like mother, like son?'

She switched on Radio Five Live, and tried to immerse herself in the outside world, but Ivy Beasley's words haunted her as she drove on to winkle out Susanna Jacob. She had to get a final word out of the girl before she advertised for someone else. What a morning! It had begun to rain, and Lois set her screen wipers going. Two sweeps, and a wiper flew off and disappeared. The curse of the Beasleys! she shouted aloud, and drove on very slowly, peering through a curtain of raindrops.

And what was all this about Bill's honeymoon? Some questions to ask there.

Lois drew up outside the Jacobs' house,

and put on a stern face. At least she could assert her authority over Miss Susanna. She looked forward to it, and marched up the path with purposeful vigour.

Susanna was out. 'Out where?' said Lois sharply. Mrs Jacob flushed. 'She's gone for a walk with the dog,' she said. 'The doctor recommended a little walk each day.'

'Huh!' Lois remembered this mythical doctor of the Jacobs, who was never consulted but gave advice that suited Susanna's purposes. 'Well, if it's a little walk, I'll wait,' she added. 'I've got something very important to discuss with her.'

Mrs Jacob opened the door wider with some reluctance, and Lois marched in. She refused an offer of coffee, and said she would be quite all right on her own, if Mrs Jacob wished to get on with her work. But Mrs Jacob wasn't having that. She asked Lois to sit down, and perched on the edge of a chair on the opposite side of the room.

'Is it about the job?' she said nervously.

'It is a private matter,' Lois said firmly.

Mrs Jacob looked even more nervous. 'Can I help you at all?' she said. 'In case Susanna has met someone and stayed for a chat.' Lois considered this, and decided that the girl had probably gone shopping in Tresham, or to a movie, and would not be returning until much later. She should probably leave at once, but did not move. Maybe a conversation with Mrs Jacob would be useful.

'Would I be right in supposing you and your husband do not really like Susanna cleaning other people's houses?' Lois was blunt, calculating that this might break down defences more quickly.

'Oh! Well, of course it's up to Susanna but...'

'But what, Mrs Jacob?'

'Well, in a way, you are right. Her father, particularly, considers it not suitable for a girl coming from a good background like hers. And she had a good job ... promotion ... at the Town Hall. Plenty of opportunities for getting to the top.'

'And getting into trouble,' Lois said, risking all.

The silence seemed to go on for ever. Mrs Jacob passed a hand over her eyes wearily. 'So you know about that,' she said. 'I knew it would get out. We did our best to keep it secret, but villages are a hotbed of gossip. No chance, really.'

'It is none of my business, of course,' Lois said. 'But if it affects how she performs her job, then I have a right to know. I'll tell you straight, Mrs Jacob, I don't believe that Susanna has had flu. I don't think she is out for a short walk. I'm sure she has been lying – not to put too fine a point on it – and for one reason. So she doesn't have to work for

Mrs Jenkinson. Mrs Jenkinson isn't too keen, either. She doesn't want Susanna anywhere near her. Now, this ain't good for New Brooms, and I need to discuss it with Susanna. Not much future in her working for me, but I'm bound to give her a chance to talk about it.'

Another silence. Then Mrs Jacob seemed to come to a decision. She began to talk in a different, more confident voice. 'I see your point,' she said. 'We have been very unfair to you, Mrs Meade, and I hope you'll excuse us. We are overprotective of our only daughter. I see that. Particularly her father. But we owe it to you to give you the facts.'

'Yes, you do,' said Lois, unrelenting.

'It began when Susanna first worked in the Town Hall. She bumped into the Mayor in the corridor, and he put his arms around her to steady her. Well, that's what he said ... It went on from there, and – you probably won't believe this – she fell in love with him. She was so young, but she was certain. We did our best to show her what a dreadful mistake she was making. Then, of course, she got pregnant. Father dealt with all that, and she was terribly upset. Wanted to keep the baby. I was a coward, and kept out of it.'

Lois watched the trembling woman fumbling for a handkerchief, and felt bad. But Mrs Jacob was talking voluntarily. It was her decision. She continued, 'We wanted her to leave the Town Hall then and there, but she wouldn't. And then, to our horror, we discovered the whole wretched relationship had started up again. Father was so angry, and threatened to turn Susanna out if she didn't leave her job. So she did. But I am not at all sure this was the end of her seeing him. Then after the drowning accident Susanna went to pieces. But working for you seemed to be bringing her back to normal, and we went along with it. More or less. Now you see why she couldn't work for Mrs Jenkinson. And I can see it will be the end of her job with you. Fair enough. She'll probably have to move away – she's got friends in London, and might get a job there.' She tailed off, and blew her nose hard.

Lois stood up. 'Thanks for telling me. A pity Susanna wasn't straight with me in the beginning. Please ask her to ring me today, and we'll fix a meeting. She has to have the final word.'

After that, Lois let herself out of the front door, aware that Mrs Jacob was in tears again, and thanked her lucky stars that Josie had settled down into a responsible adult. But then Josie had not been a precious only. Nothing like a couple of brothers to keep your feet on the ground.

Susanna came to see Lois late that afternoon, and their conversation was not long.

Mrs Jacob had told her daughter that Mrs Meade knew the whole story now, and it was with relief that Susanna sat in front of Lois in her office and offered to resign.

'That would be best,' Lois answered. 'I'll make the necessary arrangements, and we'll forget all about it. I wish you well, Susanna. As for the Jenkinson affair, you'll have to deal with that in your own way. My advice, if you want it, would be to get a job far away from here. Keep in touch with your parents, who love you a lot, but make a new life.'

Susanna nodded, and prepared to leave. 'The thing is, Mrs M,' she said, 'I did love him, you know. He was not such a villain as my father thinks. And I'm not such a tramp. Howard used to talk to me. Not like he was with other people, all blustery and confident. He was gentle and kind. And he told me about himself. Said he'd always had to cover up part of his real self, because he had terrifying panic attacks that really floored him. Various things triggered them off, he said, and he'd more or less learned to avoid them. The bluster, he said, was a cover-up, and mostly worked. But he was different with me,' she repeated. 'It was real love with me. Not like anything he'd had before, he said.' Lois raised her eyebrows, but said nothing. 'Bye,' Susanna said wanly, 'and thanks, Mrs M.'

'Howard Jenkinson?' Lois said to her

empty room. There was only one person Howard Jenkinson really loved, and that was himself. And what a yarn he'd spun her! Poor, silly kid, she thought. Susanna loved him, and would not have harmed him. But her father? He must have loathed the Mayor, and would not have been the first enraged father to avenge his wronged child.

Lois considered the Slaters, remembering Ivy Beasley's parting shot, reluctantly admitting that the old bat clearly had an encyclopaedic memory, and a good nose for what was going on.

Whatever Ken Slater's mother had been, he seemed to Lois to be the very model of a respectable civil servant. He had a permanently disapproving air, and in their few meetings – more confrontations than meetings – he had looked at her as if he had a bad smell under his nose. What did she know about him? Two things: one, he was a member of the golf club; and two, he belonged to the Tresham Shooters, a gun club with impeccable credentials. Won prizes, and often had his photograph in the local paper, bearing championship trophies. The thought of Ken Slater with a gun made her shiver...

Still, Howard had not been shot, nor whacked with a golf club.

Jean Slater next. She was more interesting to Lois. A woman who had worked closely with Howard. Lois remembered that Jean had made the initial contact with New Brooms. She was getting on in years, and was apparently Doreen Jenkinson's best friend, though out of her league as far as wealth and position were concerned. Had she been closer to Howard than just a faithful secretary? It was more than likely. My God, Lois reflected, they certainly went in for wife-swapping in elevated Tresham society! But she had no proof. And in any case, why should any of this make Jean want to up-end Howard into his fish pond? Jealousy, possibly. But Howard's death would have put her out of a job – had, in fact, done so. She was probably too old to get another as well paid, and the Slaters maybe needed the money. Too many possibles and probables.

But Ivy Beasley was not one for wasting words. More ferreting was needed on the Slaters. This was difficult, as she had no obvious contacts. Perhaps she would bring them into the conversation when she went to Hornton House tomorrow morning. Risky, but she would be tactful, and Doreen might divulge something of interest.

Meanwhile, Lois remembered, there was Bill and his honeymoon. Miss Beasley could have been stirring it, but she had looked so pleased with herself at knowing something Lois did not. She would ring Bill in the morning and make a joke of it. She put out the light in her office, and quickly downed an illicit piece of Gran's chocolate cake before joining the telly-watchers. Keep it light with Bill, that would be best. After all, his private life was his own affair, and although she felt a little hurt, she was sure he would tell her in his own time.

Forty-Seven

Doreen Jenkinson sat at her desk, writing a letter to her sister. She had thought hard about what she would say, but still sat chewing the end of her pen. It was not easy to warn her that the police might be in touch, checking Doreen's story about her movements on the day of Howard's death. She had had an unexpected visit from Inspector Cowgill, asking all sorts of questions. Why now? He hadn't given much away, just hinted that they were making further enquiries into the circumstances surrounding what they now seemed to regard as a mystery. She was irritated. It had all looked straightforward, hadn't it? Howard had been drinking on his own, gone up the garden to look at the fish and tripped, too drunk to save himself. She'd told the police at the time that Howard had a weak head for alcohol. A couple of whiskies would make him more or less incapable, she'd said.

'Dear Sis,' she wrote. 'Something has come up. The police are checking some final details about that awful evening when I was on my way home from seeing you. They might get in touch, to get your confirmation that I was with you. Sorry about this, but it's not important. Just getting everything straight before they close the file. That sort of thing. How are you? Come down and see the new house soon. It's great, and I am turning into a real villager! Love Doreen.'

She addressed an envelope and stuck on a first-class stamp. Hearing a tap at the door, she guessed it was Mrs Meade, and went to greet her.

'Morning!' said Lois in her cheeriest voice. She wanted Mrs Jenkinson in a good mood, relaxed and communicative. Doreen offered her tea, and although she much preferred coffee, she accepted, taking the mug with her to start work in the dining room. There were no extra duties to do this morning, and before she moved on, she went back to the kitchen with her empty mug.

'Shall I stack the dishes?' she said, noticing

that breakfast things were still on the table. Doreen nodded. She seemed abstracted, and Lois saw that she was holding an envelope tightly in one hand. 'I'll just go over and post this,' she said. 'I want to make sure it goes today.'

'Oh, I'll take it when I leave,' Lois said quickly. 'I've got to pop in and see Josie, and the post doesn't go until this afternoon.'

Doreen hesitated, but could think of no reason to refuse. 'Right,' she said. 'Well, in that case, I'll make a phone call.'

Damn, thought Lois. She'll be on the phone for hours, and I need to manoeuvre her into a chat. She lingered in the kitchen, taking longer than was necessary to clear away the remains of a modest breakfast for one. Doreen's end of the conversation was perfectly audible, and Lois pricked up her ears when she realised she was talking to Jean Slater.

'A migraine? Oh, you poor dear.' Doreen's voice was full of concern. 'Of course you mustn't think of playing this morning. What was that? Ken's got a day off and could give me a game? Is that what you said? I can't hear you very well. It was. Right, well, I'm a bit of rabbit compared with him, but if he ... All right, then. I'll be ready at half ten. Yes, yes, she's here. In the kitchen. Take care now. Byee.'

Lois busied herself with a brush and

dustpan, trying to ignore the shiver that caught her unawares. 'She'? They must have meant her. Why would Jean Slater have asked? And why did she need to know where in the house Lois was?

Doreen called from the hall that she was going upstairs to change, and would be in the shower for ten minutes. Lois moved on to the drawing room. Her mobile rang, and she took it quickly from her pocket. She had forbidden her staff to have mobile calls while working, but when she saw who it was, she answered. 'Yes? I'm at work, so make it snappy.'

'Right,' Cowgill said. 'I'll be brief. Just a warning. Things are hotting up, and could be dangerous. Can't say more at the moment, but be very careful, Lois. Very careful indeed.'

Lois put her mobile back in her pocket and stood still, staring at nothing. 'Did I hear someone talking?' Doreen said, appearing at the door.

Lois nodded. 'It was me,' she said. 'An urgent call from one of the team. Sorry if it alarmed you.'

'Of course it didn't alarm me!' Doreen said, a little too quickly. 'Just that I wondered if someone had called. Anyway, I am expecting to go out shortly. Mr Slater will be calling for me.'

Lois looked at her blandly. 'How nice,' she

said. 'Playing golf? My Derek is threatening to take it up, but I've told him it's a very expensive game these days.'

'Too right,' said Doreen, smiling. 'But I have no other vices. Don't smoke, don't drink much.'

'I wouldn't call golf a vice,' said Lois.

'Depends what kind of game you play,' Doreen said, turning away, her smile gone. She disappeared into the hall, and Lois heard the rattle of plates as Doreen reorganised the dishwasher. Why is it that every idiot who owns a dishwasher thinks only they know how to stack it? Lois dusted the keys of the piano, out of tune because nobody ever played it, and made much of the cacophony she produced.

In due course, the front door bell sounded, and Doreen went quickly to open it. In minutes she was gone, without asking Ken into the house. Lois heard a muttered conversation at the door, and caught the words, 'She's still here, Ken.'

So I'm still here, and that matters. Lois continued to clean the house, but her thoughts were elsewhere. Golf ... depends what game you play ... what kinds of game were there? Good or bad. Slow or fast. Honest or cheating. On the fairway or in the rough ... In the rough, in the woods, with thick beds of bracken, concealed from sight? A warm, sunny day with bees humming and

299

birds busy in the trees. Lois was almost scared at the clear picture unrolling in her mind. She shook her head. Overactive imagination, my girl, she said to herself. She finished her work and locked up the house. Too much thinking about Ivy Beasley and her second sight! The thought of Ivy Beasley led her on to Bill, and she hadn't yet asked him about a honeymoon. Perhaps it should wait until the Monday staff meeting? No, she would talk to him in private.

The floor of the shop was covered in opened cardboard boxes. Josie had been to the wholesaler's, and Gran was helping her to unpack and price the stock, then stack it on the shelves. 'You can see why village shops are going out of business,' Josie said, mopping her brow. 'Supermarkets have loads of staff to do this job. Me and Gran have to do it all. The lot.'

Lois felt guilty. She had promised to help out when she could, but Josie very seldom asked her. 'Can I do something?' she said, then remembered she had to get back to meet Bill.

'No, it's all right,' Gran said. The truth was that she loved helping Josie, and didn't want Lois muscling in, telling them what to do and organising everything.

'Well, I wanted a loaf, Josie, if you've got one left.'

'It would be better if you asked me to save you one regularly,' said Josie grumpily. She went into the back room and returned with a small wholemeal loaf. 'You can have this,' she said. 'Daisy Forsyth asked me to keep her one, but she's not been in. She always collects it at half ten promptly, so I guess she doesn't need it. You're in luck.'

Not the time to ask Josie anything, Lois concluded. In any case, she had only wanted to see if Josie remembered handling letters with handwriting like the one in her pocket. It was a long shot, and not worth risking Josie's sharp tongue. She posted the letter and made her way home.

Daisy Forsyth had not been in to collect her bread because of an almighty family row that was still going on. Fergus had shut the shop and arrived in the middle of the morning with a long face. 'What's wrong with you, boy? And who's looking after the shop?' Rupert had said crossly.

'Are you ill, dear?' Daisy had said, pushing Rupert to one side, and reaching up to kiss Fergus's pale cheek.

'No,' he said. 'I'm not ill, and the shop can look after itself for one morning. Trade is not that brisk. In fact most mornings not a single punter comes in. So can we sit down. I need to talk.'

'Talk about what?' Rupert was angry and

301

impatient. What on earth did the boy think he was doing?

Daisy led the way. 'Shall we have a coffee and calm down?' she said soothingly. Whatever Fergus said, she knew that something was very wrong.

Rupert and Fergus sat hunched in their chairs saying nothing, while Daisy made coffee and brought it in on a tray. 'Biscuit, dear?' she said to Fergus. He shook his head. 'Let's get this over with,' he said.

'Right,' said Rupert firmly. 'Get going, and then we can get back to the business that keeps us all in food and drink, and a roof over our heads.'

'Bull's eye, Dad,' Fergus said. 'It's the business. And my life in the business. I hate it, if you want the truth. I hate the goods, the customers, the shifty looks and sideways smiles of my so-called friends. I hate sitting in that cramped little shop, nowhere near the centre of town, wasting my life doing bugger-all most of the time. No, don't interrupt, Dad. You can – and, I am sure, will – have your say in a minute. I want out. The way things are going, we'll be losing so much business anyway, and it won't be enough to do all those things you just listed so pleasantly.'

Daisy looked at him admiringly. This was a new, more confident Fergus. He sat up straight and looked his father in the eye. 'I

302

suggest,' Fergus continued, 'that we either sell the business or wind it up and you and Mum can retire. I mean to get some training to do something completely different. A new start, Dad. Before it is too late.'

He sat back, and waited. Daisy took a deep breath and looked at Rupert, who seemed to be stunned into silence. 'Excellent, Fergus!' she said. 'Just what I've been thinking myself. We can all have a new start.'

Rupert came alive. 'And what shall we bloody well live on?' He glared at Daisy, as if it was all her fault.

'Our pensions, and we shall get some money from the sale of the business ... or the property.' She felt a rising excitement at the prospect.

Fergus nodded. 'The area is going up,' he said. 'Prices of houses round there are rising all the time. I was talking to Hazel and Maureen—'

Rupert leaned forward and interrupted him with venom. '*If,*' he hissed, 'you spent less time talking to those stupid women, we might be gaining business instead of losing it. The shop always looks a mess, and your sales talk is pathetic. You're a waste of space, and the answer to your ridiculous proposition is No, No, No!' His voice had risen to a shout, and his face was apoplectic.

Fergus stood up. He looked at his parents, squared his shoulders, and marched out, slamming the front door as he went. Daisy heard his car driving off and put her head in her hands.

'Stop that blubbing!' Rupert yelled, and raised his fist. At that moment, the doorbell rang. And then the knocker rapped several times.

'Morning, sir.' A man in a well-cut suit stood there. 'Inspector Cowgill, Tresham police. May I come in? Just a few more questions I'd like to ask you and your wife.'

Forty-Eight

Later that day, when not a single customer had crossed the threshold of Rain or Shine, Fergus Forsyth considered shutting the shop early. He had returned after his abortive conversation – if you could call it a conversation – with his father, and had spent the rest of the day planning his future. If his father would not co-operate, then Fergus had decided to carry out what he planned, regardless of what happened to the business. He would wash his hands of his father, and start straight away on applying for further education courses and grants. He had a fair amount of money put safely away, and he had hoped his father would reward his years of faithful service with a share of any sale. Ha! Those hopes were dashed this morning. But no matter, he would stay afloat whatever happened.

He looked out of the window. The lights were on in the New Brooms office, and he could see Hazel talking on the telephone. She was a good listener. Maybe he'd walk over and have a chat. He needed someone to confide in. The day's events had left him very determined, but at the same time he felt shaky when he thought of how Rupert would take it out on Daisy. Fergus was fond of his mother, but had never found a way of helping her. She always laughed away his concern, saying she was tough, tougher than his father any day, and Fergus was not to worry.

Just as he was locking the safe and preparing to leave, a car drew up outside. Ken Slater. Fergus looked at his watch. Still a quarter of an hour to official closing time. He sighed and went back inside the shop, switching on the lights.

'Ah, good lad!' said Ken. 'Thought you were shut, for one awful moment...'

He walked not too steadily behind Fergus, and sat down on a stool, narrowly missing falling off the edge. Oh my God, thought Fergus. Ken Slater the worse for wear. He was a boring enough companion sober, but drunk...

'Been playing golf with a lovely lady,' Ken said happily. 'Thought I'd pop in for a chat. You going to the gun club tonight? There's the big competition, and you'd stand a good chance. I shall be there – give you a lift if you like?'

Ye gods, Fergus muttered. If Ken turned up in this state, he'd be shown the door and probably exit into the arms of the police bearing breathalyser. 'Not sure, Ken,' he said. 'Better go under my own steam. I shan't decide until later.'

'Well, let me know if you change your mind,' Ken replied expansively. 'Plenty of room in the old Audi...' He swayed on his stool, and his eyelids drooped. Then he snapped awake. 'Did I ever tell you,' he began in a portentous voice, 'about the time I took Howard to the club? Not golf ... no, the gun club, I mean.' Fergus nodded, but Ken continued anyway. 'Disaster!' he said. 'The bugger's hands shook so hard he nearly dropped the gun. Terrified! Never got anywhere near the ranges. Had to take him home, shaking like a jelly. Luckily Doreen was there. Took his hand like he was a kid. Knew just what to do. He asked me – well, paid me, if you want the truth – to keep quiet about it, and I did. You're the first person I've told, and I know you'll keep mum. Good old Fergus!' He began to laugh, and couldn't stop.

Fergus said, 'I'll get you a glass of water,' and rushed out to the back room. He pulled out his mobile and dialled the Slaters' home number. No reply. Sod it! He got the water and considered throwing it over Ken to sober him up.

When Fergus returned the laughter had stopped, and Ken sat up to the counter with his head resting on his hands. 'All right now,' he said morosely, all his good humour evaporated.

There was a short silence, whilst Fergus wondered what on earth to do. He couldn't let the fool drive his car, but he was sure that Ken wouldn't agree to a taxi, or a lift from Fergus. He had the supreme confidence of a man fuelled by far too much alcohol, and anyway, he was bigger than Fergus.

'Came in useful, later on,' Ken muttered, as if to himself.

'What did?' Fergus was still thinking desperately, not really concentrating on what Ken had said.

Ken turned and looked at him. 'What did you say, young Fergus?'

'What did?'

Ken looked puzzled. 'You're talking in riddles, boy,' he said. 'Riddle, diddle, dee ... I need a pee!' This sent him off into another fit of uncontrollable laugher, and Fergus looked around desperately for the mop bucket.

At this inauspicious moment, just as Fergus found the bucket, the door flew open and Jean Slater appeared, followed by Doreen Jenkinson. They ignored Fergus completely, and positioned themselves either side of a surprised Ken. 'Come on, you fool,' Jean said. 'Ready, Doreen?' Doreen nodded, and they frog-marched him out of the shop and into the back seat of his car. A swift consultation between the two women, and then Jean drove off in the Audi without once looking back.

Fergus stood motionless, staring after the car. Doreen took his arm and propelled him back into the shop. 'Sorry about that,' she said. 'Doesn't happen often, but oh boy, when he does go on a bender he does it thoroughly. Funny thing was,' she added lightly, 'I was playing golf with him this morning. He did seem a bit abstracted, but otherwise the same old Ken. Still, we had a drink after the game, and when one of my friends offered me a lift home, he said he'd stay for a while and get some lunch. A liquid lunch, I reckon. Jean got a call from the club after he left, and we finally tracked him down. Something must have upset him...'

'Perhaps he was celebrating,' said Fergus.

Long after closing time now, but the lights were still on in New Brooms. Fergus felt even more the need to unburden himself to Hazel, and after locking up, crossed the road and greeted her with relief.

'Hi,' he said. 'Can you spare a minute to listen to a desperate man?' He was smiling, and Hazel offered to make him a coffee.

'No thanks,' he said. 'I just need a sympathetic ear, and who better to come to than the lovely Hazel?'

'That's quite enough of that! Just get on with it,' Hazel said, and leaned back in her chair.

'Well, it has to be kept very confidential. Not repeated to anyone. Is that all right with you?'

He must be barmy, thought Hazel, but nodded in agreement.

Fergus began at the beginning and related in a neatly chronological order all the events of his day. By the time he had finished, Hazel was sitting up straight, listening hard. 'I feel much better now, thanks,' he ended. 'Everybody should have a Hazel to talk to,' he ventured.

He got a caustic reply. 'Try finding a girlfriend,' Hazel said, and looked at her watch. 'Time to shut up shop,' she said, and ushered him out.

She watched him safely across the road, and then switched off most of the lights. Then she lifted the telephone and dialled. 'Mrs M? Hazel here. Have you got a few minutes? I've just heard some stuff that might be of interest to you. Fine. Here goes, then.'

Forty-Nine

Jean and Doreen sat in Jean's small kitchen, with a defeated-looking Ken on the opposite side of the table. Jean had made quantities of strong, black coffee, and replenished Ken's mug as soon as he emptied it. 'Steady on, Jean,' Doreen said. 'He'll be having the heebie-jeebies with all that caffeine.'

'Serve him right,' Jean said.

After a moment's silence, Doreen said, 'How's your head?'

'Migraine's gone,' Jean replied. 'It's like that. Some sudden unexpected shock can do it. Only silver lining to this particular cloud,' she added, glaring at Ken.

'Oh, for God's sake leave it, Jean,' Ken muttered. 'I've said I'm sorry ... what more do you want? Grovelling? I'll grovel, if it will shut you up. And I don't want any more sodding coffee!'

He rose unsteadily to his feet and emptied his mug down the sink. He was no longer drunk, but had the shakes, and stumbled back to his chair.

'So you had a matey chat with Fergus?' Jean said. 'And what was it about? How you were still mourning your best friend, and every time you went on the golf course you were reminded of him? Especially when you landed your ball in that wood, in the thick bracken? So you'd decided to drown your woes?'

'Jean...' Doreen said softly. She felt sorry for Ken. But if he'd blabbed to Fergus, then it was serious. She doubted if he remember-ed any of the conversation, but that didn't deter Jean.

'Come on, then,' Jean said. 'Tell us all. Mind you, we know most of it already, don't we. You're a fool, Ken Slater.'

Ken made an attempt to sit up straight. 'Thanks very much, wifey dear,' he said. His eyes were like stones. Pinkish stones. 'I don't see why I should tell you anything. Or why the pair of you had to come bustin' in like a couple of Valkyrie. Well, I don't intend to be carried off to Valhalla just yet, and I could quite easily have found my way home.'

Doreen raised her eyebrows. 'I don't see you in the home of the Gods, Ken dear,' she said. 'More the other place, given the circumstances. Anyway, this is getting us nowhere. And it's WI tonight, so I'd better get on. I'll leave him in your capable hands, Jean.' She left quickly, patting Ken's shoulder lightly as she passed him on her way out.

Doreen was not going straight home. She drove through the narrow lanes at speed, narrowly missing one or two oncoming vehicles, and squashing a small creature rashly crossing the road in front of her. Instead of heading for Hornton House, she turned down a side road and came to a jerky halt in front of the Forsyth house.

Daisy saw her get out of the car and open the garden gate. 'Rupert!' she yelled. But he was upstairs in the little office, with Wagner turned up loud, and did not hear. The doorbell rang twice, and then again, impatiently. Daisy opened the door.

'Ah, yes,' said Doreen, 'I'd like a word.' She walked past Daisy and into the sitting room. 'Is your husband in?' Daisy nodded mutely. 'Then ask him if he can spare me a few minutes. I need both of you.'

Rupert appeared, silent for once, and sat next to Daisy on the sofa. Doreen settled herself in an upright chair, in a commanding position over the other two. She stared at them for a couple of minutes, until Daisy stuttered, 'H-how can we help you, Mrs Jenkinson?'

'I doubt if you're even willing to help me,' Doreen said sharply. 'But I don't need your help. It's the other way round. I can help you.'

The Forsyths exchanged startled glances. 'What do you mean?' Rupert said.

'Well, as you must know, and as your wife certainly knows, my late husband was a jolly man. Loved jolly parties and jolly times with pretty ladies. I never minded. Worked off some of his surplus energy, and saved me the bother. And anyway, it was all in the past. But then it came to my ears that Howard had paid Daisy Forsyth a visit, right under my nose, in the village where we intended to live. Now, this was too much. I'm sure you'd agree with that, Mrs Forsyth?'

'Where is all this leading us?' Rupert said in an even voice. He moved a few inches away from Daisy, disassociating himself from her goings-on.

'To your son, Fergus.' Doreen smoothed down her skirt and clasped her hands together. She almost smiled. 'I understand he is a great gossip. Quite a lot to gossip about, in a shop like yours, I imagine. A friend of mine, as it happens, was talking to him this afternoon. He was not quite himself, unfortunately, and could well have burdened your son with things which were on his mind – things which had nothing to do with Fergus, of course.'

'Get to the point, Mrs Jenkinson,' said Rupert. 'I am rather busy.'

'I think you'll want to hear the rest, Mr Forsyth,' Doreen said comfortably. 'The point is, you do something for me, and I'll do something for you. You ask – no – tell Fergus to forget anything my friend told him, erase it; and I'll make sure Daisy's little interlude with Howard does no harm to her reputation in Long Farnden.' She sat back in her chair and waited.

Daisy looked at Rupert, and back at Doreen. 'Your husband, Mrs Jenkinson, was an old friend of mine,' she said. 'I don't know and don't care how "jolly" your marriage was, but I am not in the habit of turning away old friends who find my company congenial.'

She paused, and then stood up. 'As for your proposition, my husband and I will discuss it with Fergus, and let you know.' She walked towards the door. 'Come this way, please,' she said. 'We are both rather busy, and I am sure you are, too. WI tonight, isn't it? Have a good meeting. Goodbye.'

Doreen drove home slowly. She had been so sure of her strategy, but now felt oddly discomforted. Had Daisy one-upped her? That middle-aged scrubber? She turned into the garage, and was dismayed to hear a scrape as she drove too near the wall.

In a thoroughly bad temper now, she let herself into the house and stepped into three inches of water. The dishwasher had stuck on filling up, and flooded most of the ground floor.

Fifty

Jean and Ken sat in silence on opposite sides of the breakfast table, which, for all the contact between them, could have been a wide chasm. Ken was pretending to read the newspaper, though the print blurred before his eyes. Jean stared into a cup of cooling coffee and reviewed the last few months.

Since Howard had died, she had enjoyed her freedom, though she was missing the extra cash. With Doreen and Ken, she had picked up the pieces of their lives, and had looked forward to a future without the ever-present grey cloud of Howard and all the trouble he had caused them. She had to admit that her affair with him had been exciting, and had been conducted with a kind of licence from Ken and Doreen, who were at it like rabbits at the same time. She supposed it was that vulnerable time of their lives, when middle age had suddenly been a reality, and dangerous liaisons seemed a good way of keeping the future at bay. Oh, come on, Jean, she said to herself, half-smiling, we were all randy as hell. Simple as that. And it *was* good while it lasted.

'What are you smiling at?' Ken broke the silence at last. 'Doesn't seem much to smile at just now.'

'Thoughts,' Jean replied dully. 'But really I was thinking about all the mistakes we have made. Me and Howard, you and Doreen. Feelings out of control. That sort of thing.'

'At least we shared it all,' Ken said, looking hopefully across the table.

'Not all of it,' Jean said quietly.

'Like what?'

'Like how Howard died. I think you know, Ken. You and Doreen, perhaps. I have an idea, but I don't know exactly.'

Silence settled over them once more. Then Ken put down his newspaper and stood up. 'I'll make some more coffee,' he said. 'Then I'll go over it with you, step by step, and you'll see that whatever your husband's faults are, he is not a murderer.'

'Convince me,' Jean said, and glared at him.

Lois walked out into Derek's vegetable garden and studied the neat rows of cabbages, carrots, parsnips and onions. Good, old-fashioned English vegetables, increasingly popular in Josie's shop, where they were sold on the day Derek had lifted them, fresh as a daisy and unsullied by sprays or plastic wrappings. She walked on to the little

gate in the hedge and through to the footpath by the river. She needed to think, and
with the flowing water and clear air, no telephone or Gran chattering to disturb her.

She had not yet heard from Cowgill about
Doreen and the letters, but was sure it had
been she who blackmailed Norman Stevenson. She had probably had some hold over
him from the past, when he had worked in
Tresham and had that big row with Howard.
Possibly an affair? The Mayor's Parlour
seemed to have been a hotbed of how's
y'father! Why the wealthy wife of Howard
Jenkinson should need to blackmail for
money was a mystery, but one that Cowgill
could easily solve.

Willow branches swept over the footpath,
and Lois walked round them, feeling the wet
grass cool around her ankles. It had rained in
the night, but now the sun was shining and
everywhere sparkled. Why am I mixed up in
all this? she asked herself. I could be thinking about the business, planning expansion,
all that ... Maybe this would be the last time
she'd be persuaded to help Cowgill. Well, she
could postpone that decision. But for now it
was back to the fearful foursome. Doreen
and Howard, Jean and Ken, linked by so
many connections. School, business, sex,
Norman, Susanna. Hotbed was probably a
good description. A hotbed that overheated
somewhere. And now Cowgill's warning for

her to be careful. That meant that one or more of the foursome suspected she knew too much. Perhaps Doreen, alerted by Lois's questions. Or Jean, who had had access to all Howard's secrets, more than likely including the Susanna catastrophe. Susanna and New Brooms. It didn't take much to put two and two together and make five, to add Lois to the foursome – an unwelcome intruder. If Norman Stevenson had known of Lois's amateur sleuthing, ten to one the Slaters and probably Doreen knew too.

Right. Lois turned purposefully around and headed back to the house. She was due at Hornton House this afternoon, and – watching her back – would quietly open a few drawers and, if she got the chance, ask a few innocent questions. She was pretty sure now that one of them was in some way responsible for Howard's death, but exactly why and how was still unclear. Doreen had an alibi, but the others did not. They claimed to have been at home, but had no witnesses.

Before she left for work, she rang Cowgill. He was out, but she left a message to say that she would be working at Hornton House that afternoon. That was all. She hoped he could mind-read, but doubted it. She would just have to be extra careful.

The breakfast dishes were now stacked on

the draining-board, and Jean washed while Ken dried. It had not taken long for Ken to give his account of what happened, and Jean was numb. Now she paused, resting her gloved hands on the sink. 'Is that really all there was to it?' she said. 'Just an accident? You'd both had too much to drink? Too foozled to go to his aid? And why didn't you tell me all this before? You weren't that drunk when you arrived home...'

Ken sighed. 'Scared,' he said. 'That's why I lied to you, said I'd been at the gun club. I'd been with Howard all the time. After golf, we watched some blue movies in his den, then went down and had a drinking session. It was him that suggested a walk in the garden. The cold night air didn't help. Hit me like a wet sheet, and it was all I could do to walk. He'd gone on ahead of me, up to his bloody pond. Then it happened. By the time I got there, I could see he was dead, and I sobered up and scarpered, like a fool.'

'And persuaded me to say we were both at home all evening, convincing me we'd be the first to be suspected.' Jean shook her head. She muttered, 'Now where is it all going to end,' and continued blindly washing the dirty dishes.

Ken said no more, and half an hour later arrived at his office, shutting the door firmly and sitting down at his desk. He took out his mobile and dialled. 'Doreen? We need to

talk. Well, what time does she come? Fine.
Right. Yes, I can make it – but just a sandwich. Not very hungry. See you later then.'

Fifty-One

After Ken had gone out, Jean tidied up and
had a hot shower. She dressed carefully,
choosing the dark grey suit she had bought
before Howard died, in a last-ditch attempt
to update her image in the face of Susanna
Jacob's youth and beauty. She looked in the
long mirror, and decided the general effect
was good. Responsible, sensible and confident. She had a call to make, and needed all
the ammunition she could muster.

Ken had taken the car, of course, but she
waited for the bus into town. Her neighbour
looked at her curiously as they waited together at the bus stop. 'You all right, Jean?'
she said. 'Fine, thanks,' said Jean. She was
not. She felt remote from everything but her
determination to carry through what she had
planned. Her neighbour said something else
that Jean did not hear. 'Sorry?' she said.

'Shall we have a coffee together in town?'
repeated the woman.

Jean shook her head. 'No, thanks, I've got an appointment as soon as we get there. In fact, I wish this bus would get a move on.' Another lie. She had no appointment, but was sure she would be seen, when she explained.

Finally they reached the bus station, where passengers disgorged and vanished in different directions.

'Which way are you going, Jean?'

Why doesn't she leave me alone, thought Jean, but shook her head politely and said she was not heading for the shops, not at first. 'Hope you find some bargains,' she said, and strode off. Screaming red SALES notices were everywhere, and the streets were crowded. But soon she was out of the bus station and walking fast down a back alley that came out exactly where she wanted to be. She climbed up stone steps, waited for the automatic doors to open, and went in.

The reception area was full of people waiting for attention. A dark, plump girl was sobbing into her handkerchief, and a kindly grey-haired man tried to comfort her. Finally it was Jean's turn. The young man behind the reception desk apologised for keeping her waiting. 'Handbag thieves are out in force today,' he said. 'It's the sales, you know. People come in from the villages, not vigilant enough.'

'Doesn't matter,' said Jean, looking at her

watch. 'As long as I can be seen right now.'
The young man listened to what she had to
say, nodded, and spoke quietly to someone
at the other end of an internal line.

'Yes sir, it's urgent, apparently. Very well,
we'll bring her up.'

Doreen also dressed with care, but more
frivolously, to please Ken. He liked her to be
feminine. It was a chilly morning, but she
decided on a frilly blouse and close-fitting
skirt. High heels, of course. Then she spent
the morning preparing. She made notes and
crossed them out. Should she leave the
talking to Ken? No, not entirely. She had
important things to say. In the end, she
decided to wait for the way things went, and
act accordingly. Safer to prepare sandwiches!
She cut wholemeal bread, placed smoked
salmon on the buttered slices and squeezed
lemon juice. Then she remembered Ken
liked horseradish with his salmon sandwiches, and made a stack of these as well.

He might arrive early, and she was ready.
She had opened a bottle of chilled white
wine, and set out the sandwiches on the
kitchen table. Sun poured through the windows, and the view down the trim garden
and out across the shining water meadows
filled her with optimism and confidence. It
would go well. She could trust Ken. In fact,
she had always trusted Ken more than she

could Howard. Howard was a lying toad most of the time. He wasn't very good at it, and she had almost always found out the truth. After a while, she'd decided it was either divorce or putting up with it, and had decided on the latter. She had found ways of coping, and Ken was one of them. As for Norman Stevenson, he had been like one of those flies that persist on landing on your bare arm no matter how many times you brush them away. He would never take 'no' for an answer. He had declared undying love, threatened to reveal what he knew about Howard, but she had never let him come near. Ken and Jean had helped keep him at bay. They knew him well, and Jean had felt sorry for him. Doreen had not, and the letters had been a pleasure, as well as a way of settling her bank balance. She hadn't asked for much, after all. She hadn't wanted him dead, but could not raise much sympathy for him now that he had been finally swatted.

A knock at the door. Doreen's pulse quickened, in spite of herself, and she walked nervously to open up. Ken stood there, frowning. He pushed past her, without the usual peck on the cheek, and went straight into the kitchen. 'What's all this?' he said, looking at the table, the sandwiches and bottle of wine. 'Nothing to celebrate, is there?'

His voice was harsh, and Doreen quaked. Surely it was not that bad? It could all be sorted out, no question about that.

'Won't you take off your coat, dear?' she said.

Ken shook his head, and slumped down into a chair. 'What time is she due?' he said.

'Two o'clock. There's plenty of time for us to have a bite. And I need a drink, even if you don't.'

Ken said, 'We need to talk first.' Doreen felt irritation rising. This was her house, and she expected guests – even Ken Slater – to be at least polite.

'Are you suffering, then?' she said sharply. 'Still got a hangover? It wouldn't be surprising after your little exhibition yesterday.' He looked at her with bloodshot eyes, and said nothing. She relented, and said, 'I wasn't going to mention it, Ken, but you are such a bloody misery...'

He nodded. 'Sorry, sweetheart,' he said, and sighed. 'And yes, I am feeling grim. Still, hair of the dog. But I'll keep my coat on. Feeling shivery, and I know that serves me right, so you needn't say so. Here, shall I pour?'

She persuaded him to have a sandwich and the atmosphere lightened. He began by telling her all that had been said between him and Jean the night before, and this morning. 'I just hope she believed me,' he said. 'I told no lies.'

Doreen said sagely, 'There's ways and ways of telling the truth, Ken dear. I'm sure Jean is with us all the way. It is the matter of Lois Meade we have to talk about.'

'Yes, well, it may be that we are too late. She fancies herself, you know, as a kind of Miss Marple in the village. Been involved in several crimes, ferreting about and informing that Hunter Cowgill. Time he retired,' he added glumly.

'Still, that wouldn't necessarily stop our Lois,' Doreen said. 'Wretched woman, why can't she mind her own business and stick to cleaning? Ideas above her station, if you ask me.'

'In that case,' said Ken, 'we have to remind her. She has to be stopped. Things had quietened down nicely before she started poking her nose here and there. I didn't like the look of her that day you moved in. And Norman said she'd been very narky with him. Denied anything to do with being a private eye. Mind you, I can't think why he ever rang her ... he must have been desperate, poor sod.'

Doreen had a sudden impulse to tell him about the letters, but wisely held back. She had to keep Ken thinking she was a brave little woman who had done her very best in a bad situation. He would have to know eventually, of course. It was Lois Meade's insistence on taking that letter to the post that made her certain the woman knew too much. And then the call she took on her mobile. She lied about that, Doreen was convinced. She was used to a lying face. Could tell in an instant.

The sun had gone in, and the kitchen clock ticked relentlessly on to five minutes to two. Doreen felt a sudden pang of fear. Was this a good idea? Lois Meade didn't seem the type who would agree to keep her mouth shut, not even for the wad of notes in a brown envelope in the kitchen table drawer. Ah well, Ken seemed to know what he was doing. Silence had fallen between them, and then suddenly there was a tap at the door, and she heard Lois's key in the lock.

Fifty-Two

Lois knew something was wrong the minute she stepped into the hall. It was there in the air. Mrs Jenkinson clattered towards her on high heels, and said, much too brightly, 'Good afternoon! How are we today?'

'I'm fine,' Lois said. 'I don't know about the rest of us.'

Mrs Jenkinson's smile disappeared instantly. 'Well, good,' she said. 'Just go on into the kitchen, please. We have to have a little talk before you begin.' As Lois walked down the hall, she heard Mrs Jenkinson turn the key in the mortise lock in the front door. She turned around and said, 'Why did you do that? Not expecting burglars, are we?'

'I'm not,' Doreen said sharply. 'I don't know about the rest of us.'

Well, sod you, thought Lois, who was not used to being outsmarted. She strode into the kitchen and saw Ken Slater sitting at the table. 'Oh, sorry!' she said. 'Don't let me disturb your lunch. I'll just get some things.'

'Sit down, Mrs Meade,' Ken said, without ceremony. 'Sit there, and listen.'

'What did you say?' Lois glared at him. She raised her eyebrows and turned to Doreen, who nodded briefly.

'Do as he says,' Doreen said.

Thoughts of leaving at once crossed Lois's mind, but Ken was ahead of her. 'Give me your keys to this house,' he said. Once more Lois appealed to Doreen, and once more received a curt nod. She handed over her keys, quite sure that she could escape by the scullery door. It was almost never used, and they would have forgotten about that.

But Ken's chair was placed so that he could easily intercept her on her way to the scullery.

'Go on, Mrs Jenkinson,' she said, feigning reasonableness.

'Well, dear,' Doreen said, 'it's just that since my husband died, I'd been hoping for a peaceful time to grieve, to try and build a new life. I had thought that with the passing of time Howard's memory would take its place and I'd be able to remember the good times without bursting into tears all the time.'

My God, thought Lois, she should have been an actress. Even the chin was wobbling! What about the bad times? Would she mention those?

Ken cleared his throat, but Doreen began again quickly. 'And now, unfortunately, old wounds seem to be opening up. The dreadful accident had been thoroughly investigated, and I was perfectly satisfied with the explanation. Of course, I wasn't there, and if I had been it would never have happened. I shall never forgive myself for that.'

Ken Slater's face was a study. If she hadn't been tense with alarm, Lois would have laughed. Disbelief was written all over his grey pallor and heavy eyes. But Doreen hadn't finished. 'Now the police have started asking questions again. Insinuating things which upset me. And we were wondering, Jean and Ken and I, whether it was something you had said, something on your mind which you had mentioned to your friend

Cowgill?'

Ken had had enough. 'The woman knows exactly what we're talking about,' he said. 'She's a snoop, a cheapskate who takes money for information. This cleaning business is a cover for getting into people's houses. It's got to stop, and right now, as far as we're concerned!'

Lois stood up furiously. 'You can go to...' Her voice petered out. Ken had pulled his hand from his pocket and was holding a pistol, aimed straight at her.

'Sit down!' he said. 'This is the real thing, and I know exactly how to use it. You will sit there and say nothing, and listen to our proposition. After I let you go, you will contact your masters and tell them you want no more to do with them. Use some excuse – husband, kids, too dangerous ... which it will be, if you don't do what you're told.' He waved the gun with an unpleasant grin that sent a shiver down Lois's spine. The man was a loony, driven to it by all the twists and turns of the web of lies they had woven between them. If he was trigger-happy, she would have to watch every move.

'And then,' he continued, 'you will take this package,' he reached into the drawer and held a fat brown envelope towards her, 'and book yourself and your husband a luxury holiday far, far away from here. Perhaps you might be persuaded not to come back. We have been thinking about that, haven't we, Doreen? Ways of making you disappear, maybe temporarily, maybe permanently.' The gun held steady.

Lois gulped. She looked over Ken's shoulder at the garden and the water meadows. It was early afternoon in Long Farnden, just down the road from her house, and across the road from Josie's shop. Was this really happening? Just as she looked away from the window, back to the outstretched hand with its evil bribe, a flash caught her eye. It was in the corner of the window, and she was certain it had been a face. A white face, that was gone at once.

'I'm not sure what you mean,' she said, making a huge effort. 'Could you explain it a bit more clearly. What exactly are you saying? If I don't shut my mouth, you'll bump me off?' She laughed then, and this was the most difficult thing of all. 'But I know you didn't mean that,' she said. 'After all, what chance would you have of getting away with it? No, you must have meant something else.'

'Just watch it, Mrs Meade,' Ken said slowly. 'And don't be too sure about what I would or would not do. Everything we have done, Doreen and me, has been carefully planned.'

Lois looked hopefully towards the corner of the window, but there was nothing. She had to keep them talking somehow. 'Why should I bother about you lot?' she said. 'You've got it all wrong. I know you were his best friend an' that. And Mrs Jenkinson was so upset when he ... when he died. I'm just sorry for you all, and New Brooms has done its best to help Mrs Jenkinson through bad times. If the poor man hadn't had too much to drink that night ... it was a tragic accident, wasn't it?' She couldn't help her voice rising in a question.

Doreen spoke again, soothingly, and without looking at Ken. 'Of course you and Bill have been a great help. It was just that we've heard things. Our friend Norman Stevenson...' Ken darted a furious look at her. 'He had told us about you,' she continued. 'Said he'd asked for your help in a certain matter, but you'd refused. So we know your reputation, dear.' Lois managed a half-smile, and willed her to continue. 'As for that terrible night,' Doreen went on, as Ken leaned across the table and held the gun ever closer to Lois, 'there were unfortunate things that were best kept untold. You see, Ken was there, keeping Howard company. They were such good friends. And both were pissed as newts!' Doreen turned and laughed at Ken. He turned around slowly towards her, the gun moving with him.

'You stupid bitch!' he said, and Lois looked again at the window, praying that help was out there somewhere. This is what it must have been like that night, she thought. Howard faced with this terrifying idiot. What was it Susanna had said? Her lover had been scared of lots of things? Had he found a way of coping? But maybe not that night. Maybe he was *too* scared. Guns were scary enough, but for a man in a panic attack? Perhaps he could do nothing to save himself. Fear would have been enough.

'Ken! For God's sake!' Doreen's wide eyes stared at him. 'What the hell are you doing?'

His colour rose until his face was purple. 'Is there anything else you'd like to tell her?' he shouted at her, all control gone. 'Like how I pointed the gun at him and forced him up to his precious pond? Why don't you blurt it all out? Tell her he could hardly walk, and that I grinned when I saw he was in one of his crazy attacks, not to mention the drink. But I got him there ... I was more than ready to trip the bugger into the water, but he did it all by himself! Thrashed about a bit, and I was ready for him with the gun if he made it, but no need. All quiet in no time. Just like we'd planned, you and me, Doreen ... why don't you tell her *that*?' His voice had risen to a scream.

This delivered the final blow to Doreen, and she threw herself forward at him. 'But Ken – I love you!' she yelled. But as she embraced him, the gun went off and she slid slowly to the floor. He did not look at her, but, instantly subdued, stood up quickly as Lois made for the scullery door.

'Get back, else you'll join her,' he said.

Lois retreated to her chair. This is it, then, she thought. I've always been lucky before, but my luck's run out. She desperately fought back tears, sensing that this would enrage him more. 'Mr Slater,' she began, with little idea of what she would say next. He nodded at her, gun still pointing at her, but not so steady now. 'How about a bargain?' she improvised. 'I sit here and do nothing, and you get away. I'll give you an hour – nobody expects me to leave yet anyway – and then I'll go home and say nothing ... ever. I know you mean what you say about my family's safety, and that's enough to keep my mouth shut. Permanently.'

Ken said nothing, but stared fixedly at her. 'Is it a deal?' Lois said, trying to keep her voice steady.

He slowly lowered the gun, stood up and fastened his coat, having trouble with the top button. Without saying another word, he walked out of the kitchen, out of the front door, and straight into the arms of Chief Inspector Hunter Cowgill. At the same time, the scullery door opened, and Jean Slater appeared, crossed to where Lois still sat, frozen in her chair. Jean looked down at the lifeless body, and collapsed on to the chair so lately occupied by her husband. 'Oh my God,' she said, and tears streamed down her cheeks, unchecked by her shaking hands.

Lois came to life. 'Sorry,' she said. But that wasn't enough, and she mustered all her strength. 'Mrs Slater,' she stuttered, 'he didn't even look back at her. What he'd done to her. He was a devil.'

Fifty-Three

After a few minutes, Cowgill walked into the kitchen and went straight to Lois, who was still sitting at the table, holding tight to Jean Slater's shaking hand.

'For God's sake, Lois, are you all right?' His hand on her shoulder was warm, re-assuring. 'Why didn't you tell me what was happening?'

'I tried,' she said. 'I left the message to say where I was, hoping you'd come. But I didn't know,' she added, finally turning to look at him, 'I really didn't know Ken Slater would be here. Did you get him?'

Cowgill nodded. 'Gone to the station with the lads,' he said. He sat down. 'Mrs Slater,' he said, looking at Jean, but she seemed not to hear him. 'I'm afraid we have to take Mrs Jenkinson away soon. And you will have to come with our policewoman so that we can ask you some more questions. She'll be here in a few minutes. We'll wait together, if you can spare us a little time, Lois?'

She nodded. 'It might help ... help Mrs Slater ... if I just told you a couple of things now. Ken and Doreen were lovers, but I expect you knew that. They planned to kill Howard ... Seems they relied on his phobia for guns, and scared him to death. That's what people say, don't they ... scared to death. Never actually come across it before...'

Cowgill reached out and took Lois's hand, connecting the three of them. 'You're a bit shocked, Lois, and no bloody wonder.'

She had never heard him swear before. 'No, I'm okay, I think ... but I'd like to get home to see Derek, an' that.'

A small frown briefly appeared on Cowgill's face, but was quickly gone. 'Not much longer,' he said.

Jean suddenly looked up. 'No, Mrs Meade,' she said. 'It wasn't just because they were lovers, wanting Howard out of the way. Although I thought all that was finished.' She passed a hand across her eyes and resumed. 'It was Doreen started it, when she saw Howard on the golf course in the summer. Doreen and me were playing together. We'd fixed up a game on the spur of the moment, so Howard wouldn't have known we were there. She hit her ball into the rough, underneath the trees. She went in after it, and when she came out she was pale as a ghost. I thought she was going to faint. We sat down on the edge of the fairway, and when she'd recovered a bit, she told me she'd seen Howard, deep in the bracken, with that Susanna Jacob. At it, they were. No mistaking that, Doreen said. Bare bums an' all. After that, we used to fantasise about ways of getting our own back on the bugger. And this is how it ended. Ken would do anything for her, you know. Anything.'

She looked down at Doreen's body, and the spreading pool of blood. 'Except that,' she said, beginning to shake again. 'I never thought he would do that...'

'I'm not sure he meant to.' Lois was feeling sick, and wondered how much longer. At that moment the door opened, a policewoman came in, and then everything was organised and dealt with. After a while, Lois walked out of Hornton House, and saw Josie waving to her from the shop doorway. She hesitated, then went across the road. 'Got time for a cuppa?' Josie said. 'Nothing much happening at the moment. A really quiet afternoon, unfortunately!'

Lois stared at her. 'Well,' she said, 'there's

something to be said for that.' She shivered, and visibly pulled herself together. 'Now,' she began firmly, 'I promised Dad tinned rice pudding tonight. Gran disapproves, but Dad likes it better than hers. Got any left? And yes, I'd love a cup of tea, hot and sweet.' She bit her lip, keeping a hold on herself.

'You all right, Mum?' Josie looked closely at her.

'Yep, I'm fine, thanks, love. Shall we get that tea, before the queue of customers arrives?'

Josie laughed. This was more like her Mum. Perhaps she'd had a bit of indigestion. Too many chocolate biscuits over at Mrs Jenkinson's. 'Mrs J had visitors this afternoon, didn't she?' she said. 'I saw those Slaters, and was it your cop friend, with henchmen? I had to answer the phone and missed most of it.'

'Just a social call, I think,' Lois said. Josie would know it all soon enough.

When Lois returned home, there was a message to ring Bill. 'He sounded excited,' Gran said. 'Are you going to ring him now?'

'Might as well,' Lois said, and went into her office.

'Bill? You rang,' she said, and he replied at once, 'Yeah, I've got some news. But first tell me what's wrong with you, Mrs M.'

'What d'you mean?'

337

'You sound awful. We've known each other a long time, and I know something's up.'

'Tell you later,' Lois said, and then remembered. Bill and Rebecca. 'Hey, Bill!' she said, her spirits rising rapidly. 'Is it...?'

'Yeah, it is – at last! Rebecca can't resist my charms any longer, and has agreed against her better judgement to marry me in six months' time. Seems it takes that long to make arrangements. What d'you think?' He sounded anxious for her approval.

Lois found a tissue and blew her nose hard. 'She must be mad,' she said, and then laughed. 'Oh, Bill, I'm so pleased. What wonderful news! You can't imagine how glad I am you rang me. Bless you both. Give her my love, and we'll talk later.'

She didn't mention having heard the news first from Miss Beasley. She didn't care. All she could think of was being at home, with Gran in the kitchen making supper, and Derek on his way back, full of news of the day and leaving muddy footprints all over the floor.

Epilogue

'Red sky in the morning, shepherd's warning,' Derek said darkly. 'It'll rain, me duck, before breakfast.'

'Rain before seven, fine before eleven,' Lois one-upped him. 'You'll see, by the time Rebecca arrives at the church, the sun'll be shining. It always shines on the bride.'

'Rubbish! Anyway, better take umbrellas. And we should get up. It's a long way to the Rogers' ancestral home.'

'Don't be daft.' Lois gave him a shove. 'You go to the bathroom first, and I'll go down and help Gran. Do you think we'll all squeeze into Josie's little car?'

'Have to,' Derek said, disappearing into the bathroom. 'Don't fancy turning up at a society wedding in New Brooms van. Even if you do sweep cleaner...'

They did after all arrive in plenty of time, and Derek suggested a drink in the pub to shelter from the rain. He managed to avoid sounding smug. There they found many others fuelling themselves for the momentous event. Some of the lads joshing each other were clearly Bill's friends from York-shire. Two elderly ladies sitting decorously in a corner, sipping dry sherries, bore a faint resemblance to Rebecca. 'Aunties,' whispered Gran to Lois.

The small village church was full of flowers, and the scent of white lilies made Gran sneeze. It was full of guests, too, with not a spare seat. Lois looked around, and saw her girls, Bill's colleagues, were there in force. She smiled, proud of their loyalty. Then the organist began the dramatic music signalling the entrance of the bride, and all heads turned to the door. Bill, who stood at the front, handsome in his morning suit, upright and serious, did not turn. Nervous, thought Lois. Poor Bill, first time I've ever seen him nervous. Then Rebecca appeared on the arm of her father, veiled and majestically mysterious. As she approached Bill, she pushed back her veil and, like the sun coming out, she smiled at him.

Lois and Gran held hands and sniffed. The service began, and it was, as always, a solemn and moving time. Then they were man and wife, and walked down the aisle triumphantly surrounded by goodwill and love.

As Lois opened her front door and stepped into the hall, she could hear the telephone ringing. If she left it, the answerphone would click in. She sighed. It would have to be attended to sooner or later, so she went into her office and lifted the receiver. 'Hello? New Brooms here. Can I help you?'

There was a slight pause, and then a voice she had all but forgotten said, 'Mrs Meade. Jean Slater here. You may not remember me ... but I am able to look for a job now. I was wondering if you had any vacancies. I do actually need the money, and jobs are a bit difficult, so I'd be grateful...' She tailed off into silence.

Lois took a deep breath. 'Of course I re-member you,' she said. 'Best if you come and see me. I'll give you a ring tomorrow and fix an appointment. And by the way,' she added. 'Glad to hear you're okay. Bye.'